Finding Her Dad
Janice Kay Johnson

TORONTO NEW YORK LONDON
AMSTERDAM PARIS SYDNEY HAMBURG
STOCKHOLM ATHENS TOKYO MILAN MADRID
PRAGUE WARSAW BUDAPEST AUCKLAND

Recycling programs
for this product may
not exist in your area.

ISBN-13: 978-0-373-78455-4

FINDING HER DAD

ABOUT THE AUTHOR

The author of more than sixty books for children and adults, Janice Kay Johnson writes Harlequin Superromance novels about love and family—about the way generations connect and the power our earliest experiences have on us throughout life. Her 2007 novel *Snowbound* won a RITA® Award from Romance Writers of America for Best Contemporary Series Romance. A former librarian, Janice raised two daughters in a small rural town north of Seattle, Washington. She loves to read and is an active volunteer and board member for Purrfect Pals, a no-kill cat shelter.

Books by Janice Kay Johnson

For my own,
much loved daughters, Sarah and Katie.
May they always find what they seek.

CHAPTER ONE

"SEE, I DIDN'T WANT TO just, like, email him or something. I thought I should really go talk to him. In person. You know?" Earnest and wide-eyed, Sierra twirled one lock of indigo-blue hair around her finger. Elaborately casual, she finished, "It would be cooler if I had my driver's license, but since I can't drive myself with only a permit…"

Permit. Driver's license. Email him. Him who? Lucy Malone realized, as she stared at her foster daughter in bewilderment, that her mind seemed to be scrolling backward through what had been a fairly lengthy recitation. Back to the beginning, which had been…

"I found my dad." Perfectly timed, the sixteen-year-old said it again, hugged herself and did a small end-zone dance. "Is that amazing or what?"

Lucy pressed her fingertips to her suddenly aching temples. "Wait. No. You don't *have* a father."

Sierra rolled her eyes as only a teenager could. "Of course I have a father. What do you think? Mom managed an immaculate conception? I mean, sure, it was *close,* but…"

Oh, Lord, Lucy didn't want to believe Sierra knew anything at all about conception, especially the kind that *wasn't* immaculate. Which was foolish in the extreme. What else did girls—and boys—her age think about, if it wasn't sex?

Fathers, apparently.

What Lucy did know was that Sierra's mother had never married and had decided to have a child on her own. She'd gone to a sperm bank; yes, the closest thing to an immaculate conception that a woman could achieve. From what Sierra said, all her mother had ever known about Sierra's father was what he'd chosen to share about himself for the women shopping for sperm. Catalog copy. And how accurate was that likely to be? No guy selling sperm was likely to admit that his IQ was really eighty-five and his best skill was belching louder than his buddies.

Lucy sank onto the stool behind the cash register. "Explain," she ordered.

Thank God there were no customers in the store at the moment, a fact that wouldn't normally make her grateful. She'd opened her gourmet pet food supply store only a year before, and although business had been steadily climbing, she still sweated through paying the bills every month. But this was definitely not a conversation she wanted overheard.

"I told you!" Sierra complained. "Weren't you listening?"

"You know me. My idea of high-tech is ultrasonic teeth-cleaning equipment. I know zilch about DNA." Lucy was a licensed veterinary technician who'd gotten tired of taking orders from other people. But if there was one thing she knew, it was animals, so her choice of business made sense.

"I sent in a swab from the inside of my cheek to a lab for DNA testing," the teenager said with exaggerated patience.

"Isn't that expensive?"

"Not that much. Anyway, I was saving all the money I made babysitting and working for you."

"Okay." Lucy closed her eyes briefly. "Then what?"

Then, Sierra said, she had compared her DNA results to millions of others on a variety of online databases.

Lucy frowned. "Surely you couldn't get

on— I don't know. Whatever one law enforcement uses. Isn't that the main one?"

Sierra's sky-blue eyes gave a betraying flicker. Lucy recognized it. Aghast, she whispered, "You didn't."

Her foster daughter was going through a Goth phase. Currently her hair, shoulder length and blunt cut, was dyed blue, a change from last year's jet-black. A tattoo of a dragon twined around one slender ankle. Her nose and one eyebrow were pierced. More piercings climbed the rim of each ear. Lucy had nixed the idea of a tongue piercing until, at a minimum, Sierra turned eighteen. Fortunately, she'd taken the refusal in good humor.

The thing was, she was brilliant. Scary smart. At home she was rarely without her fingers on a computer keyboard. She carried her laptop everywhere. Screens constantly popped up as friends sent instant messages. They didn't seem ever to talk; they communicated in a sort of bizarre shorthand via the internet. Lucy knew that Sierra was very, very good at hacking in to forbidden websites; she'd gotten into big trouble while in eighth grade for changing a friend's marks in the school records. When telling Lucy about it recently, she'd said blithely, "It was easy.

Hey, I did them a favor! They've at least made it a little harder now."

Lucy had not pursued the subject. Had there been more recent incursions into the school district personnel or student records, she didn't really want to know about it. What worried her were Sierra's exact capabilities now, almost three years later.

Now gazing sunnily back at Lucy, Sierra said, "Um...I didn't have to. I bet I could, though. It's called CODIS. Combined DNA Index System. You can do partial-match searches in it, too. Haven't you read about it? The American Civil Liberties Union doesn't think cops should be able to compare, like, some guy's brother's DNA to the sperm taken from a raped woman."

Lucy grappled with that. "You mean, if I had a brother who'd raped a woman, *my* DNA could be matched to his sperm?" She heard her voice rising.

"Sure. I mean, it wouldn't be a perfect match. That's what a partial match is. See, that's what I did."

She went on to explain that there were DNA databases for all kinds of reasons. Some were medical, for people trying to find a match who might donate an organ, or bone marrow. Others were for people into genealogy. DNA was a new way to track family and ancestors.

"So I found this woman in Seattle." Her pretty face was aglow with enthusiasm. "She's a really close match. Then I did more research, and I found out she and her husband had two kids. One was a girl, one a boy. He's the right age, and he went to college at the UW."

Lucy found herself nodding numbly. The University of Washington was in Seattle, less than an hour northwest of Kanaskat, where Lucy had her home and business. Sierra's mother had grown up in the Seattle area and never left, and had presumably used a local fertility clinic.

"And…this man. He's still around here."

"Yes!" The teenager indulged in another delighted dance. "It's just *got* to be him. I know it is."

Lucy couldn't argue on a factual basis, given her relative ignorance of DNA testing and profiling and online databases. And, heck, genealogy.

Maybe I could find my father.

A little shocked that the thought had even flitted through her mind, she almost snorted. Like she'd *want* to find him.

"Sierra," she said, "this man gave sperm

with the understanding he'd remain anonymous. The deal was never that he'd actually take any kind of parental responsibility."

For a timeless, stricken moment, Sierra's crystal clear eyes held Lucy's. Then the girl ducked her head and her blue hair swung down to hide her face. Lucy felt cruel.

"I know," Sierra said in a small voice. "I just, um, want to meet him. And *see*. That's all." She lifted her face, a pleading expression on it. "He might like to meet me. I mean, wouldn't you think he'd be curious? It's not like I expect him to actually want me."

"I want you," Lucy said quietly.

Her foster daughter gave her a tremulous smile and her eyes filled with tears. "I know. I know how lucky I am. I love living with you, Lucy. It would just be nice to have family who would, like, call sometimes. Care if I get accepted into college. You know?"

A lump filled Lucy's throat. She knew.

Sierra's mother, Rebecca Lind, had died in a head-on car accident eight months ago. She'd never had any other children. She did have a brother, who lived in Albuquerque, New Mexico. When social services contacted him, he'd said there was no way he and his wife could take on a teenage girl. The social worker had privately told Lucy that his exact words had been "For God's sake, I haven't seen Becky in twenty-five years. We didn't even try to stay in touch after Mom died. It's too bad about the accident, but I can't take on some kid of hers."

The last thing a grief-stricken fifteen-year-old had needed was to be rejected by the only relative she had left in the world. At the time, Sierra had begun working on Saturdays for Lucy, cleaning and stocking shelves. After her mom died, she'd stayed temporarily with a friend. She had come by midweek to tell Lucy she wouldn't be able to make it to work anymore.

Lucy hadn't seen her since the funeral. She'd looked awful. Her hair had been dyed black at the time, but the pale roots were showing. A tall, skinny girl, she looked as if she'd dropped ten pounds in two weeks. She was gaunt, and her eyes were puffy, and her fingers writhed together while she talked.

"I'm being sent to a foster home in Midford," she said. Even her voice was dull. Her thin shoulders moved in a listless shrug. "They tried to find one here so I could stay in the same school, but I guess there weren't any."

Lucy was still in shock that the aunt and uncle had said no. Hearing that they had refused made her mad. No, worse than that. It made her ache inside for this gawky child-woman who had already been so very vulnerable, even before the only person in the world who loved her had been stolen from her by a drunk driver.

Sierra might have a little barbell through one eyebrow and a ring in one nostril, her hair might be dyed pitch-black, her clothes black and the dog collar she wore around her neck spiked, but she was a sweetheart. She was smart, and funny, and oddly innocent. Lucy had already thought that she would like nothing better than to have a daughter like Sierra.

Which was probably why, that day, her mouth had opened and she heard herself say, with no forethought whatsoever, "Would you like to live with me?"

So now here they were. Although at twenty-eight she was too young to actually be a mother to a girl Sierra's age, she'd gotten properly licensed as a foster home, and now *she* was Sierra's family.

Which meant, of course, that there was no way she could let the girl go by herself to see this man who might or might not be her father. Clearly, stopping her wouldn't fly. Look at all the effort she'd gone to finding him in the first place. And, face it, the chances were really good that he wouldn't believe Sierra's claim, even if he had given— or did the men sell?—sperm when he was in college. If he did believe her, he probably still wouldn't want to admit he was her father.

Were she honest with herself, Lucy couldn't even entirely blame him. He probably had a wife and children. It would be more than slightly awkward for him to admit that not only was this teenager who'd appeared out of the blue—and had blue hair—his daughter by a woman he'd never even set eyes on, but he might have other daughters and sons running around. Not might; probably did.

Nightmare city.

She waited until Sierra met her eyes, and then she said very softly, "Are you sure you want to do this, honey? You know he might want nothing to do with you." Especially after he took in her clothes and her piercings and her tattoo.

In Lucy's experience, men tended not to look beneath the surface.

Sierra squared her shoulders, held her head high and said, "Yes. I'm sure."

Lucy nodded. "Then I'll take you to see him."

The teenager grinned. "Cool! I already

have an appointment with him. Except I made up an excuse."

"You've what?" Alarm filled Lucy. "What does he do for a living?'"

"He's a cop." She made a face. "Jeez. My dad the cop. But he's one of the ones in charge, I think. He's a captain."

Alarm metamorphosed into dread. Lucy had this sudden, terrible premonition. Yesterday's *Dispatch* had carried a front-page article on the electoral race for county sheriff. The incumbent was retiring. One candidate was the police chief of Willis, the county's largest city, the other the captain of Investigative Services for the Emmons County Sheriff's Department. She had stared for a long time at the photo of that candidate, her attention caught for reasons she hadn't quite been able to pin down.

"Oh, no. Please tell me he's not…"

Sierra nodded, as if to confirm Lucy's suspicions. "His name is Jonathan Brenner. He's running for sheriff. I found tons of pictures of him online. I look like him," she said simply.

Dear God, she did, Lucy thought. That was why she hadn't been able to look away from his photo.

Well, it was one of the reasons. The other

was the disquieting fact that simply looking at him, even in black and white, had made her heart do an odd little skip and bump.

And she hadn't been able to help noticing, in the article, that he wasn't married.

As if, she'd told herself, folding the newspaper up and determinedly depositing it in the recycling bin, *she* would ever meet him.

"When I'm wrong," she murmured, once Sierra had wandered away to the pair of cages that held two shelter cats awaiting adoption, "I'm wrong. Really wrong."

Lucy had a strong suspicion that her role in the upcoming meeting was not going to endear her to the very upright, conservative Captain Jonathan Brenner.

"I'M NOT LETTING HIM BACK on the street until the investigation is complete," Jon Brenner said flatly.

Eddie Prindle, the police union representative, said, "You don't have grounds to put Deputy Chen on suspension. At this point, you have no evidence that the incident was his fault."

They'd already said this. Several times. Jon abruptly lost patience.

"Then file a grievance." He rose, but stayed

behind his desk. "I'm afraid you'll have to excuse me. I have another appointment."

Prindle didn't like him. The feeling was mutual. Jon didn't hold out a hand. After a moment the other man stood, too. "You've gone too far," he said. "Are you afraid voters will think you're colluding to excuse a deputy's malfeasance if you don't come down hard enough on Deputy Chen? Whatever the truth of the incident?"

Jon didn't allow his expression to change. "The election has nothing to do with this. Chen screwed up. I don't know how badly yet. When I do, I'll make a decision. I can tell you this. It's to his benefit for me not to make that decision prematurely. You're not doing him any favors, Prindle."

"You'll be hearing from us," the union rep said. He turned on his heel and stalked out of the office.

Jon swung away to gaze out the window. On a clear day he had a glimpse of Mount Rainier from here. Today the mountain was wrapped in puffy clouds.

He was pissed off enough to mutter a couple of obscenities. At the very least, the young deputy had been hotdogging. At worst, he'd been criminally careless. No one had died in the incident that had resulted in his suspension, but that wasn't thanks to him. Right now Jon was inclined to fire him, but there might turn out to be extenuating circumstances. And Chen was, while not a rookie, far from seasoned.

After a minute Jon rubbed the back of his neck and turned to his desk. There was a name on his calendar for three o'clock—Sierra Lind. A high-school kid, apparently. Something about the school newspaper. Which was strange in August, when school wasn't in session. Probably she was an eager beaver who wanted to have an article on the election ready for the first issue. Jon didn't have time for this kind of thing and he wasn't in the mood right now, but it wasn't optional. Community relations were too important.

Election or no election.

He touched the button on his intercom and said, "Dinah, is my next appointment here?"

"Yes, sir."

"Send her in, please."

He walked around the desk as the door opened. Two people entered, a girl and a woman. The girl caught his eye first, thanks to hair dyed a ridiculous color and a bunch of piercings. Nothing unusual there, but a shame all the same. She'd be prettier without metal impaled on her face. Unusually tall for a girl, maybe five foot ten or eleven, she was skinny and long legged. Had long arms, too, that hung awkwardly as if she wasn't quite sure what to do with them. Blue eyes, strangely intense.

The woman who came in behind her didn't look like any relation. The teacher in charge of the school newspaper, maybe? She was a good six inches or more shorter, with long wavy black hair, chocolate-brown eyes and a curvaceous figure. Plump by modern standards. Just right by his, he couldn't help thinking, even though lusting after random visitors to his office wasn't exactly appropriate.

Both of them were looking him over with unusual gravity. The girl seemed nervous, maybe even a little scared. The woman was wary, edging into hostile.

What the hell? he asked himself, even as he held out a hand to the girl, who was in the lead. "Welcome. I'm Captain Brenner. Are you Sierra Lind?"

"Yes." Her voice squeaked, and she flushed. "Yes," she repeated. She looked from his hand to his face and then back again before tentatively reaching out.

They shook, her long, slender fingers icy enough that he glanced down in surprise.

She retrieved her hand, and he smiled at the woman. "And you are…?"

"Lucia Malone." Her voice was pleasantly husky. It didn't go with a persona that seemed to bristle. "I'm Sierra's foster mother. And chauffeur."

"Ah." He wanted to shake her hand, too, but she was gripping a large purse fiercely enough he had a feeling she might ignore his hand if he proffered it. Instead, he gestured toward the seating area separated from his desk by only a few feet. "Please."

They sidled that way, not taking their eyes from him. Rather like a cautious doe and fawn unsure whether the other visitor to the water hole was a predator or not. Ruefully amused, he stayed where he was until they'd sat side by side. Then he chose a seat on the far side of the coffee table. No point in panicking them.

His gaze wanted to linger on Lucia Malone's pretty face. Her first name, brown eyes and black hair suggested that she had Hispanic blood.

He dragged his attention to the teenager. She was the one who'd made the appointment.

"What can I do for you, Sierra?" he asked.

She gulped, then cast a panicky look at her

foster mother. When she looked back at him, he thought idly that her eyes were as blue as his. They were several shades lighter than her hair dye.

In a rush she said, "I'm not really here to do an article for my school newspaper." When he didn't say anything immediately, she hurried on. "That's what I said when I called. Because I thought then they'd let me in to see you."

Feeling considerably more cautious now, he studied her. "All right. Why did you want to talk to me?"

She gnawed on her lower lip. After a moment Ms. Malone reached out and squeezed one of her hands. Jon's gaze dropped to those clasped hands, one small and competent and warm skinned, the other very white and longer fingered. And yet, from the way those two hands clung, he could feel a connection beyond the physical. Reassurance. Love.

He met the girl's eyes again and waited.

"The thing is," she said, so fast the words tumbled over each other, "I think you're my father."

He stared. Either she was delusional or his recurring nightmare had just become real. He couldn't seem to think. To figure how old she was. Whether she could be… But, goddamn it, how would she have found him?

The silence stretched, became painful.

"I know you may not want anything to do with me," she said hurriedly, "and that's okay. Really. I just, well, wanted to meet you. And *see*."

He cleared his throat. "To say you've taken me by surprise is an understatement. Forgive me, but…do I know your mother?"

She shook her head. "No. Mom is— She died." The girl—Sierra—sucked in a huge breath. "Mom went to a sperm bank."

God help him.

Voice hoarse, he said, "How old are you?"

"I'm sixteen. I turned sixteen in July." She paused. "I'll be a junior this year."

Sixteen. Jon had quit breathing. Sixteen years ago he was a senior in college. Oh, damn.

He could feel the foster mother watching him. He didn't let himself look at her.

"What makes you think I'm your father?" he said finally.

"I compared DNA in a whole bunch of databases. I came up with a partial match. To a Linda Brenner. Then I did some research and found out she had one son, who was the right age."

"Me," he said slowly.

Her head bobbed.

His mother had become obsessed with tracing her family heritage, lord knows why. He did vaguely recall she'd sent off a DNA sample at one point. Jon had argued against it; once something like that was out there, you lost a piece of your privacy. She'd laughed and said, "What do I have to hide? The only people I'm likely to hear from are relatives. Imagine finding cousins I didn't know I had."

Imagine, he thought grimly, *finding a granddaughter you didn't know you had.*

He cursed. Lucia Malone gave him a reproving look.

"You did this on a whim," he said to the girl.

Her teeth closed on her lower lip again. Her eyes slid from his, then came shyly back. "It was after Mom died that I thought…" She gave a little shrug. Her shoulders stayed slightly hunched after that, as if she were braced for a blow.

When she didn't say any more, he did look at Ms. Malone. "She doesn't have any other family?"

"An uncle in New Mexico." Her voice was repressive. "He wasn't able to take Sierra."

Jon couldn't remember the last time he'd been staggered like this. He didn't know what to think. There was supposed to be no way he could ever be traced. DNA testing had been around, but in its relative infancy. The idea of partial matches, of people casually sending off spit so they could track down unknown relatives, had been unimaginable.

No longer.

He made himself study the girl and immediately thought, *hell*. Her eyes were the same color as his, an unusually crystalline, pale blue. Her hair…well, who knew? No, that wasn't true. Her eyebrows were light brown. Which meant she was likely a blonde. He'd been blond as a kid, but by his twenties his hair had darkened to a medium brown that bleached easily in the sun. This summer, between work and politicking he hadn't gotten outside enough for that to happen.

He was tall—six foot three. His sister was five-ten. Fine boned like this girl, too. The nose and Cupid-doll mouth weren't his, but the shape of her face…yeah, she could have gotten that from him.

Desperately he wondered what the voters would think of this. Was there any way to keep Rinnert from finding out about Sierra? He had a horrifying vision of what his opponent could make of the stunning appearance of an unknown daughter.

"Do you have any proof at all," he said, his voice harder than he intended, "or did you pick me out of the phone book?"

Lucia Malone let go of her foster daughter's hand—he hadn't noticed until now that she'd continued to hold it in silent reassurance—to pluck a file folder from her capacious bag. She glared at him as she handed it over.

He opened it and took a quick glance, barely keeping himself from swearing aloud again. He'd seen enough DNA typing on the job to know he was screwed.

He closed the folder. "I'll need to study this."

Ms. Malone's eyes narrowed. "You did donate sperm, didn't you? Or you'd have kicked us out by now."

His jaw muscles flexed. "I don't have to answer that question."

They stared at each other, her expression angry and contemptuous. At last she stood.

"Sierra, I think it's time we go." Her voice was astonishingly gentle, considering the way she was vibrating with outrage. "We've put Captain Brenner on the spot. I think it's fair to give him time to think."

"Oh." The girl scrambled to her feet. Her

cheeks were flaming red. "Yeah. Sure."
She didn't want to meet his eyes anymore.
"My phone number's in there if you want….
But if you don't, that's okay. I really didn't
mean…" She squeezed her eyes shut. "I didn't
mean…"

Oh, hell, she was going to cry. He almost
groaned.

But she pulled herself together and looked
at him with sudden dignity that gave him an
odd, burning sensation beneath his breastbone. "Thank you for your time, Captain
Brenner. I'm sorry if this felt like I was at-
tacking you or something. I promise I won't
tell anyone." Then she inclined her head, as
regal as a princess, and walked beside her
foster mother to his door. She carried herself
proudly, and he felt like scum.

"Sierra." His voice emerged rough.

She paused without turning. Ms. Malone
did.

"I'll be in touch," he said.

The lips that had spoken so softly to the
girl tightened. Ms. Malone nodded, and the
two of them left, carefully closing the office
door behind them.

He didn't move; just stood there, stunned,
and saw his chances of becoming sheriff
implode. And knew he was a son of a bitch

to even let that cross his mind after looking into the eyes of a girl tossed into the foster-care system because she had no family who wanted her—a girl, he had no doubt, who was his daughter.

CHAPTER TWO

JON DIDN'T KNOW how he got through the day. He had several other appointments, and had to attend a potluck dinner at a seniors' center and then, later in the evening, a volunteer fair at a community center. The brief talks he gave to the seniors and the volunteers came by rote, for which he was grateful. He was getting good at running for office, which these days seemed to matter more than whether he'd be an effective sheriff. He could tell his tough-on-crime stance went over better with the old folks than it did with the activist kinds at the fair. They were inclined to be softhearted. He found their suspicion of him ironic, considering his core belief was that every person should take responsibility for his or her own actions. He believed in a kind of morality that was very personal. Wasn't it that same sense of morality, a need to take responsibility, that had driven all of them to give of their precious time to some cause?

The whole time he talked, listened, smiled, shook hands, he felt as if he was having an out-of-body experience. He would have sworn he was standing outside himself watching critically.

Knowing the guy he watched was a hypocrite.

He argued for a morality that should govern every choice a person made, a sense of responsibility that wouldn't let you look away when it was convenient to do so.

Responsibility. Now, that was funny, coming from a man who'd sold his sperm. Who might have a whole bunch of unacknowledged kids out there. Kids who were deeply wanted, he'd told himself back when he was twenty-one and saw the sperm donation as a quick and easy way to bring in bucks. He was doing the world a *favor.* After all, he was healthy, smart, athletic; he carried no genetic booby traps of which he was aware. What was wrong with helping women have babies, if their husbands were sterile or they'd chosen to go the single-parent route?

He'd returned to the clinic two or three times, hating the sordid feel of the process itself. But he'd been working as many hours as he could and still keep his grades up, and yet struggled to pay his tuition and rent and buy food and books. He'd been damned if he would take a cent from his father. He would do anything not to have to surrender his pride enough to ask for help from his parents.

He worked his butt off. And, when necessary, he'd sell sperm, and he'd sell blood. He had done both.

Personal responsibility wasn't the strong suit of twenty-one-year-old boys. He'd been blithe enough about jacking off and handing over the tube of milky liquid, until one day he was waiting for a bus near a medical clinic. A pregnant woman came out and sat on the bench near him. He remembered looking at her sidelong. He didn't know how pregnant she was. She was round, but not waddling. Five or six months, maybe. No husband with her. He'd wondered a little disapprovingly why not. A pregnant woman shouldn't have to wait for the bus. What if it was full and she had to stand? Or she got jostled and bumped hard against the sharp edge of the seats? There were punks who hassled lone women on buses. And then he'd thought, *Oh, my God. She might not have a husband, or a boyfriend. She could be pregnant with my baby.*

He'd sat there in shock, trying not to stare but unable to help sneaking looks. Of course the kid she was carrying wasn't his; that was stupid even to think. What were the odds? The sperm bank supplied fertility clinics all over the country and even abroad. Not just locally.

But it could be.

Man, that had given him cold chills. After that he'd stuck to donating blood when he was desperate. It wasn't as if the money had been that fabulous. He pretended to himself he didn't even notice the pregnant women who seemed to be everywhere.

It was a couple of years before an obviously pregnant woman didn't seem to light up like a neon sign to him, and before he succeeded in putting from his mind the fact that probably some of his sperm had been put to use, that at least a few babies had been born that were blood of his blood.

And now, he thought as he stood outside himself and watched while he went through the motions of politicking, he'd met one of those children. Sierra Lind.

The question was, what was he going to do about it? About her?

Had she meant it when she said she didn't expect anything? That she wouldn't tell anyone he was her father if he didn't want to acknowledge her?

Maybe. He thought she did mean it now. Which wasn't to say she wouldn't change her mind.

It would matter less later, once he'd won the election, if he could put her off.

He felt cold-blooded even thinking that.

Even if Sierra kept her mouth shut, what about her foster mother? Ms. Malone had started dubious and moved right along to mad because all she could see was that he was hurting her precious chick's feelings.

And he had. Jon didn't like to remember the wounded look in those blue eyes or the pride with which Sierra—his daughter—had carried herself when she assured him that he had no obligation to her. Sierra might even believe that she'd been operating on mere curiosity, that she had no secret wish for him to hold out his arms and gather her into the bosom of his family. But he knew better. She'd lost her mother, and her only other relative didn't want her. She'd gone to extraordinary effort to find him. Of course she hoped, desperately, that he would feel an immediate bond. Curiosity to match hers.

So…what did he feel?

He had no idea.

No surprise, even after having downed a

shot of straight Scotch while watching the late-night news, that he couldn't sleep.

The day had been muggy enough that he'd left the ceiling fan running. He slept naked, the moving air cooling the sweat on his body. Lying on his back, arms crossed behind his head, he gazed at the pale square of moonlight that fell through the open window onto the bed. Most of him was in the dark, leaving only his knees, calves and feet exposed by that cool light.

He wondered if she was able to sleep tonight. What had she felt, meeting him? Anything in particular? Had there been some sort of recognition, on a cellular level, or did she imagine there was? Was she lying awake right now, too, hungrily remembering his face or the pitch of his voice and the set of his shoulders, deciding which bits and pieces of him had been echoed in her by the genes that had imprinted her?

He muttered a soft imprecation. Those long, skinny arms and legs… He'd gone through that phase. In middle school he'd taken to hunching and hunkering low in his chair, because he towered over everyone. He'd been ridiculously, embarrassingly skinny. PE was a nightmare for him, when he was required to wear shorts that exposed stick-thin legs. Jon smiled a little, thinking about the boy he'd been. A boy with size-thirteen feet that sometimes seemed to be only loosely attached to him. Getting interested in girls, and knowing he looked ridiculous to them.

Sierra's body still wasn't quite finished, but she hadn't looked as if she was clumsy, not the way he'd been. But maybe she had been when she was younger. He wouldn't be surprised. By sixteen, he'd finally been gaining some muscle, some coordination. By twenty, he guessed Sierra would be a beauty, model-slender and graceful. Did she know that, or still despair?

She had to be smart, or she wouldn't have been able to track him down. He had a feeling Ms. Malone hadn't helped. She'd radiated too much disapproval. So Sierra was enterprising, too. Creative. He'd never heard of a kid using DNA to find a sperm-donor father. And she must be a dreamer, or she wouldn't have embarked on her plan in the first place. He'd been driven, but he wouldn't call himself a dreamer. At that age, he'd been engaged in ice-cold warfare with his father. Sometimes he thought his every decision had been made in anger and rebellion. He'd been consumed by that anger.

Sierra's decisions were being made in grief and loneliness.

"Damn," he whispered to the moonlit room.

His mind drifted. *What would Mom think of her?* He knew. His mom would be shocked at first, that he'd sold sperm, that she had unknown grandkids out there. She would look as disapproving as Lucia Malone had. But she would love Sierra, given her innate dignity and vulnerable eyes the exact color of his.

His sister, Lily, would, too. Although it would be awkward explaining to her two kids why they'd never met—or even heard of—this cousin.

After the election…

Jon gritted his teeth. That was almost three months away. Three months, during which Sierra would believe her father didn't want anything to do with her.

He *wasn't* her father, not in any meaningful sense. There had never been any such expectation of him. Her mother had known the deal when she purchased sperm. He should be able to feel detached.

He couldn't.

She might not be his. There was clearly a relationship to his mother—the DNA test confirmed that. But he probably had dozens of second and third and fourth cousins he didn't know. Either he'd have to give a DNA sample, or they'd go to the sperm bank or fertility clinic together and ask for confirmation.

But he knew. He knew.

And he also knew he couldn't live with himself if he turned away from that girl.

Election or no election.

"It's okay if he doesn't call." Sierra sat on one of the two tall stools at the breakfast bar in the kitchen, watching as Lucy put together a salad to go with the leftover casserole she was reheating. The teenager's arms were akimbo on the tiled bar. Lucy heard her feet lightly bumping the cabinet as she swung her legs. Sierra was always in motion, even when she was at rest. "Really," she said, convincing neither of them.

Chopping a carrot, Lucy said, "Give him time."

Behind her reassuring facade, she roiled. The son of a bitch had *better* call. Or she was personally going to hunt him down.

Wham. She wielded the knife with unnecessary force. *Wham.*

No, she didn't blame him for being shocked. She did blame him for being so careless with something as personal as sperm. She couldn't imagine giving away her eggs. Men, of course, were a whole lot more likely to strew their sperm hither and yon with no thought for consequences. Except he'd known darn well that his *would* produce consequences. That had been the whole point, after all.

She didn't even know why she was so mad. Her sympathies had—somewhat—been with him when this started. What Sierra had done was outrageous. It should have been impossible. Because of the publicity about his campaign, Lucy knew that almost seventeen years ago, when Jonathan Brenner gave/sold sperm, he'd been only twenty-one. Hardly older than Sierra was now. Lucy had done stupid things herself at that age. Who didn't?

But she'd felt things when she first saw him stepping out from behind his desk, smiling at Sierra and holding out his hand. A quivering inside. Because he was perfect. Not perfect-perfect—his nose was too big for his face and looked as if it had been broken, his hair was cut shorter than she liked, to suit his law-and-order persona, and she couldn't imagine that smile was sincere. And yet her first idiotic thought was that he would win the election because he embodied strength and razor-sharp intelligence and a gritty determination to protect.

She had done her best to convince herself that he could just as well be a cardboard cutout, with no more substance.

Except that he did have an excellent record on the job. The current sheriff had endorsed him rather than his opponent.

But then she saw the shields he erected when Sierra told him she believed he was her father. There was an instant of understandable shock, then…nothing. Blank. Except Lucy had the sense that he had immediately begun to calculate the pros and cons and develop a strategy. Would this pretty daughter be an asset or a huge detriment? His gaze had flicked over Sierra's piercings, lingered briefly on her bright blue hair. None of which could be good, in his view. If he admitted he was her father, could the fact be kept secret? Would she go away if he made no admissions?

So okay. *Wham. Wham.* Lucy didn't actually *know* that he'd thought anything of the sort. He was a cop. Of course he was good at hiding what he was thinking. She shouldn't succumb to her own prejudices.

But oh, it was very hard not to.

Sierra had been watching in silence, but now she said wistfully, "How much time should I give him?"

"As much as he needs. Unless you plan to pester him?" Lucy took the salad dressing from the refrigerator, then handed it and the bowl of salad over the breakfast bar. "Put this on the table."

Sierra took the bowl. "I said I wouldn't," she said, looking offended. "Just because he's probably my dad doesn't mean anything. Maybe he never wanted to have kids."

Then he should have kept his sperm to himself, Lucy thought but didn't say.

"I was hoping," Sierra said. "That's all."

Lucy set the casserole dish on the table. She half wished she'd heated some rolls or a baguette, but she didn't really need bread, too. She must have put on ten pounds in the past year. The financial risk and long hours required to get a small business off the ground added up to stress. Lots of stress. Lucy ate when she was stressed. She'd vowed to lose those ten pounds this year. One pound a month. How hard could that be?

The phone rang. Sierra quivered, but didn't move.

"Do you want to get it?" Lucy asked.

"It's probably for you." Head bowed, Sierra stirred casserole around on her plate.

Lucy looked at her thoughtfully. Sierra was

boisterous, cheerful and bold. Vulnerable yes, but she hid it well.

Usually Lucy ignored calls during dinner. Although she carried a cell phone, she didn't believe everyone should be available 24/7 to any demands. But if there was a chance the caller was Captain Brenner...

"Excuse me," she said, and went to the kitchen. She caught the phone on the fifth ring, before it went to voice mail. "Hello?"

There was a momentary silence. "Ms. Malone?"

Oh, Lord. It was him.

"Yes?" she said cautiously.

"This is Jonathan Brenner. I called to speak to Sierra."

Lucy kept her back to the dining room and her voice low. "I hope you intend to be kind."

After another pause, he said, "You weren't predisposed to like me, were you?"

She hesitated, a little embarrassed to have been so obvious. "That's not it," she said finally. "I'm sorry if I've given that impression. I actually, um, felt a little bit sorry for you, blindsided that way."

"Then why the hostility?"

Because my father was a sperm donor of

a different kind. A one-night stand. But she wasn't going to say that.

She felt herself making an apologetic face, which, of course, he couldn't see. "I'm scared for Sierra. I suppose I was…"

When she didn't finish, he did it for her. "Striking preemptively?"

Chagrined, Lucy admitted, "Something like that."

He sighed. "I hurt her feelings. I lay there in bed last night thinking about the expression on her face. When you were in my office, I was too stunned to be as sensitive to her feelings as maybe I should have been. Part of me was thinking it all might be nonsense, or even a con. Maybe I wanted to think that. I don't know. But…" He was the one who didn't finish this time.

"She looks like you."

"Yeah. Enough that…it's possible. I looked at the DNA results, and she's definitely a close relation to my mother."

"Does your mother have siblings?"

"Three. Two of them have sons somewhere in the right age range. And there are probably second cousins. I don't know."

"So Sierra jumped to conclusions," Lucy said slowly.

This silence shimmered with tension. His

voice was tight when he said, "But seventeen years ago I gave sperm. What are the odds that any of my male cousins did?"

Startled at the admission, Lucy only murmured, "Oh."

"May I speak to Sierra, Ms. Malone?"

"Lucy," she heard herself say. "You can call me Lucy."

"Not Lucia?"

"No." She'd never gone by Lucia, although it was her legal name. Her mother told her it was a tribute to her Hispanic heritage. She didn't want anything to do with the father who didn't want her. Lucy wasn't sure why she'd said Lucia and not Lucy when she first met him.

"I go by Jon," he said, sounding…gentle, as he hadn't been earlier. Less wary, anyway.

She took a breath, on the verge of asking what he was going to say to her foster daughter, but instead said, "I'll get Sierra."

"Thank you."

She took the phone with her to the dining room. She mouthed, "It's him," and handed it to Sierra, who had a deer-in-the-headlights look. In a normal voice Lucy said, "If you want to take the phone to your room, that's okay."

Sierra sat frozen. The hand gripping the

receiver was white-knuckled. After a moment she gulped. "No, that's okay. I—I don't mind you listening." She visibly girded herself, then put the phone to her ear and said, "Hello?"

She listened. Lucy could hear the low rumble of his voice, but not his words. Surely, surely he wasn't brushing Sierra off, not after admitting to her that he might be Sierra's father. Not after the way his voice had softened.

She ate a few bites, chewed and swallowed, and she might as well have been putting foam packing peanuts into her mouth. Expressions washed over Sierra's young face with such rapidity, Lucy couldn't pin any one down.

"I— Yes." She nodded. "Uh-huh." Listened some more. "No, Mom never said." Pause. "Okay. I—" More rumbles from Jon. At last Sierra said shakily, "Thank you. Okay. Um, bye."

She dropped the phone, which clunked on the tabletop. Tears welled in her big blue eyes. "That was him!"

Smiling, Lucy said, "I know."

"He…he… Oh, Lucy!" Her mouth trembled.

Oh, Lord. He hadn't rejected Sierra after all, had he? Lucy jumped up and circled the table to hug the teenager. "What did he say, sweetie?"

Sierra buried her face against Lucy's shoulder and hugged her fiercely. "That he's going to call the clinic," she mumbled. "He thinks that, with both of us giving permission, they'll tell me who my father is. At least, they will if it's him."

Lucy laid her cheek against Sierra's bright hair and closed her eyes in relief. Mostly relief. She was surprised to discover some other emotion tunneling beneath. It felt furtive, as if she should be ashamed of herself. In astonishment, she wondered if she could be jealous.

"Oh, Lucy," Sierra whispered. "I'm so happy. He was really nice."

The position was awkward, but Lucy held her tight as she sobbed. *Maybe,* she thought, *I am a little jealous, but mostly I'm glad.* If Sierra really had found her father, if he accepted her—no, *wanted* her—that was the best thing in the world for a girl who eight months ago had been left with no one at all.

JON HALF EXPECTED TO GET the runaround when he got in touch with the sperm bank. Probably he should have started with the fertility clinic Sierra's mom had gone to, but Sierra didn't know what one it was. Why would she? So the next morning he looked up the phone number of the sperm bank on his BlackBerry and called from his car, where he could be sure no one would hear.

He explained his mission to three different people; he wasn't surprised when the first two hastily passed the buck. All three expressed shock and dismay, which he fully understood. If they couldn't guarantee anonymity to donors, how many men would be willing to give? Jon had no trouble imagining what his own reaction would have been if he had a wife to whom he'd have to explain the teenage daughter who'd shown up unexpectedly on his doorstep. Yeah, this wasn't the 1950s. Times had changed. He still doubted that most women would be thrilled to find out their husband might have God knows how many children out there who could come a-knocking.

The final person he spoke to, a woman, conceded that they did indeed keep such records. The circumstances were unusual…. Unprecedented was what she meant. The mother was deceased? They would require proof of her death, as well as his and the child's identification before releasing the requested information. However, assuming he *was* the father, she didn't see why they couldn't then give confirmation.

Lucy answered that evening when he called. Sierra was at a friend's, apparently. Jon tersely explained what Sierra would need to produce.

"Doesn't a doctor or the medical examiner or somebody have to sign a certificate of death?" she asked.

"Yes. Sierra wouldn't necessarily have that, but we could get it. I suspect a newspaper article would do as well, though."

"She has clippings." Lucy was quiet for a moment. He pictured her face with its soft, round chin and a mouth that had struck him as feminine rather than sultry. For some reason, he imagined her biting her lower lip. "She put them in her photo album after the last picture she has of her and her mother together."

Well, damn. He didn't like to think of the girl sitting alone in her bedroom—in a foster home, no less—flipping through that album. He wondered if she did often. Every night? Gazing at her mother's face, desperate to be sure she never forgot it. Turning the last, stiff page to the black-and-white newspaper clippings. Had the paper printed a picture of Sierra's mother?

"How did she die?" he asked.

"Drunk driver. Middle of the afternoon, not even nighttime. He pulled out to pass someone who was daring to go the speed limit and hit Sierra's mom's car head-on."

"Hell."

"He wasn't even badly hurt." Outrage was evident in her voice.

"Too often, drunk drivers aren't." He hesitated. "What was her name?"

"Rebecca Lind. She went by Becky."

Jon vaguely recalled the accident. County deputies had responded and arrested the other driver. He was engulfed again by the stunning feeling of unreality. What if he'd known at the time that Becky Lind might be the mother of his child? A woman he'd never met. He shook his head. He'd made...what? Two hundred bucks over the course of his several donations? A pittance. Not worth it.

But then, Sierra wouldn't exist if he hadn't. Or she wouldn't be Sierra—she'd be someone else, with a different father. And he suspected she was a remarkable girl. So maybe it wasn't so bad, what he'd done. He felt weirdly...protective. As if he hadn't liked the notion that *he* could have been responsible for her failing to be born. Jon heard himself make a sound that might have been a laugh, but came closer to the sharp exhalation of air a man made after a fist to the gut.

"Sierra has a birth certificate?" he said finally.

"Yes, of course. She had to produce it to get a driver's permit."

"She's driving?" He didn't know why that shocked him.

"With me. She didn't get into driver's ed last semester, so she's taking it this fall. That's the only reason she doesn't have a license."

"How's she doing behind the wheel?"

Lucy's chuckle tripped down his backbone like dancing fingers. It was closer to a giggle—young, yet just husky enough to remind him she was a woman. "Not well. She scares me to death. She's, um, not as co-ordinated as she could be. She always looks down when she moves her foot to the brake or the gas. I can't seem to break her of it."

He grinned, even though he was wincing, too. "You're a brave woman."

"Not brave enough to let her out on the highway yet." There was a tiny silence, and her laughter was gone. "Especially after what happened to her mom."

After a moment he said, "She's brave, too,

to be willing to drive so soon after her mom was killed behind the wheel."

"That's probably part of the reason she's so stiff driving. She wants the independence, but…"

But. He got that. Warring impulses. Sierra Lind, he thought, was indeed courageous. He was more than a little surprised to realize a part of him half hoped she was his child.

"Poor kid," he said softly.

"Yes." Stoutly Lucy said, "I can drive Sierra to Seattle tomorrow afternoon. She can show her ID and the newspaper clippings. It would be awkward if the two of you went together, especially if it turns out you're not her father."

He supposed it would, but found that he was a little disappointed. He would have liked to see both woman and girl again.

Jon frowned when it crossed his mind that Lucy might be married. But wouldn't she or Sierra have referred to the husband if there was one? There wasn't a live-in boyfriend, or she couldn't have gotten licensed as a foster parent. Did she have other foster kids, or had she known Sierra and gotten licensed specifically to take her? He wanted to ask his questions, but knew the timing wasn't right.

If Sierra was his daughter, he'd be getting to know Lucy, too. If she wasn't…

Determination firmed in him. He would find out whether Lucy was single, and if she was, he'd ask her out.

He was both thoughtful and irritatingly aroused when he said good-night and ended the call.

CHAPTER THREE

WHEN HIS CELL PHONE RANG, Jon was in the middle of a conference with two commanding officers of the SWAT team, who were requesting new-and-improved weaponry and body armor. After glancing at the screen on his phone, he said, "I need to take this," and stood, walking to the window to answer the call. "Brenner."

"This is Lucy Malone. I just wanted to let you know that Sierra and I have done our part."

"Good," he said. "Did you have to take the day off work?"

"I got someone to cover for me."

He realized he didn't know what she did for a living. If he hadn't had two men waiting right behind him, he might have asked. "All right. I'll be in touch."

Ending the call, he walked to the table. "Let me look at the budget. I don't know if I can okay your whole shopping list, but I'll do what I can. Now I'm afraid you'll have to excuse me."

Lieutenant Stevens looked faintly surprised at the abrupt dismissal, but said only "Good enough."

Stevens, Jon thought, was an ambitious man, but also fair with his officers, smart and diplomatic. He was Jon's choice to take over his own current position if he won the election. He was less sure he believed Sergeant Clem Hansen had what it took to be in charge of the team as Stevens's replacement.

Jon was still mulling over the problem ten minutes later when he drove out of the multilevel county parking garage. SWAT members had to make tough decisions. He wanted someone with a cool head and a good sense of public perception to be leading them. The men respected Hansen, but he made Jon uneasy. For one thing, he seemed to enjoy being deliberately crude in front of female officers. Stevens had called him on it, and he'd excused himself by saying they should be treated the same as the men. If they weren't tough enough, they didn't belong on the job. Plainly, he didn't think they did. There were no women on the team; the sheer physicality of the requirements had so far kept the few women who'd applied from qualifying. But if

Hansen felt contempt for women in general, it would affect his decisions as commanding officer.

Thinking about Clem Hansen led Jon into consideration of some of the other personnel shifts he had in mind. He'd passed Boeing Field on I-5 before he let himself think about why he was taking a couple of hours in the middle of the day to drive into Seattle. His fingers flexed on the steering wheel and he realized he had a ball of tension lodged in his belly.

He was opening a can of worms here. Once he'd pried the lid off, they'd start wriggling out. Once he heard the words *Sierra Lind is your daughter,* he'd have to face the fact that the news would spread. He could ask Sierra to keep their relationship quiet for now—but if he did that she'd think he was ashamed of her.

It would help if she wasn't into that Goth look. She'd present better to voters if he could get her to take out the eyebrow and nose piercings. Her hair…well, hell. His mouth curved in a reluctant smile. At least the color was cheerful.

And the truth was, she wasn't really the problem. He was. Choices he'd made long before he had ever considered running for electoral office. Maybe that would make a good addition to high-school life-skills classes. *Always keep in mind that your behavior now may disqualify you in future from public office. Do you want to close that door?*

His campaign manager wasn't going to be happy when he told her. Edie Cook wouldn't appreciate being kept in the dark this long.

Tough. There was always the chance he'd learn today that, in fact, he was *not* Sierra Lind's biological father. He'd be off the hook. He wouldn't have to confess the sins of the past to anyone.

Jon drew a ragged breath that did nothing to ease his tension. He parked outside the modern building not far from the University of Washington campus and got out, locked and went in without letting himself dawdle.

The woman he'd spoken to on the phone was willing to see him immediately. Afraid he'd sue?

Miranda Foley was an attractive woman in her fifties, at a guess. She was pleasant and poised as she led him into her large, elegantly furnished office. He took a seat on the other side of her desk and handed over his driver's license.

She scrutinized it for a moment, then gave

it back. "This is an unfortunate situation. Are you quite certain you want an answer? You were guaranteed anonymity, and I'm very willing to be the bad guy here."

Temptation showed its ugly face, but he didn't let himself forget his mantra. *Personal responsibility.* Sierra deserved better of her father.

"I take it Sierra is my daughter," he said quietly.

Miranda's gaze dropped to the single piece of paper that lay squared in the center of her otherwise bare desktop. "Yes."

He sat still for a moment, absorbing the news. The ball lodged in his gut didn't unknot…but neither did whatever reaction he'd braced himself for happen. It seemed he'd already achieved acceptance.

"She explained how she found you," Miranda said. "If word gets out, women's access to donor sperm could be severely curtailed. I imagine there are a great many men who would live in fear that they'll be tracked down as you've been." She hesitated. "I'm a little surprised at how calmly you're taking this."

He was momentarily amused. If only she knew what was churning inside him.

"The circumstances are somewhat unusual,"

he pointed out. "I doubt Sierra would have ever set out to find me if her mother hadn't been killed, or even if she'd had other family who cared. It was finding herself completely alone that apparently inspired her...quest."

"Yes, so I gathered." She sighed. "You do intend to acknowledge her, then?"

"Yes." He stood. "May I have a copy of that?" He nodded at the paper on her desk.

"This is for you." She handed it to him.

He thanked her and walked out. He'd gone numb again, he realized. Or something. He found himself sitting in the driver's seat of his car with no recollection of getting there, and he was a cop. He was *always* aware of his surroundings. Jon groaned and pressed the heels of his hands against his eye sockets. The pressure grounded him. He heard himself breathing hard. Maybe he wasn't numb after all.

I'm a dad. Break out the cigars.

She'd be waiting to hear from him. She and Lucy. He hadn't told them he was coming up to Seattle right away. He didn't have to call this minute. He could wait until evening. Tomorrow, even.

But that would be cruel.

After a long sigh, Jon took out his cell

phone. He went to Received Calls, found Lucy's number and hit Send.

It rang only once. "Captain Brenner?" she said warily. So she'd either memorized his number or entered it in her phone.

"Yes," he said. "Is Sierra with you?"

"Right here." There was a murmur of voices. Then a different one, young and full of nerves, said, "This is Sierra."

"They confirmed to me that I'm your biological father," he said bluntly.

"Oh!" This was almost a squeal, followed by a more subdued "Oh," probably after she'd taken in how stilted he sounded.

"I'd like to sit down with you this evening, if you're free." It was the first evening in nearly a week that he had been.

"Um, sure. Do you want to come to my… to Lucy's house?"

He felt a pang that she couldn't confidently claim ownership of her home. Kids needed to feel safe. Rooted.

"Yeah," he said. "Can I talk to her for a minute?"

She came on, gave him her address, which he scribbled on the notepad he kept in his breast pocket, and they agreed on seven o'clock. All very matter-of-fact. He ended the call, but made no move to start his car.

Instead, he kept staring blindly through the windshield at other parked cars and at the passing traffic on the cross street.

What was he going to say to his daughter tonight?

LUCY TRIED TO LEAVE THEM in privacy. She was eaten up with curiosity, of course, about what Jon was thinking, but he and Sierra were entitled to share things that would remain private.

But Sierra gripped her hand when Lucy tried to excuse herself shortly after letting him in the front door. "I—I'd like you to stay." Her gaze darted to Jon. "If that's okay."

His eyes met Lucy's. She told herself she was startled because she was used to seeing eyes that color in her foster daughter's face, not in a man's. But she knew better. It wasn't just the stunningly clear, pale blue, it was what she saw in them. His eyes betrayed a rueful acknowledgment of his bemusement at being in this position. And—she thought— some attraction to her.

"It's fine," he said. "Lucy will be involved with any plans we make."

Her knees weakened and she sank onto the sofa beside Sierra, still holding her hand. *Plans.* Oh, thank goodness. He wasn't going to try to weasel out of any relationship with Sierra.

Lucy had already offered coffee or tea. He'd pleasantly declined. She had shown him into the tiny living room of her tiny house. He was simply too big for this room, she couldn't help thinking. He chose the easy chair that was sized for him, but his knees bumped the coffee table. On the other side of it, she and Sierra were ridiculously close to him. Much closer than they'd been in his office. She could see every weary line on his face. His eyebrows and lashes were considerably darker than Sierra's, making the clear blue of his eyes all the more surprising. There was the faintest hint of a cleft in his chin, and the shadow of a beard on his hard jaw and cheeks. His fingers drummed a staccato beat on the upholstered arm of the chair, but otherwise his composure was absolute.

"Sierra," he said, "maybe you'd better tell me what you're hoping for from me."

A flush rose from the collar of the girl's black T-shirt, blotchy by the time it reached her cheeks. Her fingers tightened on Lucy's. "I don't know." Lucy could feel her struggle for dignity. "I guess… I thought…maybe you wouldn't mind having a daughter. Not…

not to live with you or anything, but, I don't know—"

"To pay your college tuition?" he said mildly.

Despite the vivid color in her face, she swiftly lifted her chin and met his eyes. "I never expected money from you. I just wanted..." Her mouth worked. Her voice had gone so soft, he leaned forward, as if afraid he'd miss the rest of what she had to say. "Family," she finally whispered.

His eyes closed for a moment. Some powerful emotion crossed his face. Lucy couldn't be sure what it was. Finally he took a deep breath and looked at Sierra. "You have that now." His voice was kind. He was even smiling faintly. "Not just me. You'll meet your grandmother and an aunt and uncle and two first cousins, too."

She stared. "Have you...*told* them about me?"

"Not yet, but I will. I feel confident they'll welcome you, Sierra."

The wonder on her face scared Lucy. It couldn't possibly be this easy. She hated watching Sierra's hopes rise like shimmering soap bubbles, all too fragile and certain to pop. Lucy didn't believe that he was prepared to joyously embrace a teenage daughter's arrival in his life. There had to be a catch. Probably a whole bunch of them, little traps she imagined closing, *snap, snap, snap*, until Sierra was dancing fearfully to miss them.

Her own voice was harsh when she said, "Do you intend to tell anyone else about Sierra?"

His dark eyebrows rose. "Do you mean, do I plan to go to the *Dispatch* or KOMO TV?"

His sardonic tone was probably meant to embarrass her. In her defense of Sierra, Lucy didn't let it. "I'm asking if you'd rather her existence stay private."

"Secrets are hard to keep, and this doesn't have to be one." The gaze that met hers now was hard. "Would I rather the press not catch wind of her right away? Yeah. I want my campaign to focus on my ability to do the job, not on the surprising appearance of a daughter I didn't know I had. Is that unreasonable?"

Of course it wasn't. She wasn't entirely willing to back down, though. "I'm asking whether Sierra can tell her friends about you, or if you want her to keep quiet for now."

He noticeably hesitated for a moment. Sierra couldn't miss that any more than Lucy did. Then he grimaced. "She can tell her friends." He sighed and met Sierra's gaze again. "I won't pretend I'm not concerned about the impact on the election. My opponent will probably try to make something of this if he learns about you. But we're not going to sneak around, Sierra. You're indisputably my daughter. I want to get to know you."

She gave a tremulous smile that made her momentarily radiant. The sight seemed to transfix him. Watching their faces, Lucy felt the oddest lurch in her chest that almost—but not quite—hurt. It felt a little bit like envy.

Jon's voice was huskier than usual when he said, "Perhaps I can take you both out to dinner Friday night."

Wouldn't he be recognized? She imagined him shaking hands with people who paused at the table. The speculative glances.

"Why don't I cook instead?" she suggested. "Sierra can make dessert. She's becoming quite a baker."

If she hadn't been looking so closely, she wouldn't have seen how he relaxed. "That sounds good," he said, smiling. "In the meantime, I'll talk to my mother. We'll figure out a time for you to meet her."

"O-kay!" Sierra all but sang. "A grandmother." She let go of Lucy and hugged herself, making no effort to hide her delight.

Lucy saw him watch Sierra, then unexpectedly turn his gaze to her. His eyes flickered, the color momentarily deepening. He'd recognized her worry, she suspected. She didn't care.

"What do you do for a living?" he asked.

"I own a pet-supply store," she told him. "Barks and Purrs."

"Ah." He glanced around. "No pets of your own?"

"Two cats. They disappear whenever we have visitors. You?"

He shook his head. "I work too much. I had a dog growing up. A mutt. Moby lived to be sixteen." His mouth wasn't exactly smiling, but his eyes were. "Is there a Mr. Malone? I've had the impression not."

"No. It's just Sierra and me."

"No family?"

She didn't like how perceptive his eyes were. "Only a mother," she said. "We're...not close." She didn't talk about her mother. Ever. She didn't let herself think about how soon that would have to change. "Sierra hasn't met her." Yet. "I take it your father has passed away?"

"Massive stroke a couple of years ago."

"He couldn't have been very old."

His look became quizzical. "Worrying

about what kind of genetics Sierra carries?"

Flustered, Lucy began, "No, I—"

He grinned, the effect both wicked and astonishingly sensual considering how unrevealing and almost grim his face usually was. "It's all right. Dad's parents lived to be eighty-nine and ninety-one respectively. My father spent most of his life angry. I figure he worked himself up to the stroke." He transferred the smile to Sierra, although it was softer for her benefit. "You wouldn't have liked him. My mother is a nice lady, though."

She smiled shyly back. "How old are my cousins?"

"Younger than you. Reese is ten and Patrick twelve. You'll be the only girl."

Still shyly, she asked, "You don't have any other kids?"

His mouth quirked, and Lucy knew what he was thinking. He almost certainly did have other kids, ones he'd never know. She wondered if he felt regret now.

"I've never been married," he said. "I was engaged years ago, but she was killed. It hasn't happened since, despite my mother's nagging."

Killed. That made Lucy wonder, but she didn't ask. They didn't have that kind of relationship.

He made I-need-to-be-leaving noises, and Lucy stayed where she was so that Sierra could walk him out. They talked for a few more minutes on the porch, his quiet bass in counterpoint to Sierra's soprano bursts. She heard the sound of his car starting, the slam of the screen door and then Sierra burst into the house.

"Lucy! Isn't he *amazing?*" She went *sur la pointe* and spun. She was astonishingly graceful, although she'd given up dance lessons at age twelve when she grew so tall. "He wants to be my dad! I can't believe it. Oh, Lucy." Eyes drenched with tears, she flung herself onto the couch and into Lucy's arms, where she wept quietly and happily against her shoulder.

Lucy said the right things, and she wanted to believe in Captain Jonathan Brenner, that he was as decent and kind as he seemed, but she knew that people rarely were. She loved Sierra too much to lower her guard.

What scared her most was knowing how little she could do to protect her foster daughter's too-vulnerable heart.

EDIE COOK WAS NOT PLEASED. She paced the confines of his campaign office after staff and volunteers had gone home, her indignation making her steps choppy.

"We couldn't have discussed this *before* you walked out on a limb?"

"No." He half sat on a desk, his legs stretched out and his arms crossed. "This is personal. I had to do what was right. To hell with politics."

She glowered at him. Edie was small and stocky, her graying hair cut severely short. She had the energy of a hyperactive kindergartner. She could be running campaigns of far more significance than his, but she had a daughter with multiple sclerosis, and she needed to stay close. He knew he was lucky to have her. Even so, he wasn't going to let her shape him with her nudges and prods the way she'd like to. He wasn't clay that could be molded into a pretty face. He was a cop. A man on a crusade begun to avenge Cassia.

Jon was honest about his own motivations. Along the way, it had all become more complex, but he'd gone into law enforcement out of anger. He had fallen in love with Cassia Winterbourne the minute he met her during his first year of grad school. They had been engaged and living together six months later when one night she closed the coffee shop where she worked part-time as barista, started for the bus stop and never made it. She was raped and murdered by a man released from prison the day before.

Rage and grief had consumed Jon, to the point where he'd scared himself. He'd almost dropped out of college. He'd taken incompletes on several courses and had to finish the work later, after the rage froze into a solid chunk of ice that lodged in his chest where his heart had once beaten. He had vowed never to let himself feel so intensely again. He'd never come close to falling in love since.

And when his mother came to Cassia's funeral but his father, who'd never liked her, didn't, Jon had severed the last bitter ties with him. He never spoke to his father again, and went to his funeral for his mother's sake, not his.

Edie knew about the estrangement, in case it became an issue in the campaign. She knew about Cassia, too. She'd wanted him to use the tragedy as the lodestar of his campaign. He'd refused. His heart beat again, and the ice had receded, but the rage remained. He could tap into it too easily. That didn't mean he would use the horror of her death or his feelings for her as something cheap to sway voters.

"I'd rather keep Sierra out of the public eye," he said, his head turning as Edie stomped by.

She snorted. "Fat chance."

"If we don't make any announcement, how will Rinnert find out about her?"

"It wouldn't surprise me if he already knows. Hell, he's probably got a P.I. trailing you."

His jaw firmed. "That's ridiculous."

"Don't kid yourself. He's behind in the polls. But really, he doesn't have to go to those lengths. Are you telling me no one saw you walk into the sperm bank? Wait in the lobby? Your race is a hot one. Your face is on the local news often enough—you're all too recognizable."

"You *want* my face to be recognizable," he said sardonically.

"That was before you did something stupid like visit a sperm bank."

"Most people would assume I had questions relating to an investigation."

She stalked by again. He felt like a spectator at a tennis match, his head swiveling.

"You don't do investigations. You supervise other people who do them."

That was true, but he doubted that the common voter realized he was pretty well trapped behind a desk these days. When he pointed that out, Edie snorted again.

She eventually wound down, conceded they might get lucky and no, it probably wasn't the end of the world if Sierra's existence became public knowledge.

"Will she be living with you?"

He hesitated. "I don't know. Not right away. We need to get to know each other."

"You found your daughter, and have left her living in a foster home? That may not play well."

"You know how seldom I'm actually home these days." He hadn't realized how tired he was until he said that. But he was. The exhaustion wasn't physical, but it was real, and went bone deep. "I can't be an adequate single parent right now, even if that was the right thing to do for other reasons."

Edie, grudgingly, supposed he was right. She made noises about Sierra going to live with his mother or sister. He still hadn't told either that he had a daughter. Even if they'd been eager and willing to have Sierra with them, he wouldn't insult Lucy that way. Remembering their clasped hands, he knew it wouldn't be right anyway to separate them.

He and Edie made the decision to keep quiet about Sierra for now, but Jon warned her that he'd answer questions honestly if they came to be asked.

"This woman she's living with? Is she an asset or a detriment?"

In a flash that startled him with its vividness, he saw Lucy Malone sitting on that couch watching him with the spark of suspicion in her chocolate-brown eyes. He saw the lush curves of her petite body, her pretty face, the thick, glossy, wavy black hair that to his disappointment she'd worn in a fat braid last night. And he hated himself for, however briefly, actually giving some consideration to Edie's question.

"Asset," he said finally, shortly.

Edie gave him a startled glance, opened her mouth as if to say more, then visibly thought better of it. "All right," she said. "Keep me informed."

She left, but he lingered in the deserted campaign headquarters. Usually he focused on his goal—becoming sheriff. Finally being in a position to make the decisions that counted. But he was unsettled tonight, and he found himself looking around at the half-dozen desks where volunteers would sit making phone calls on his behalf, at the stacks of campaign posters and the placards stacked in corners waiting for supporters to jam them into their lawns or beside well-trafficked roads. Jonathan Brenner for Sheriff. Hard Decisions Made with Integrity.

That was him, so defined by integrity that he could weigh a woman's worth only as it related to him. How would it look that he was spending time with her?

A phone rang at one of the desks, the sound shrill in the otherwise quiet storefront.

Jon muttered a profanity, scrubbed a hand over his face and let himself out, locking the door behind him. He wasn't often ashamed of himself, but there were moments, and this was one.

CHAPTER FOUR

"I'M TOTALLY INTO COMPUTERS," Sierra told her father. "But I don't know if I want to work in software or anything. I might decide to be a doctor. Or maybe a veterinarian." Her expression became eager. "Did Lucy tell you she helps finds homes for cats that end up in shelters? I've been spending lots of time with the ones she has at the store right now. And with Rosemary and Magnolia, too. Those are Lucy's cats."

There was a smile in Jon's eyes when he looked at Lucy over the dinner table. "I noticed you're a gardener. I gather that's where your inspiration came from."

"Yes," she said ruefully. "Only, the cats are really Rosie and Maggie. Every animal I've ever had ends up with a name that ends in an *ie* sound."

Jon thought about it. He'd grown up with Moby. His mother had a fluffy, yappy little excuse for a dog whose name was Renoir, but who had come to be called, of all things,

Really. It was a joke at first—yes, he's really Renoir—but it stuck. Jon grinned every time he heard his mother stick her head out in the backyard and shout, "Really! Come to Mommy!"

"Maybe there's something to that," he had to admit.

"We convert children's names that way, too. Jimmy, Stevie, Katie, Susie."

"Becky," Sierra said softly.

Her flash of sadness came and went so quickly, he'd have missed it if he hadn't been looking.

Lucy smiled at her. "I like to think that softened ending is affectionate. Think how often it sticks. It did for me." She reached for her wineglass.

"Were you ever Johnny?" Sierra asked him.

Lucy sputtered and had to slap a napkin to her mouth.

Jon pretended to glower. "You're laughing at me."

"No…yes. Oh, heavens. You just don't look like a Johnny."

He loved the way merriment danced in her eyes and puckered her cheeks. It sure beat the chilly stare of suspicion she also did well.

"No, I was never a Johnny. I think you have

to be cuddly to deserve having your name softened. Me, I was born long and skinny, and only got longer and skinnier."

"Me, too!" Sierra exclaimed, her face bright. She wrinkled her nose, looking down at herself. "I think I've quit growing." Her tone said she wasn't betting on it.

Lucy smiled at her. "You probably have. Girls usually reach their full height long before your age. It's boys who still keep growing into their twenties."

"Oh, yeah." Jon began constructing another taco from the selection of ingredients laid out in the middle of the table. He chose the shredded chicken and heaped on the salsa Lucy made herself. It seared the mouth and opened the sinuses. He'd seen the challenge on her face when she first offered it to him. He had been damn careful not to react when he took his first bite. On his third taco now, he'd developed a taste for it. "I added another couple of inches in college. Mostly I got broader, though. I was a rack of bones until then." He smiled at Sierra. "Remind me to show you some pictures. Forget it," he said ruefully. "You won't have to remind me. Mom will whip out the family albums the minute you walk in the door."

"She really wants to meet me?" Her voice was wistful.

"She really wants to."

His mother had reacted exactly as he'd predicted. She was stunned to think she had grandchildren she would never meet. He thought she would have been angrier yet if she hadn't known why he had scrabbled to raise money any way he could back in those days. She felt guilty that she hadn't been able to persuade his father to treat him more decently. Jon didn't like knowing that his mom lived with more regrets than he had. In this case, though, guilt served a purpose; she'd forgiven him faster than he deserved.

"She expects me to bring you to Sunday dinner, if you're free." He transferred his gaze to Lucy. "She'd like to meet you, too."

"My feelings won't be hurt if you only take Sierra," she said. "I'm not family."

She was so composed, he was willing to bet it was a facade. She'd wanted him to accept Sierra as his daughter, there was no question of that. But he couldn't help wondering if her feelings weren't a little hurt, too, that Sierra had set out to find her biological family. It would be one thing if Sierra had been assigned to her, a licensed foster parent.

But he'd learned that she'd taken the teenager in out of affection.

The teenager. No, he told himself, *my daughter. Get used to thinking it. My daughter.*

Aware of Sierra watching them both, he said quietly, "You're family."

Lucy stared at him for a moment that stretched. He forgot about Sierra. He lost himself in those warm brown eyes that seemed to darken with emotion, and lighten and shimmer with laughter. Right now they were the color of Belgian chocolate, rich, dark and somehow stunned. Her lips were slightly parted, as if she'd started to say something and forgotten what it was.

She blinked. "I suppose I am." Her mouth curved into a heartbreakingly sad smile, although he doubted she knew it was. Very softly, she finished, "I'm family as long as Sierra needs me."

Now he felt like a heel. Would every wish of Sierra's he fulfilled hurt Lucy? Damn, he hoped not.

"Will you come Sunday?" Sierra begged. "Please? I'd…really like it if you would, Lucy."

This smile was more natural. "If you'd be more comfortable, of course I will."

"Is the store closed on Sunday?" Jon asked.

"Sundays and Mondays," she confirmed. "Although I have to go in to take care of the cats."

He asked questions, and found out that she had two part-time employees, one of whom was Sierra. Lucy had been a licensed vet tech. She told some stories from her years working in veterinary clinics. He had the impression her last boss, at least, had been an ass. Sierra was wide-eyed not at the tales of eccentric owners or animals run amok, but at the notion the clinic hadn't been computerized.

"A wall of file folders?" she said, as if Lucy had been describing a holdover from the Edwardian age. Maybe even Jurassic. "How did you ever find *anything?*"

Lucy chuckled. "Easily. As long as it wasn't misfiled. And I might point out that a misfiled folder is still more easily recovered than a computer file with a locator name misspelled."

"That's not true!" Sierra launched into a passionate explanation of search functions. Jon and Lucy listened with amusement.

At the end of her lecture, Jon said only, "The world did run precomputer, you know. America was settled, railroads spread, manufacturing changed society, wars were conducted. Nobody knew what they were missing."

Sierra sputtered a little, but tongue in cheek.

Lucy rescued her. "Sweetie, why don't you bring out your dessert? I'll start clearing the table."

The teenager jumped up. "Okay."

"Can I help?" Jon asked, starting to rise.

"Don't be silly," Lucy said comfortably. "This isn't a three-person kitchen." She had picked up a couple of the serving bowls and almost bumped Sierra when she turned. Over her shoulder she made a face at Jon. "It's not even a two-person kitchen."

No, it wasn't. The snug eating area was tucked in what he suspected had once been a glassed-in porch. One more could have sat at the table, but wouldn't have been able to get in or out once everyone was seated. Like the rest of the house, though, the room was charming, the windows that wrapped it small-paned and looking out at roses and tall, daisy-like flowers in deep blues and purples that he thought might be asters. Walls were painted a buttery-yellow, woodwork snowy-white, the floor tiled. A small watercolor painting of tulip fields hung on the one stretch of wall not filled with windows.

Jon examined his feelings of contentment as he watched woman and girl work in the kitchen in a seemingly practiced dance of steps that kept them from colliding. Sierra was more graceful than he'd thought at first; she made him think of a blue heron, with those long limbs and initial awkwardness overcome when full flight was achieved. And Lucy... His gaze tracked her, small and pleasantly rounded, her waist tiny and the glossy black braid swaying seductively as she moved, emphasizing the supple line of her back and the equally seductive sway of her hips in neat chinos.

Lucy Malone wasn't a beautiful woman, exactly. Jon couldn't even have said why she attracted him so powerfully, but she did. She was really too short for him, he mused; he'd have to bend over to kiss her. He contemplated the kitchen counter. No, he wouldn't stoop, he'd set her butt up on the counter and stand between her thighs. That would work. And lying down, height didn't matter much, did it?

Oh, hell. He was getting aroused thinking about it. Wondering how firm or soft her generous breasts were, whether her skin, a pale cocoa, was ivory colored where the sun didn't touch it. Would she have small, pert nipples, or ones with broad aureoles as generous and womanly as her breasts themselves?

He almost groaned aloud. This was—what?—his third meeting with her and in his mind he already had her in bed with him. Although he wanted to think she was attracted to him, too, he doubted she was anywhere near as far along in her thinking about him. She was still too suspicious of him, for one thing.

As well she should be. He had no idea whether he could meet this unexpected daughter's needs. Whether he really wanted to. He'd accepted responsibility, acknowledged that she was his, but that might not be enough, whatever Sierra insisted to the contrary. She wanted what she'd lost: a parent who loved her, completely and absolutely. He'd never felt that way about anyone.

He refused to feel guilty yet. He had to get to know her first. As smart as she was, she probably had a personality more complex even than the average teenager. He saw the sweetness, the quick leaps her mind took, the eagerness and yearning. But he knew there had to be considerably more. How did she feel growing up without a father in a world where most kids had one, even if they saw him only every other weekend? Had her mother been enough? Were they closer than usual, given the need teenagers had to push away from their parents? How much did she still grieve privately? Did she have crushes on boys? Have one especially good friend? Feel rage or self-loathing that she hid for fear she'd be rejected by Lucy or her newfound father?

Thinking about Sierra had given his body time to relax. He was able to smile naturally at Lucy, who brought dessert plates, and Sierra, who produced a cheesecake.

"I hope you like it," she said anxiously. "I was going to bake a pie. Lucy has an apple tree in the backyard. But I've been experimenting with cheesecake, so I thought I'd make that."

"I love cheesecake," he told her. "I'm afraid I have a sweet tooth."

Her face lit in that way she had. "Me, too. I must have gotten it from you. Mom didn't care about desserts at all. Mostly we had store-bought cookies. Like Oreos and Fig Newtons. But it was fun when we made, like, Christmas cookies, so I started baking when Mom would let me. I don't like regular cooking that much. Mom said I was her pastry chef."

Sierra cut the cheesecake, which she said was layered with tiramisu. Jon took the first bite figuring it would be good—this was a kid bright enough, after all, to manufacture a nuclear bomb if she put her mind to it—but he hadn't anticipated pure nirvana. He actually closed his eyes to savor the pure, melting flavor on his tongue. After he swallowed, he said with complete honesty, "I think that tastes better than anything I've ever put in my mouth."

Sierra grinned in delight. "It is good, isn't it?"

"Heavenly," Lucy murmured around her first bite.

Jon's body stirred again at the sight of her face. He'd have sworn color had risen in her cheeks, and her eyes had closed as his had. Her mouth was moist, and as he watched the pink tip of her tongue flicked out to sweep over her lips. Damn, he thought. Would she look like that when he touched her? When he suckled her breast?

He wrenched his gaze from her and took another bite, good enough to be distracting. After a minute he said to Sierra, "Tell me about your mom. What did she do for a living?"

"She was a bank manager. She'd just gotten promoted to having her own branch not that long ago. She was good with math and computers, like me."

She was silent for a moment, seemingly having forgotten her own serving of cheesecake. She'd withdrawn somewhere inside, and he could tell she was no longer really seeing him or Lucy. He hoped asking her to talk about her mother hadn't been a mistake.

"I think sometimes Mom felt bad that I'd had to go to day care and after-school care and all that. I mean, that she couldn't ever be stay-at-home. You know?" Her eyes briefly focused on him, and he nodded. "But the thing is, she wouldn't have been any good at that. She wasn't into stuff like sewing or crafts or really even cooking. She hated mowing the lawn and we didn't have flowers like Lucy does."

Jon was conscious that Lucy, too, had stopped eating and was watching her foster daughter. He wondered if, like him, she'd tensed at the unconscious comparison between her and Sierra's mother. He wondered, too, where Sierra was going with it.

"I guess, like, when I was really little I

wished Mom was more like some of my friends' mothers. You know? But later I was glad she wasn't. Because she didn't just *have* to work. She liked her job. That made me want to do something I'm as happy doing. Some girls I know want to have babies, or get married, or take some classes at the community college. But you can tell they think jobs are just something you do to make money. Mom was different. She talked to me about anything." She shrugged finally, and looked at the two adults. "I love Lucy's garden, and the cats, but now I know that everyone has different things that make them happy."

To Lucy she said, "I see how you like to touch. I mean, you run your fingers over the cats, or smooth my hair, or stroke that antique bookcase you bought, or the petals of a flower. Mom lived more in her head. She wasn't so…" Her face reflected her struggle to find the right word.

"Tactile?" Lucy suggested gently. "There have been studies, you know, about different ways of learning. Some people learn best by touching, some by reading, some by hearing information."

Sierra nodded vigorously. "Yeah. Tactile." Jon could tell she was sampling the word.

"Mom and I weren't that huggy, but I knew she loved me."

As if she couldn't help herself, Lucy reached across the table and squeezed Sierra's hand. "I know she did. I could see it when you were together."

Jon looked at their hands, briefly flexing and then separating, and realized he'd noticed Lucy's need to touch. He thought perhaps it had been good for Sierra, even if it wasn't what she was used to. He wouldn't mind if Lucy would reach for his hand, too. He knew how small it would feel in his, but suspected her hands were strong. She'd spent years containing frightened, struggling animals that were in pain; she worked hard in her garden and her business. This house was relaxed but spotlessly clean. Lucy was a hard worker, he could tell. Somehow very feminine in a way he suspected Sierra's mother hadn't been, and yet Lucy was strong, too.

Tactile was sexy. He'd never been with a woman who could convey so much with a simple touch.

Sierra. You're here for her, not Lucy.

"I'd like to see a picture of your mother," Jon said.

"Sure." Sierra leaped up, abandoning her dessert again, and dashed from the room.

He laughed low in his throat. "I didn't mean right this second."

Lucy laughed, too, shaking her head. "For all that she does like her sweets, Sierra isn't a very big eater." She grimaced. "Not much makes me push away from the table."

"You don't need to," he heard himself say roughly.

Her eyes widened. "What?"

Suddenly embarrassed, he said, "I thought you were implying that you eat too much. You don't."

Lucy sighed. "I am trying to lose weight. Even five or ten pounds really show when you're my height."

"You look…just right to me."

"Well…" Now her cheeks were definitely pink. "Thank you."

"You're welcome." He cursed himself. There had to be a better response than that, considering he wanted to make her see him as a man, not just Sierra's father, not just as a threat. *That's right, be formal, distancing. Way to get the girl.* He didn't have a chance to say that *skinny women weren't sexy.* Sierra had returned, holding a framed photo.

Just as well.

His daughter thrust the photo at him, then plopped into her seat with that somehow ungainly grace that made him think of the way the giraffes at Woodland Park Zoo moved.

He accepted it in the spirit it was offered and sat for a minute gazing at the face of the woman whose genes had blended with his to create a child. It unsettled him, looking at her, grappling to understand how they'd made a baby together without ever meeting.

The picture had been taken of her and Sierra together. They might not be "huggy," but their arms were about each other and they were laughing when the camera had captured them. It looked as if they were in a park, Becky Lind wearing shorts and a mint-green camp shirt, Sierra jeans and T. She was younger. Twelve? Thirteen? He wasn't any judge, but could see that she was skinnier and lacked the slight curve of hips and breast that she'd since acquired. Her hair was not just blond, but the pale, somehow childish shade that most people grew out of. Moonlight. Jon felt a peculiar squeezing sensation in his chest as his eyes moved from Sierra's face, happy in an uncomplicated way she'd lost, to that of her mother, a plain woman with ordinary brown hair, eyes that were… hazel or gray, he thought, behind glasses that sat a little crookedly. She had a neat figure.

She wasn't a homely woman, but he knew that he'd never have been attracted to her and that made him feel bad. Shallow.

He wished suddenly, passionately, that she hadn't died. Not for his sake, but for Sierra's. Some drunken son of a bitch had stolen Sierra's mother from her, and that made Jon angry. He found himself gazing into Becky Lind's eyes and wishing she could see that he was there. That Sierra had found him. That Lucy had taken her in. He hoped her last thought hadn't been despair for her daughter, left parentless.

"I can see you in her," he said finally, feeling oddly reluctant as he handed the framed photo to Sierra. "Your mouth, and something in the way you hold yourself."

He saw the pleasure in her face. "People said we looked alike. Except I was way taller than Mom."

"You're way taller than me, too," Lucy pointed out.

She rolled her eyes. "I've always been way taller than practically *all* the girls. And most of the boys, too, in grade school. And even middle school. I was always in the back row when pictures were taken."

"Me, too," Jon said. "It's not hard to spot me in class photos even if I was in the back."

"Mom knew you were tall when she, um, picked you. She liked the idea."

Had she? Would Becky have found *him* physically attractive? Jon found himself wondering. It was another weird thought.

"I'm glad she picked me." His voice had come out gravelly from that same odd sensation in his chest. This girl was making him feel unfamiliar emotions. Which maybe answered his earlier questions to himself. He might be coming to it late, but he was beginning to suspect that loving Sierra Lind might not be hard.

Sierra blushed and ducked her head. Lucy, he saw out of his peripheral vision, was watching him with slightly narrowed eyes as if she was trying to judge his sincerity.

Did her lack of trust have its roots in her deeply protective instincts toward Sierra? Or was it something about him? Maybe she didn't like cops, or the fact that he was running for office, or was damn near a foot taller than she was. She obviously didn't like the fact that he'd given sperm seventeen years ago.

And maybe she was suspicious only because he was a man.

Finding out would be interesting. Convincing her to trust him, a challenge.

Jon let his eyes meet hers and he smiled. They stared at each other for a sizzling moment, Lucy bristling with suspicion and perplexity and he didn't know what else. Sierra remained oblivious.

Jon let his smile broaden. "So on Sunday, to meet my mother, I'll pick you two up at eleven, if that works."

Lucy didn't even blink. "We'll be counting on you." The warning was unmistakable.

Jon took it to heart. If he was to have any chance with Lucy, he couldn't screw up.

"Understood," he murmured, and she gave a sharp nod as if satisfied.

JON BRENNER HAD GROWN UP with money. They weren't rich, but his mother's home was a handsome, two-story house with a view of Lake Washington in a neighborhood of dignified homes that weren't ostentatious but were well cared for. The clapboard was painted white, the trim and shutters black, the front door fire-engine red, which Lucy especially liked. The color was like a saucy wink from an otherwise gracious, elegantly dressed lady. The yard was large, with smooth lawn and old trees, including a couple of big maples with leaves beginning to turn color. And flower beds, curved swaths out of the lawn. Lucy thought she might like Mrs. Brenner.

He'd parked in the driveway beside a blue Volvo station wagon.

"My sister's here," he commented.

Sierra didn't say anything. She was staring wide-eyed at the house. She'd been quiet the entire drive. Lucy didn't blame her for being terrified. Having a lifelong wish fulfilled would scare anyone. And she had to be wondering if this new family would like her, or would stare and wonder whether the stork had brought the wrong child.

Jon got out and turned, waiting for them to join him. Lucy said quietly, "Shall we?"

Sierra gulped. "Oh, wow."

"Aren't the flower beds beautiful? Your grandmother must be a gardener."

Through the windshield, Lucy saw Jon look surprised.

"Come on, honey."

Sierra took a deep breath. "Okay." She still didn't move.

Lucy laughed and got out. After closing her door, she opened Sierra's. "Chin up."

"Right." She did get out, moving stiffly. Her eyes were huge. She walked up the driveway beside Lucy.

Jon reached out and squeezed her shoulder. "You okay?"

"Sure."

The front door swung open before they reached it. The woman who appeared was medium height, slender and with blue eyes. No, Lucy saw as they got closer, her eyes weren't merely blue, they were that pale, crystal shade of her son's, and of Sierra's. Jon's height and breadth might have come from his father, but he'd gotten his coloring from his mother. Mrs. Brenner was groomed in the way of someone who'd never lacked money— her hair was short and chic, her slacks and silk blouse simple but expensive.

Her gaze had found Sierra immediately. "Oh," she said. Then another, long-drawn-out "*Ohh.*"

Sierra had stopped in her tracks. She wrapped her arms around herself protectively, her elbows sticking out. Lucy had thought she looked pretty this morning, wearing a filmy blue shirt over a darker blue T along with a flowery skirt. In a fierce surge of protectiveness, Lucy decided she was going to hate all the Brenners forevermore if this woman didn't say the right thing.

Whatever that was.

Mrs. Brenner suddenly had tears in her eyes. "If I'd seen you at the mall, I'd have known instantly that you were my Jon's daughter. Oh, my dear, you're lovely."

Of course, that was absolutely the right thing for her to say. Sierra's cheeks flushed with color and tears sparkled on her lashes. "Thank you for...for inviting me," she said. "You must have been surprised to hear about me."

"Surprised, and delighted." Definitely weeping, the older woman gave her son a quick hug and Lucy a smile, then held out her hand to Sierra. "Sierra. Such a pretty name. Come and meet your aunt Lily and your cousins. They're as excited as I was."

Jon and Lucy followed. Somehow, as she climbed the porch steps and went inside, his hand came to rest on the small of her back, as if she needed guidance. She was dismayed by how very good that large hand felt touching her.

She told herself this peculiar melting feeling was really relief for Sierra's sake, because today was going to be everything she'd dreamed about. It had nothing to do with the tall man who stayed close to her even as they entered the living room, where the rest of the family waited.

But she lied, and she knew it.

JON'S MOTHER TURNED the page of the photo album. "Oh, this is a favorite of mine."

Watching from across the family room, Jon winced. Some of his mom's favorites were more embarrassing than others, but there were a few he'd considered slipping out of the album and shredding to avoid future blackmail attempts. Knowing her, though, he figured she had the negatives neatly filed somewhere and would simply print new copies of any pilfered photos.

Sierra giggled and clapped one hand over her mouth. His mother laughed with pleasure. The two sat together on the sofa, close enough for their shoulders to touch, and the big album that held pictures of Jon from newborn to college graduation lay open across their laps. Sierra lifted her head to let him see the merriment in her eyes.

"You were skinny."

"Yeah, I was."

Beside him, Lucy laughed. "Ooh. I'm going to have to go look at this one."

He grabbed her upper arm. "Not a chance."

"Spoilsport."

"You can't tell me your mother doesn't have a few pictures of you tucked away somewhere that you'd rather never saw the light of day."

The laughter disappeared from her face—click, a light turned off.

Why?

"Maybe," she said politely, and settled beside him on the love seat.

Dismayed and somewhat intrigued, Jon released her. "I was kidding. Look if you want."

"I wouldn't want to embarrass you." She shifted so that she was facing his sister. Very politely she said, "It was nice of you to come over today, too. Sierra was nervous."

"Jon would have had to point his Glock at me to keep me away." Lily cocked an eyebrow at him. "The boys and I were really excited. To think Jon has a daughter he never knew about."

The two women chatted, while his nephews sprawled on the floor and played a Nintendo game that wasn't engrossing enough to keep them from stealing peeks at this fascinating and exotic creature he'd introduced into the family. A cousin. A teenager. A girl. Jon sat there taking it all in with a tangle of emotions he hardly understood.

A part of his mind played with what Lucy's odd reaction to his teasing remark about her mother had meant. At the same time, he kept looking from Lily to Sierra, comparing them and seeing even more clearly the familial resemblance. His sister and daughter were near the same height and build. Lily still had something of the lankiness combined with unexpected grace that characterized Sierra.

His mother and Sierra laughed and looked up at him at the same moment, giving him a jolt. How had he doubted even for a fleeting moment that Sierra was his child? She took after his mother far more than Reese or Patrick did. Having her here felt good, but... unsettling.

The good part was seeing the happiness that shone from her. The first ten or fifteen minutes, she'd been painfully shy, responding to questions but carrying herself stiffly and looking frequently for reassurance to Lucy. His mother, though, had had the sense to wipe away her tears and back off, chattering cheerfully, introducing Sierra to her cousins, who were uncharacteristically shy, too, and involving both Lucy and Sierra in preparations for the big meal.

When they first sat at the table and his mom suggested they all hold hands and give thanks, not only for this meal but for finding each other, Jon suspected he wasn't the only one who had a lump in his throat. He'd held Lucy's hand in one of his, Sierra's in the other, and had seen the expression on his mother's face when she reached a fine-boned hand out and took Sierra's. Joy and wonder.

As glad as he was that his family was accepting his daughter with such generosity, he'd been startled by a shaft of anger. He'd clamped down on it right away, but it hadn't left him. Like a rancid undertone, it flavored the brew of emotions that clogged his belly like an undigested meal.

And he couldn't understand it. His father was gone. Who cared what he would have thought of the choices Jon had made sixteen years ago, or the ones he was making now?

No. That wasn't what was eating at him.

He thought it had more to do with his mother. She had welcomed Sierra with grace and love. He'd wanted that. He had.

Would she have been as generous if Dad was still alive?

Jon pictured her casting anxious looks at her husband and timidly trying to keep the peace while pleasing him. Pleasing him always came first, no matter how hateful he was.

Still looking at grandmother and granddaughter together, his mother exclaiming over another photo, Jon understood the anger. Mothers should fight as fiercely to protect their children as he suspected Lucy would for Sierra, even though she wasn't her own. A mother shouldn't claim to love, then pretend not to see when her son was beaten.

Yeah, he wanted his mother to give everything to Sierra, who was so hungry for family. Jon was glad he had family to give her. But he'd never lie if she asked. Her grandma was a nice woman. But what he'd have to say was "Don't count on her if you need her."

The churning in his belly calmed. His feelings about his mother would never be straightforward. He didn't know why he'd let himself be bothered, even briefly.

He laid a hand along the back of the sofa, behind Lucy's head, and smiled at the way she tensed, at the awareness that made her hesitate midsentence and made her fingers bite into her thigh.

At the sound of Sierra's laugh, he looked at his daughter.

"And you were my age!" She chortled. "You were so…" She tried valiantly to repress the laugh and failed. "So not hot."

He grinned at her, his ego intact. As long as Lucy thought he was hot now, he could live with the memory of the flagpole-skinny kid he'd been.

"I wish," Sierra said, her voice softer, "that

I'd seen these pictures back when I was so ridiculously skinny. So I knew."

She didn't say what she would have known. She didn't have to. Linda Brenner hugged her, and Sierra hugged back.

Jon glanced at Lucy, who was watching, too, and knew exactly why her expression was both happy and sad.

Strangely, he felt the same.

CHAPTER FIVE

"FETCH, MAGGIE!" Sierra tossed the wadded-up paper ball across the living room. It bounced, skittered and disappeared beneath a side table.

The cat had been intrigued by the crackle of the paper. Maggie's eyes followed the ball's path. The rest of her didn't. She continued to lie placidly on the rug, her middle-age spread…spreading.

Undeterred, Sierra bounded up and crossed the room, dropping to her knees to reach the ball. Maggie seemed to enjoy watching Sierra fetching.

Lucy did, too, in between turning the pages of her book. She was laughing when her phone rang, but as soon as she recognized the caller's voice, she excused herself to Sierra and went outside to talk. On her rear patio, she closed the French door before she said cautiously, "Mom. Hi."

"Lucy. Was that Sierra I heard?"

"Yes." Lucy's heart was pounding hard.

Her mother, Terry, was allowed a phone call every other Sunday. This was Tuesday evening. "I didn't expect to hear from you."

"I've been given a release date."

Jon's face flashed before Lucy's eyes. She hated the idea of him meeting her mother. Of course Mom couldn't stay with her, not now that Sierra was here, but he might not approve of her being around at all, corrupting his daughter.

As if he had any rights, she thought suddenly, furiously. He hadn't cared what became of his sperm. He was involved in Sierra's life now only out of a sense of duty. Or maybe he was afraid she and Lucy would go to the press and he'd look bad in the last two months leading up to the election. No matter what, Lucy wasn't going to let him make her choices for her.

"When?" she asked, throat tight.

"The first of October."

Her fingers squeezed the phone. "That's... soon."

"Yes."

They were both silent for too long. Light spilled through the small panes of the French door onto the dark patio. Lucy could smell the roses and a whiff of lavender, so elusive. A car passed on the street, the growl of the engine deepening and then fading. The moon was barely a sliver.

"I can go to a halfway house."

She ached to say, *Yes, that might be best, Mom.* How many times had she been waiting when her mother got out of prison? Feeling hope so sharp she could taste it, even as she should have lost any semblance? Too many times. Her mother was an addict who would do anything to feed that addiction. Steal, spread her legs for creepy men, lie, cheat.

Only then, back in Purdy or whatever correctional institute she was sent to, she got off the drugs and was Lucy's mother again. She lived with terrible guilt and regret and pain at her own weakness, and Lucy always…not forgave her, but pretended to. Never forgot, but pretended to do that, too.

But she was tired of pretending, tired of hope. This time she could barely taste it. She wasn't at all sure she loved her own mother anymore. What she felt was closer to the sense of obligation that Jon probably felt for his newly discovered daughter.

"Let me see what plans I can make," she said finally. "Now that I'm licensed as a foster home for Sierra, I doubt I can have you stay here." She managed a sort of laugh. "Not that the house is big enough for three of us anyway. And I can't turn my back on Sierra now. I can't."

"I understand, Lucy," her mother said quietly. "I'd be disappointed in you if you did."

"But if I can find you a place to live… Maybe a room for now. I can help you get a job."

"Do you suppose the library has any openings? I like working in the library here."

The local library was part of the county-wide system, a government entity. Did they hire ex-cons? Lucy couldn't imagine.

"I'll start watching their job postings," she promised. "There's a secondhand bookstore in town, too."

"All right. Let me know." She paused. "If you don't think it'll work, I can make other plans."

Lucy closed her eyes against the longing. Why couldn't her mom have called and said, *I've leaned on you too many times, I won't do it again?* But she hadn't. Despite everything, Lucy thought, *She's been in for a lot of years this time. Maybe she doesn't feel the craving anymore. Maybe…this time…*

Sure. That was happening.

But…people *did* change.

Her eyes burned as if she was going to cry,

but she refused to let herself. "Can you call me next Sunday, Mom?"

"Of course I can. I love you, Lucy."

After a minute Lucy whispered, "I love you, too," even though that wasn't quite true. Even though she was pretending, because if she didn't she wouldn't have family at all. She would be like Sierra before she'd found her dad.

Remembering some of the men her mother had been involved with, Lucy almost shuddered as she closed her phone and stood breathing in the scented night air. Her own father had been one of those men. One of those men best left forgotten in the mire of her mother's past.

She and Sierra differed here. Because even if Lucy lost her mother, even if she were suddenly alone, she would never, ever want to find her father.

IF HE DIDN'T HAVE an obligatory luncheon of some kind, Jon usually ate lunch—if he ate it at all—at his desk. Today, in the absence of a commitment, he decided to fire an opening salvo in a different kind of campaign than his electoral one. He couldn't get Lucy out of his mind, and he was ready to do something about it.

He stopped at a great lunch place in Kanaskat and carried out two bowls of chili, two sandwiches and drinks, thinking that he was going to look like a fool if he arrived at Lucy's store to find she wasn't working today, or had already left for lunch with a friend, or was plain too busy to stop and eat with him.

But he had to start somewhere, and this seemed less awkward than calling and asking her out. Easier for them both to retreat from if she wasn't interested.

He found street parking half a block from her store and entered it carrying the white paper bags containing their lunch. He saw her immediately, behind the counter ringing up a sale. A bell on the door tinkled and she glanced up, her eyes widening when she recognized him.

"That'll be $39.29," she told the customer, an older woman who had a placid mongrel on a leash at her side. As Jon approached, he saw the dog's big brown eyes fixed hopefully on Lucy, who laughed as she leaned over the counter.

"I've spoiled you, haven't I? What will it be today? Peanut butter or liver?"

"He does love those peanut-butter treats,"

the owner said. "Who'd have thought? Dogs are carnivores."

"Well, think of some of the strange things we eat." She chose a great big bone-shaped dog treat from a basket on the counter and proffered it. The Lab mix took it with surprising delicacy, then sank to his belly to crunch contentedly.

Shaking her head, his person said, "You know what else he loves? Carrots. Maybe it's the crunch."

Lucy glanced at Jon and murmured, "I'll be with you in a minute." Then she smiled again at the customer. "A friend who grows a huge vegetable garden told me that one year her carrots kept disappearing. Pop, pop, pop, part of the row would be gone. She thought it must be moles, until she saw her dog out there pulling one up, eating it, then going back and pulling up the next. She fenced her garden after that."

CHUCKLING, CUSTOMER and dog left the store, the bell on the door ringing again. Lucy closed the cash register drawer.

"Jon. I didn't expect you."

He couldn't tell from her expression how she felt about his surprise appearance.

"Didn't feel like eating lunch by myself

today," he said, setting the bags on the counter. "I was hoping I'd get you at a slow moment."

She looked ruefully around. "Well, you succeeded in that. I even adopted out the pair of cats I had here in the store and the shelter hasn't brought me new ones yet. It's you and me."

He smiled. "Good."

He loved the way color rose in her cheeks. How many women her age blushed so readily? It made him wonder how experienced she was sexually. And *that* made his body tighten, which was lousy timing.

Patience, he told himself. Too damned bad that he hadn't felt patient from the first time he set eyes on Lucy.

"I did bring a lunch," she said, then wrinkled her nose. "Yours smells better."

"Chili." He circled the counter and discovered a pair of stools back there. He sat on one, hooking a heel over the lowest rung and keeping the other foot on the floor. "Sandwiches. You get first dibs. I didn't know what you'd like."

"Picky I'm not."

Unlike him, she had to hop to get her butt up on the second stool, after which she tucked both her feet on one of the rungs. He'd have said he liked his women to be tall, but Lucy's petite stature charmed him, as everything else about her seemed to.

She unwrapped the first sandwich, said, "This looks yummy," and took a bite.

Jon popped the top on one of the cans of soda, then peeled the lid off a bowl of chili.

No one came into the store, although several people passed on the sidewalk out front. This downtown core had what so many towns had lost: a main street lined with small businesses that seemed, for the most part, to be thriving. In the half block between his car and Barks and Purrs, he'd passed a beauty salon, a bakery, a brokerage firm and a fabric store. A nice mix. Across the street were several antiques stores. Midday on a Wednesday, most of the angled parking was full.

"Do you have more parking in back?" he asked.

"Hmm?" She swallowed. "Oh. Yes, only two spots, but regulars know to come in that way, especially if they're going to be hauling out heavy bags of food or litter. Or if they're buying something like a cat climber." She nodded toward several good-size specimens near the front of the store.

He looked around in appreciation, liking what she'd done in here. The building was old, and the interior walls were exposed brick. The floor was gleaming wood, the planks wide and scarred from the years, which gave them character. Displays of cans and bags of dried cat and dog food sat on shelving units toward the back. Otherwise the layout avoided the symmetry and boredom of grocery-store-style aisles. The effect was mazelike, drawing the customer in, tantalizing with glimpses of cat beds in exotic fabrics, bins of toys, racks of treats and dog sweaters and holistic shampoos, brushes and combs and backpacks for the hiking dog.

"Halloween costumes?" he said.

She grinned. "Yep. Just put them out. Last year they sold like hotcakes. And not only for little dogs. Big ones, too. And cats."

"Good God."

"Yes, I'm pretty sure Rosie would slash me to ribbons if I tried to stuff her into that jack-o'-lantern getup." She contemplated the display. "Or the angel wings. She wouldn't like them."

Jon hadn't yet met a cat that would like playing dress-up.

"Costumes for Christmas are big, too. I have a Santa come in and people bring their pets to sit on Santa's lap for a photo. The proceeds go to various shelters. I choose a different one every year."

He nodded.

"*My* profit—" Lucy sounded smug "—comes from the happy sound of the cash register ringing. Even if the owners don't buy food, there's usually something they can't resist. And lots of them buy a costume for their little darling. Or a headpiece. Reindeer horns are big."

"You have the soul of an entrepreneur."

"Yep." Satisfaction glowed on her face as she looked around the store, as if measuring her accomplishment.

She ate in silence for a minute, then swiveled on her stool to face him. "Was there something you wanted to talk about?"

"You mean Sierra? No." To give himself a moment, he crumpled the paper that had been wrapped around his sandwich. "I wanted to get to know you."

"Because your daughter lives with me." Her voice was more uncertain than usual—she wasn't quite asking a question, but almost.

"No," Jon said again, bracing himself. "Because I'm attracted to you."

"Oh." She ducked her head in a gesture of shyness that he suspected was unusual for her. The Lucy Malone he knew tended to be forthright.

"If you're not interested, say so. I don't want to make it…difficult for you, when we're together because of Sierra."

He saw her gather herself. She set her can of soda on the counter and lifted her head to meet his eyes. "I don't want to hurt Sierra's feelings."

"You mean if she thinks I'm hanging around because I want to see you and not her."

She bit her lip and nodded.

"I like her."

Lucy waited, clearly puzzled.

"I'm also gaining a good deal of respect for her brains. No," he corrected himself, "not just brains. Her perceptions about other people, her honesty regarding herself. I think Sierra would be able to tell if I was faking it with her. Don't you?"

After a moment she dipped her head in agreement, or at least acknowledgment.

"I can't spend as much time with either of you as I'd like until after the election. But I won't cheat her, I promise you."

Emotions, doubts, thoughts cast shadows in her eyes. He couldn't identify any of them for sure. But finally Lucy nodded again. "Okay."

He gave a laugh that frustration made

closer to a groan. "What's *okay* mean? If I ask you out to dinner, will you say yes?"

A smile flickered on her lips. "Why don't you ask and find out?"

Jon gave in to the desire to touch her, reaching for one hand, loving the way it turned in his to grip him, too.

"Lucy, will you have dinner with me Friday night?"

"How thoughtful of you to ask," she said demurely, the dimples in her cheeks betraying the smile she was trying to suppress. "Thank you. I'd like that."

He eased himself from the stool, stepping so close to her that her knees bumped his thighs. He let go of her hand to tip up her chin. "I've been wanting to kiss you since you walked into my office looking belligerent."

"I wasn't!"

"Okay, slitty eyed and suspicious."

She thought about that. "Maybe," she admitted.

"This seems like a good time…."

The bell on the door tinkled. Voices and a high-pitched yap and the scrabble of claws on the hardwood floor told him they were no longer alone. His fingers tightened on her chin, then relaxed as, reluctantly, he let her go.

He couldn't look away from her, and her warm brown eyes didn't leave his. Jon wasn't sure he could breathe, either. The moment stretched until he made a ragged sound and backed up.

He was a cop, for God's sake, and he hadn't even turned his head to see who had walked in. He did so now, noting that two women, each with a dog on a leash, had separated to shop for different things. The one with a powder-puff gray toy poodle was looking hopefully toward Lucy, as if she had a question.

Time for him to go.

"I'll call Sierra tonight," he said. "Maybe take her out for pizza tomorrow?"

Lucy's smile was approving. "I'm sure she'll like that."

"Then I'll probably see you tomorrow, too." Regretting that they hadn't had another couple of minutes, he turned and left. Outside on the sidewalk, he looked through the front window and saw her engaged in conversation with the customer. But as he was about to keep walking, she moved her head and her eyes sought him. Neither of them smiled; their eyes met, and finally he nodded and walked away.

"YOU'RE SURE you don't mind?" Lucy asked for at least the third or fourth time.

Sierra, sprawled on Lucy's bed watching her get dressed, heaved an exaggerated sigh. "Why do you keep asking? Do you *want* me to say yes, I do mind, so you have an excuse not to go? What, are you freaked about the idea of a guy actually taking you out?"

Um…yes? But Lucy was the adult here, and not about to admit that she wasn't nervous because *a* guy was taking her out—it was because Sierra's father was. How did you say *your father is the sexiest man I've ever met?*

You didn't.

What she did say was "So, okay, I haven't been dating recently. That doesn't mean I don't."

Sierra expressed major skepticism with a sidelong look.

Poking in her jewelry box for earrings, Lucy insisted, "I haven't met anyone in ages who was interested me."

"Uh-huh."

"And you know what long hours I work."

Suddenly sounding young again, Sierra said, "It's not because of me, is it?"

It was true that Lucy might have hesitated

to get involved with someone right now, but... She made a face, knowing that Sierra could see her reflection in the mirror above her dresser. "No. Until your dad came along, I haven't been tempted in..." She tried to remember. "A year?"

"You're supposed to have *fun* when you're in your twenties."

"I guess I'm picky where men are concerned." Which was one way to put it, she thought ruefully. A girl had to rebel against her mother somehow, didn't she? Lucy's version meant she'd never done drugs, hardly ever drank and had had sex with exactly one guy. And at the time she'd thought that they were in love and would end up getting married. One of her major priorities was *not* becoming like her mother. Having fun? Low on her list.

The doorbell rang, and she jumped. "Oh, do I look okay?"

Sierra rolled off the bed, gave her a once-over and said, "You look amazing."

"And you're positive you don't..."

The teenager clapped her hands over her ears. As she left the bedroom, she said loudly, "La, la, la, la. I'm not listening. You didn't ask that *again*."

Lucy giggled, probably sounding younger

than her often-too-solemn foster daughter. She stole one more glance at herself in the mirror, then followed Sierra. She reached the living room as Sierra let Jon in the front door.

He spotted Lucy, his gaze arrested. "Hey," he said softly. "You look beautiful."

Sierra grinned at her. "See? I tried to tell you."

"Thank you both" was the only response Lucy could think to offer. She hadn't made this much effort on her appearance in a long time. She rarely bothered with much makeup, and hadn't worn a skirt except to church in ages. Tonight she'd gone for a sort of Gypsy look—snug-fitting black knit top and a layered skirt in a kaleidoscope of bright colors. She'd left her hair down and worn big gold hoops in her ears and strappy heels on her feet.

Jon wore a dark charcoal suit with a white shirt and conservative navy blue tie. Presumably he'd come straight from work. His suits were always beautifully cut for his big, rangy body.

"Do you ever wear a uniform?" she asked, then answered herself. "You must, because I've seen pictures of you a couple of times wearing one."

"Mostly for speaking to the press. The detective division goes plainclothes."

"Oh. I suppose so." Of course they did—on TV shows, homicide cops were always wearing rumpled suits or even jeans and running shoes. She supposed a police captain had to think more about appearances.

Sierra watched them leave with a vaguely maternal air that made Lucy laugh. "So much for worrying about her tender feelings," she muttered as Jon opened the car door for her.

"What did I tell you?"

"Nobody wants to hear *I told you so.*"

He laughed, too, a deep, husky chuckle that gave her goose bumps.

During the drive, she said, "Maybe this is the equivalent of parents going on a date night and talking mostly about their kids, but… Do you think your mom and sister liked Sierra?"

He shot her a glance. "You couldn't tell?"

"They might have been trying not to hurt her feelings."

"My mother fell in love at first sight." He paused. His fingers flexed on the steering wheel before he said in a carefully neutral voice, "Lily told me it wasn't fair that I got such a great kid without having to do any of the hard work getting her there."

Lucy couldn't read anything at all in his expression, but some instinct made her say, "You didn't exactly dodge out on being a parent." *Like my father did.*

She knew that wasn't fair. He'd probably never had the least idea that he'd made her mother pregnant. Lucy had always assumed she was an accident. The surprise, really, was that her mother hadn't had more of them.

Jon grunted. "Then why do I feel guilty?"

Lucy was mildly chagrined to realize she'd believed he *should* feel guilty. But she knew perfectly well she'd been projecting. She didn't really think Jon was being nice to Sierra to look good for voters in case his relationship with her was exposed. She suspected he was a good man with a well-developed sense of responsibility. He also gave every indication that he genuinely liked Sierra.

"I don't know," she said. "Why do you?"

Again his grip on the steering wheel gave him away. He didn't fidget, but his fingers tightened and loosened several times as he drove in brooding silence.

"The sperm thing was…stupid," he said

finally. "I only did it a couple of times. My father and I didn't get along—you've probably figured that out."

"You did tell Sierra she wouldn't have liked him."

His laugh was short, harsh. "No. She wouldn't have." He shrugged. "I refused to take a penny from him. Worked my butt off to get through college on my own. It took me an extra year, working damn near full-time along with keeping up the grades, but my pride wouldn't let me back down. I was pretty damn broke sometimes. Donating sperm seemed easy."

Oh, it was easy, Lucy thought, as long as the man didn't think about the consequences. And too many of them didn't.

"Then one day I saw a pregnant woman who'd come out of an ob-gyn clinic. We were both waiting for the bus. I wondered where her husband was."

She imagined it—the college kid gaping at the big belly—and her mouth curved. "You got to wondering if she was carrying *your* baby."

Stopped at a red light, he was able to meet her eyes. He didn't look nearly as amused as Lucy suddenly felt.

"Yeah. The thought did occur to me. It was like getting cold water dumped on me. I never went back to the sperm bank."

"Wouldn't it be funny if that was Sierra's mother?" she mused.

A profanity escaped him. "Thanks for the suggestion." Now he was smiling, if wryly. "You're a big help."

"Do you even remember what she looked like?"

"Hell, no. I was too busy staring at her belly to look at her face."

"I suppose the idea of actually getting a woman pregnant is pretty horrifying to a twenty-one-year-old guy."

"You could say that." He put his turn signal on. "I should have asked. Is a steak house okay?"

"That sounds good to me."

She'd heard of the restaurant he chose. It was out of her price range, so she'd never been there. What eating out she did with friends—and now with Sierra—was mostly pizza or a favorite little Mexican place. Neither had white linen tablecloths, dim lighting and private booths.

Conversation proved to be astonishingly easy. She remembered thinking, when she and Sierra had first been shown into his office, that his charm was practiced and probably not sincere, but she'd come to believe she was wrong. Despite the guardedness that was probably natural for a cop—or maybe had something to do with whatever wounds his father had dealt him—Jon liked people. He told stories from the job that were sometimes funny, sometimes poignant, but never mean. He encouraged her to talk about the challenges of small-business ownership, about how she'd met Sierra, whether she'd known Sierra's mother. The one awkward moment came when he asked, "Did you grow up around here? Any family besides your mother?"

Had she mentioned her mother to him? Oh, Lord, she must have.

"No, I was born in the L.A. area. I never really knew my father—I think I was something of an accident." How lightly she said that. "We moved around some when I was a kid, but I did graduate from high school up here. In Tacoma, actually." She was quick to direct the conversation back to him. "What about you? Did you grow up in the same house where your mom lives now?"

He nodded. "Not so common these days, is

it? I don't know many people whose parents never moved. I didn't have any of the trauma of new schools."

"Oh, I hated the first day at a new school." She thought it might have been worse because she was a foster kid. She didn't want anyone else to know, because sometimes they made fun of her, or else they felt sorry for her. She didn't want anyone, ever, to know Terry was in prison. Although it had almost been worse when Lucy *was* living with her mother, because she was so afraid her mom would embarrass her in front of a new friend.

Even now she didn't want to talk about it. She hated the idea of Jon knowing. It felt, sometimes, as if she were hiding a stain on the tablecloth. Putting a vase atop it, so no one would see. No matter how often she'd scrubbed the fabric, she couldn't get rid of the stain. Which was stupid, of course. She wasn't responsible for her mom's behavior, but it *felt* as though she was. Inside, she was still the scrawny, always-too-small child whose clothes usually came from whatever school program outfitted the poor kids.

No, she wouldn't lie to Jon, but it was too soon to bare a past that still made her feel raw.

How are you going to keep hiding Mom when she's right here in town? Sitting at your dinner table? Job hunting and naming you as her daughter?

Lucy almost shuddered. *Don't think about it. Not right now. Don't.*

Jon was looking at her oddly. Had he asked her something, and she hadn't even heard him?

"One trouble with moving," she said, "is that you tend not to keep in touch with friends. I'll bet you've stayed close to some kids you grew up with, haven't you?"

They talked, then, about friends, and eventually about what it took to make themselves feel rooted. Jon had never considered leaving the Puget Sound area, she discovered, despite the split with his father. Or maybe because of it. This was home. As a cop, his sense of responsibility wrapped around that concept—this county *was* his to keep safe.

"It was different for me," Lucy admitted. "I think because we moved a lot, I decided somewhere along the line that I never would again. All I wanted was to own my own house and have a garden and…belong," she finished softly.

He smiled, his eyes warm. "You didn't have a chance of resisting Sierra, did you?"

"Because that's what she needed, too? Nope. I didn't." Lucy's light tone became more somber. "I was so mad when she told me her uncle didn't want her. How could he not? *Somebody* had to want her. Growing up not feeling as if anyone really wants you, or that you have a real home…" A lump formed in her throat, and she didn't even try to finish.

Jon laid his hand over hers. "The first time we met, I knew right away that you were glaring at me because you felt so fiercely protective of Sierra. I think that's what did me in."

Did him in? What did he mean by that? He was implying a whole lot more than he'd expressed when he said he was attracted to her.

Her chest hurt with the knowledge of how much she wanted to believe him. To think that there was some chance he'd keep wanting her once he really knew her, once he'd seen her baggage.

"I love Sierra," she said. "She's given me as much I have her. Don't make me out to be some kind of saint."

His eyes still had the softness that made her ache. "I won't." The grin widened, became wicked. "I promise, saintly is the last way I want to think of you."

She blushed and Jon laughed. Thank goodness the waiter brought the check then, and she didn't have to think of an appropriate response.

In disgust, Lucy thought, *I'll bet Sierra knows how to flirt.*

On the way out to the car, he said, "I'm sorry to have to cut the evening so short, but I have an early-morning breakfast I have to attend."

"Political?"

"Rotary Club. I'm the speaker."

"All the business organizations tend to have those crack-of-dawn meetings, don't they?"

"Yes, and I'm going to as many of them as I can right now. It's getting old. I'm not really a political animal." He opened her car door and stood back.

"Then why—"

"I want to be sheriff," he said simply.

Lucy waited until he was behind the wheel and they were under way before she asked, "Why?"

His sidelong glance was swift. "Why what?"

"Why sheriff?"

"I think I can make the department better." He paused, apparently concentrating on his driving. When he continued, he sounded almost reluctant. "Because I like giving orders better than taking them. I suppose I'm ambitious."

"Most of us are, on some level."

She earned another of those lightning glances. "You?"

"I wanted my own business. All mine. My own house. All mine. I don't know if that's ambitious, but it's possessive. You happen to want to have your very own police department."

Jon laughed. "The trouble is, it never will be my own in the same way your business is. I still have to contend with the county council, the unions, with voters who happen to be taxpayers, with the need to win reelection every four years. Not to mention everyone who works for me. Cops are a contentious bunch, almost as bad as those council members. I can't get complacent."

"I can't, either. I have to keep customers coming back. I have a lease on the building, suppliers, neighbors, the IRS—"

"Point taken," Jon conceded, his voice amused.

She almost wished the drive was longer.

Already he was pulling into her driveway behind her aging compact car. The porch light was on even though night hadn't completely fallen yet, but the front window wasn't lit. Sierra was probably engaged in a virtual world on her laptop in her bedroom.

The silence after Jon turned off the engine was deafening. Lucy fumbled when she reached to unfasten her seat belt.

"Let me," Jon said softly, and undid first hers and then his. "I enjoyed myself tonight."

"I did, too." So much it scared her. They hadn't talked about anything that special, they hadn't gone dancing, he hadn't kissed her yet, but she liked looking at him and listening to him. That was dangerous. She couldn't imagine that an ambitious man willing to run for public office to get what he wanted would find she suited his public image. Especially once he found out about her mother.

"There shouldn't be any interruptions this time," he murmured.

This time? Then Lucy remembered the customers who had come into her store as he'd raised her chin.

His knuckles stroked her cheek. She looked up at the shadows and planes of his face, at his crystalline eyes, narrowed now, and finally at the mouth she'd thought to be hard even when he smiled politely.

She wanted, quite desperately, for him to kiss her.

CHAPTER SIX

JON DIDN'T KNOW WHY he felt so hungry for this woman, but he was. That made him determined to be careful. Lucy hadn't gotten over her wariness with him. He'd noticed how she avoided talking much about herself. Was she cautious around all men? He sensed she would have to be coaxed into a relationship.

Sliding his hand around to cup the back of her head, he brushed his lips over hers. Then did it again. Hers quivered, parted slightly. He gently nibbled her lower lip, then flicked his tongue to taste it, to slide a bit inside to the tender, damp flesh there. Her face rose when he pulled back slightly, as though her instinct was to keep contact with him. He thought maybe he was smiling when he kissed her again.

By the time his tongue met hers, his smile was long gone and a groan rumbled in his chest. She tasted like coffee and spices. She seemed startled by the kiss. Her tongue was shy, meeting his, then retreating. But as if she couldn't help herself, she lifted one hand to his shoulder, where she gripped as if to hold him close.

Jon was bombarded with sensations: the heavy, cool slide of her hair, the fragility of her neck beneath that hair, her spicy taste, the tiny sound that escaped her when he lifted his mouth enough to let them both breathe.

He wanted to put his free hand on her breast, test its fullness and weight. He wanted to slip his hand inside her low-cut top and savor her naked breast. Hell. He wanted to take their activities into the house, feel her body pressed to his, hear that little choked gasp become a purr.

He wanted…

With the most self-discipline Jon had exerted in years, he squeezed her neck, nuzzled her face one more time and let her go.

"If you didn't have a kid inside, I might try to talk myself past your front door," he admitted, hearing the roughness of his voice.

"I'm…not quite ready for that." But she didn't sound so sure. And her voice was huskier than usual, too.

"I won't push. I'm a patient man." Even if he didn't feel that way right now.

She made a funny, choked sound. "Maybe

you are, but I'll bet you're pushy, too. In fact, you wouldn't be where you are if you weren't pretty domineering by nature, would you?"

"I'm not sure I like the word *domineering*." It made him think of his father. Still, he couldn't discard the assessment. "You could be right, though. I simply try to disguise it."

"And you do that very well." Lucy sounded more relaxed, more herself now. "I'll wish you good-night." She reached for her purse and then the door handle.

Jon got out and met her at the walkway. Escorting her to her front door gave him an excuse to touch her again. He loved the subtle shift of muscles in her back when he splayed his hand there, the sheen of her hair under the porch light. She had glorious hair, thick and shiny, that reached her waist. He imagined wrapping his hands in it, or sheets of it falling across his chest and belly when she explored his body.

Oh, hell. He was even more aroused now.

She inserted her key and opened the door. "Do you want to stick your head in and say hi to Sierra?"

"Sure." What else could he say? He'd rather have stolen another kiss from Lucy before he left.

"I'm home," Lucy called, and Sierra came out of her bedroom.

"Did you have fun?" She saw Jon. "Oh. Um, hi. I thought you'd left."

She didn't call him anything. Not *Dad*, or *Jon,* or *Captain*. They hadn't even talked about what she *should* call him. It would almost have to be Dad, but he guessed the moniker would feel awkward for a while.

"Just wanted to say good-night." He looked from her to Lucy. "Can we do something Sunday? Maybe drive up to Paradise? We could take a picnic, or eat at the lodge."

Sierra's face brightened. "A picnic would be cool. Wouldn't it, Lucy? I'll bet it's really pretty there right now. I want to climb Mount Rainier someday." Her hopeful gaze settled on him. "Do you mountain climb?"

"I've been up Rainier a couple of times. I'd have to hire a guide—I'm not experienced enough for us to go alone. But we can do it next summer if you want."

"Really?" She dashed forward, gave him an impulsive hug, then sprang back as if embarrassed. "I *really* want to do that. Lucy could go, too, couldn't she?"

Alarm flared on Lucy's face. "Lucy," she said, "has never had the slightest desire to plod to the summit of Mount Rainier. An athlete I'm not."

Jon grinned at her. "Plodding doesn't require any great athleticism. It is a slog, though, I won't deny it. But standing up there, seeing the world for miles around spread at your feet, that's pretty exhilarating. Think about it," he said. "And now I'd better get going."

Lucy smiled at him. "Good luck with your Rotarians. And thank you for dinner. I did enjoy myself."

"Me, too." He glanced at Sierra, then risked a quick kiss on Lucy's cheek. Seduced by the cushiony texture of her cheek and the satin of her skin, he straightened. "Good night."

Woman and girl chorused their own goodbyes, and Lucy closed the door behind him. He found himself alone in his car a moment later, looking at Lucy's cottage with light now falling cheerfully from the windows. He might feel like a giant when he was inside, as if he had to step carefully so as not to inadvertently smash the contents. Yet he wished he didn't have to leave. The rooms were homey. A lot homier than his own.

He wondered how Lucy, who had always wanted her own place, would feel about moving.

The thought had scarcely formed when Jon stopped it. He was getting ahead of himself. Way ahead of himself.

A whole lot about Lucy was still a mystery, and he couldn't afford to forget that. Winning this election was important to him. Staying in office once he won was important. He had to be very careful about getting involved with a woman with secrets. Allowing his dick to do his thinking wasn't an option.

What bothered him as he reversed out of the lane and drove away was the ache that settled beneath his breastbone. That felt like something more than lust.

Asset or detriment? Edie had asked, and Jon knew he had to have a firm answer before he got in over his head.

THE SUNDAY EXPEDITION to Mount Rainier was a big success. The late-August day was perfect, the sky a vivid blue. One small puffy cloud clung to the snow-covered cone of the volcano, as if irresistibly attracted.

During the drive up, Sierra was animated company in the backseat, chattering unself-consciously and exclaiming excitedly at every sight. Jon flicked an occasional, bemused glance at Lucy. She could relate—living with a teenager had taken some getting used to on her part, too.

The nice weather and the fact that summer was nearly over meant they weren't alone at Paradise; it took a while to find a place to park in the huge lot. They saw a few climbers setting off up the mountain, laden with heavy packs and ropes and ice axes. Lucy knew they would climb to Camp Muir halfway up and spend the night in the hut or in small tents set up on snowfields before leaving for the summit well before dawn the next morning. She had a bad feeling she'd find herself trudging up the mountain come next summer.

Unless, of course, Jon lost interest in his daughter before then.

But she didn't want to think about that. No. What she didn't want was to believe he'd do that.

They wandered into the National Park Inn, built in 1916, and then took a two-mile hike on the Nisqually Vista trail. Despite the number of people around, the terrain was so vast that there were moments when it seemed as if they were alone and could savor the sight of the vast, cone-shaped mountain above them, the smaller, jagged peaks around, the vivid shades of green contrasted with rock and snow.

"Too bad it's not earlier in the year," Jon commented. "The avalanche lilies are spectacular when they're in bloom."

"Mom and I never came up here," Sierra said.

Jon tipped his sunglasses down his nose to stare incredulously at her. "You grew up damn near at the foot of the mountain and have never driven up here?"

Sierra shrugged awkwardly. "Mom wasn't that much into nature."

Lucy made a face. "I have to admit I haven't made the effort to get here in…I don't know, three or four years at least. If you have out-of-town guests maybe you bother, and otherwise you don't. Which is dumb, when it's so spectacular."

Jon shook his head. "I try to make it up at least once every summer. One year with a couple of friends I hiked the Wonderland Trail that goes all the way around the mountain."

Sierra wanted to know about avalanche lilies, and marmots, and why the glaciers were retreating and what caused crevasses. And why was climbing Rainier dangerous when there weren't any precipices to cling to by fingertips, and how come all the signs about not stepping off the trail?

Lucy was able to drop back, only half listening. She was content watching the two of them, Sierra animated, all but shimmering with happiness at being the center of her father's attention, Jon answering her questions with seemingly unlimited patience.

He was impressive in his well-cut suits, but it struck her that they were a sort of disguise, a civilized veneer on a man who was more obviously rugged and powerfully built—more elemental—in today's jeans, well-worn boots and T-shirt. Bringing up the rear as she was, she surrendered to temptation and tuned out their conversation entirely, focusing instead on the easy flex of muscles as he walked, the alert way his head turned at the slightest sound, the V his close-cropped hair formed at his nape. She loved his neck, strong but not overmuscled, the beard-shadowed line of his jaw, the rough sound of his laugh in response to something Sierra said.

He glanced back to be sure she was still with them, and he must have read what she was thinking, because his pupils dilated and he paused midstep. They stared at each other. Lucy swallowed. But then Sierra, having noticed she'd gotten a couple of steps ahead, said, "Dad?" in puzzlement and he turned to his daughter.

Lucy pretended her cheeks were warm from the exercise, not from a combination of lust and embarrassment at being caught gawking, but she knew better.

Eventually they found a picnic table and had lunch. Lucy found herself blinking sleepily in the sun, letting the conversation and the voices of other nearby picnickers buzz by her as if they were no more than the splash of water in a creek.

"Sleepy?" Jon asked in a low, amused voice as they walked to their car, Sierra trailing.

"I'm afraid I'll conk out during the drive home." She glanced over her shoulder. "Sierra's finally winding down, too."

His gaze followed hers. "She seemed to have a good time."

Lucy could hear his uncertainty and said firmly, "I'm sure she did. This was a great idea, Jon."

"I'm glad." He laid his big hand on her shoulder and squeezed, then let her go and turned to say something to Sierra.

Lucy quivered even from such a brief touch.

Once in the car, Sierra sank low in the seat, put in earbuds and turned on her iPod.

When Lucy looked back at her, she seemed absorbed in her music and the view out the window.

"Tell me something I don't know about you," Jon said unexpectedly.

The question sounded deliberately casual. So deliberate, Lucy knew it wasn't casual at all. He might be trying to disguise his determination to know everything about her, but that's all it was—a disguise. Or was she just being suspicious?

Maybe to be perverse, Lucy said the first unimportant thing that came into her head. "I hate cooked spinach." She shuddered. "And cooked cabbage, and Brussels sprouts."

He gave a low chuckle. "Interesting, but I was thinking of something more profound. And, by the way, I'm not fond of any of those foods, either."

That was a dumb little thing to give her a quick squeeze in the region of her heart.

Something more profound? *My mother is in prison.* No. Lucy didn't even have to debate whether she ought to say that.

"I was a preemie," she said. "Just under five pounds. I had to stay in the hospital for my first two weeks."

"Really?" A smile came and went. "You never did grow much, did you?"

"I resent that," Lucy said with dignity. "I'm not that small. Only a couple of inches below average. *You're* the one deviating from the norm."

"True enough," he said agreeably. "Did you have health problems because of being a preemie?"

"Breathing, I guess. That's why they kept me in the hospital. I had asthma when I was a kid, too, which might have been associated with it. But fortunately I outgrew it."

From what she'd read, she had probably been born prematurely because her mother was a heavy smoker in those days. She might have used drugs when she was pregnant, too. Lucy had never asked her. She wasn't sure she wanted to know.

"Your turn," she said, instead of saying, *I went into foster care the first time when I was fourteen months old.*

Jon was silent for a surprisingly long time. Lucy looked at him curiously. She'd expected some humorous fact: *I asked a girl to marry me when I was in kindergarten.* Instead he said abruptly, "My father broke my arm when I was six."

"What?"

Muscles spasmed in his jaw. "I told him I

hated him. He slammed me into the wall of the garage."

"Oh no," she whispered.

The glance he gave her was cautious, as if he needed to see her reaction. "I wanted you to know that my childhood wasn't sit-com pretty. We had a nice home and money. I love my mother. But my father was a son of a bitch, and I got so I hated his guts."

"Did you?" She was asking, and yet not. Did anyone ever truly hate a parent, however much they deserved it? Or did anger and hate stay tangled in a child's desperate wish for love? Would he understand her complicated feelings for her mother?

Jon sighed and moved his shoulders, as if trying to ease tension. "I spent years trying to win his approval. I'm sure that's normal. Not until I was in high school did I ever tell anyone that my father was physically abusive. Certainly not adults, but not my friends, either. It was our little family secret."

"Your sister...?"

He shook his head. "He was easier on her. She was his baby girl. Maybe it was only that I was male. I don't know."

"And your mother..." Lucy hesitated over how to ask this. "She let him?" She didn't have to wonder anymore about the strain she'd sensed between Jon and his mother.

"She left him after he broke my arm. Took Lily and me. He had to talk her into coming back, and she insisted on counseling. He never broke a bone again, and I think after that she mostly convinced herself that his pounding on me was his form of tough love. Or she pretended she didn't know. I'm not sure."

Lucy nodded her understanding. After a moment she reached out and lightly touched his hand, wrapped tight around the steering wheel. He let go, leaving the other hand on the wheel, and gripped hers. Neither of them said a word for what had to be five minutes.

"That was probably more than you wanted to know," he said finally.

"No. I'm glad you told me. To tell you the truth, the *Leave It to Beaver* perfection made me nervous."

"Because of Sierra?"

She saw him glance in the rearview mirror, then smile slightly. Apparently Sierra was continuing to shut out the adult conversation.

"And me."

"You?"

She might have had the courage to tell him some small part of the whole if she hadn't read a quote from him in the *Dispatch* two days ago.

Do I believe in cutting off a thief's hand? No. But I also don't believe in apologizing to the thief because he's had such a tough time finding a job, patting him on the back and sending him out to steal again. Criminal behavior deserves swift, inevitable and harsh consequences. Talking about punishment as a deterrent has gone out of fashion. That's a shame.

She had almost been able to hear the impatience in his tone. Lucy had to wonder if *forgiveness* was in his vocabulary. If only she could talk to him about her mother, about the anger that was doing battle with love inside her, but she couldn't. She was so afraid she knew which side he'd come down on.

So, rather lightly, she said, "Telling each other one profound thing per date is enough, don't you think?"

He took his attention from the road for a moment. She felt his quick assessment. "What is it you don't want to tell me?"

"Today was supposed to be fun."

There was a momentary silence. Finally he said, "You're right. We'll call it good."

When traffic became heavy, Jon let go of her hand. Lucy balled it into a fist and pressed it against her stomach. It tingled from his touch. Holding hands with him hadn't been only physical, not for her. She'd felt connected, as if worries and comfort had flowed back and forth.

Of course, that was all in her imagination, and she felt sure he hadn't felt any such thing. Although...he hadn't wanted to release her hand. She'd been able to tell.

When he dropped them off, Sierra thanked him very nicely for taking them and said, "Yeah! Cool!" when he suggested a hike another weekend.

"I can't get away long enough to go camping," he said, "but we can do that next summer, too. Maybe you could bring a friend."

"Do you have an RV or something?" Sierra asked, wide-eyed.

He laughed. "Nope. I believe in doing it the old-fashioned way. No television, no microwave, no refrigerator. I have a tent. Sleeps six. I could set up a smaller tent for myself, so you three could have privacy."

"I've never been camping, either," Lucy admitted. These plans for next summer made some big assumptions. The important one was that Sierra would still be living with

Lucy. Had Sierra noticed? Did that mean Jon had no intention of seeking custody or convincing his mother or sister to take Sierra in? Was that good or bad?

"One more thing to look forward to," he said with a nod. He gave Sierra a one-armed hug and Lucy another kiss on the cheek, then left.

The front door open behind them, Lucy and Sierra lingered on the porch. Sierra watched him leave, a pensive expression on her face.

The girl's voice emerged very soft. "Do you think he'll really take us places next summer?"

Lucy could tell what she was really asking. *Will he still be around? Will he still want to see me?*

She hesitated before answering, not wanting to lie. "Yes. Yes, I do."

Sierra nodded, ducked her head and went inside. Lucy followed.

JON WAS FRUSTRATED by his inability to break away for most of the next week. An ugly triple homicide consumed some of his time. He had to trust the investigation to his detectives, of course, but he was on the hot seat when days passed with no arrest.

A man and his two sons—the boys twenty

and seventeen—had been gunned down in their own home. Initially there didn't seem to be a drug connection. The father owned an automobile body repair shop. The house was in a respectable neighborhood. The mother was out of the picture—remarried and living in Iowa. The younger boy was a good student who played football for his high school. He'd had practice that afternoon, in fact. Jon had toured the crime scene after the techs were finished with it and noticed the filthy uniform spilling out of the hamper in the bathroom and the cleats lying by the door from the garage. The father probably made him take them off so he didn't scar the floor. The kid had number thirty-one on his shirt. That was one of those details, irrelevant to finding the killer, that always struck Jon as poignant. Things that made the victims real, human. The investigators needed to get to know the victims as people, but had to keep their distance, too, for their own emotional well-being. Easier said than done. Every so often, every cop let something at the scene slip under his guard. A toddler's blankie, blood soaked. A family's terrified dog huddled behind the sofa. A grocery list that would no longer be needed posted on the refrigerator. It could be anything.

After a day or two the focus turned to the older son, who had been something of a screw-up in school. Supposedly he was attending the community college part-time, but he'd skipped summer quarter and during the spring quarter he'd ended up with a C- in one class and an incomplete in the other. He'd gotten fired from two recent jobs for anger problems. Rumors surfaced that he was involved with a gang.

Members of the police gang unit, also under Jon, and the investigators worked together and, six days after the murders, arrested two rival gang members. The community was shocked. People expected this kind of thing in the inner city, not in the family-friendly neighborhood of a town with fewer than twenty thousand residents.

Jon had to cancel a couple of campaign appearances, but Edie was rubbing her hands together in glee at his increased public presence, especially after the arrests were made. Every time he stepped to the podium to talk at a press conference, Jon was torn between his need to come across well and his distaste that he was, in a way, taking advantage of other people's tragedy to win an election. He kept seeing that stained football uniform half-hanging from the laundry hamper, and wondered if the school would retire the kid's number.

Friday night he called Lucy. He sat in his recliner in the living room, an unopened beer on the end table within reach. He hadn't turned on the TV even though he'd intended to watch the Mariners likely get creamed by the Detroit Tigers. Some impulse had made him reach for the telephone instead.

Once he identified himself, Lucy told him, "Sierra's out with friends."

"I mostly wanted to talk to you, anyway." He couldn't say *I wasn't thinking about Sierra at all.* "I kept hoping this week to get away long enough to bring lunch to your store again, but no such luck."

"I've seen you on the news. What an awful thing."

"Yeah." Ruthlessly he repressed the memory of the bloody crime scene. "At least there weren't any little kids involved. That's the worst."

"I can imagine." She was quiet for a moment. "Did you used to work in Homicide?"

"Yeah, eight years. It's grim, but fascinating. This week I've had a few regrets that this case wasn't mine."

"Really?"

"It's the downside of being promoted to

administration. Sometimes I think about what drew me to law enforcement in the first place and realize I've left it all behind. No more Lone Ranger riding in to save the frightened woman being assaulted. No more saving anyone. And I liked detective work. The puzzle, putting the pieces together, doing interviews and reading people. Figuring it all out. There's an adrenaline rush when you're in a dangerous spot, but there's a different kind when all those pieces click together."

Softly Lucy said, "Aren't you still figuring it all out? And now you're not saving people one at a time, you're making us all safer."

"Am I?" he asked, not necessarily liking the bleak tone he heard in his voice. "This has been a hell of a week."

"What do you mean?"

"I kept finding myself pleased because I'd be on television again. Thinking about how I look, about the impact on the polls, instead of the victims." Shocked, he stopped. What the hell was he doing, laying himself open like that, especially to a woman who wasn't willing to bare herself to him? And yet he kept going with a final admission. "I haven't liked myself much this week."

Jon tensed, waiting for her reaction. What was he trying to do, make *her* dislike him?

No. Not that. He felt a different kind of shock when he realized that he wanted—needed—her to see the real him, not the noble image he was presenting to voters.

"You're not being fair to yourself," Lucy said. "Of course you have to think about things like that. You're running for office, partly because you want to do good. Think about it. It's not really any different than any working person, half focused on a job at hand and half on what the boss will think. We all have a voice running in the back of our heads that's saying, *if the customer gives me kudos, maybe I'll get that raise I've been wanting.* Thinking that way doesn't mean we don't *want* to do a really good job, and that we're not doing the best we can. I've been ashamed of myself a few times. I remember once when a cat I'd anesthetized died on the table. I was shattered, trying to figure out if I'd done something wrong. His owner was this sweet old lady who adored him. Calling her was horrible. I was heartsick, and I felt guilty. But the bigger worry was that I'd be in trouble with Dr. Rosario, who owned the practice. I was up for a raise and didn't want a complaint to jeopardize it." She paused. "Why would you expect to be any different? You can't tell me this week you weren't thinking about the victims, too."

He closed his eyes and pinched the bridge of his nose. "I was."

"Did you…did you *see* them?"

"Yeah," he said hoarsely. "I saw."

The next thing he knew, he was telling her about the uniform and the kid's cleats. About the quart of milk that had fallen to the floor and spilled when the boy went down after taking three bullets to the chest.

"I played sports," he said. "Man, I'd be thirsty when I walked in the door. Mom gave me hell for drinking straight from the carton. That's what the kid was doing, you know. He must have had it in his hand when they kicked the front door in."

He'd lived all week with this picture in his head of that boy, still skinny but with big feet, standing there in the kitchen guzzling milk and feeling pretty damn good about practice that afternoon. About some hits he'd made, maybe a few catches. Dreaming about college scouts even if that was unlikely. Turning when the door splintered open, caught mid-dream when the bullets struck.

She was quiet for a minute. Jon started worrying again. He never talked about work. Not like this. Not to his mother and sister, not to any woman he'd ever been involved with before. Cops talked to other cops. Some to their wives, he guessed. He'd never had anyone outside the job, and he didn't have anyone on it anymore. His last couple of promotions had put a strain on those friendships. He couldn't risk telling anyone in the department that he'd been strutting like a damn rooster all week, conscious of admiring eyes.

Shit, he thought, understanding that he needed someone—just one person—to see him truly. Why her? He didn't know, only that her complexities resonated with his. His body craved hers, but what he felt wasn't nearly that simple. From her first glare, he'd wanted to know her. What she thought, what she felt. To earn her trust, he had to expose himself, one layer at a time, and hope she'd reciprocate.

"I was thinking," she said, "about how much you've seen. Do you have nightmares?"

"Sometimes," he admitted. "Mostly not. I've gotten good at tucking away the stuff I see. I close a case, I file it. I keep that mental file cabinet locked. I know where the key is, but I don't get it out too often."

"I think you're worrying about nothing,

Jon. You're human. That's all. Don't beat yourself up about it."

"I shouldn't have dumped on you," he muttered.

"Why not?"

"We haven't known each other that long."

"To tell you the truth, I think I'm flattered." Her voice held an odd note. "I like knowing you'd trust me."

Jon realized that the shame knotted inside him had loosened. *Lucy's right. I did the best I could to support the investigating officers. To reassure the public. Maybe I had some selfish motives, too, but that's natural.*

You're human.

"We aren't on a date," he said. "I cheated. I wasn't entitled to tell you anything profound."

Lucy laughed. No, she giggled. A funny, sweet little bubble of sound. "That's okay. It just puts you one ahead of me."

"I want to know you," he said. "Let me know you, Lucy."

This time the silence went on long enough to make him edgy.

"It's…hard for me." Her voice was barely more than a whisper. "But I'll try."

Instinct told him this wasn't the moment to

push. He wanted to, but he was a better strategist than that. Lucy was like a wild creature, frightened but oh, so tempted to nibble from his hand. *Patience,* he told himself, although he had to know who had hurt her. Jon was shocked to realize how much he wanted to keep anyone from hurting her ever again.

He was getting in deep. Too deep, considering how little he knew about her.

"I'll call tomorrow." It took everything he had to sound relaxed. "I'm hoping we can all do something Sunday."

"You don't have to dedicate every weekend to us, you know."

"I want to." He hadn't realized how much. He had spent all week aching to see Lucy. Wanting to talk to her. Thinking about Sierra, too, wondering whether she was still happy that she'd found him or whether in a way she was disappointed. She might have harbored fantasies that he would fill the entire hole in her life her mother's death had left and now knew he wouldn't. Couldn't.

As if reading his mind, Lucy said, "This has meant a lot to Sierra. Just don't…disappoint her. Okay?"

What about Lucy? Was she already braced for him to disappoint her, too? He hoped not.

"I'll try not to. That's all I can promise."

"Okay," she said.

They said good-night. He hung up feeling as though he had heartburn. He popped open the beer and took a swallow to relieve it. He often felt that way after seeing Lucy, talking to her. She got to him. He didn't yet know whether this thing with her was going anywhere serious, but it felt as if it might. The timing stank, but…she'd given him some balance tonight when he'd been unsteady, and he couldn't remember the last time anyone had offered him that much.

Still gazing at the blank TV, Jon wished he knew why Lucy held back so much of herself. Whether she had secrets that would turn out to matter. It made him uneasy that he even had to ask himself. He wasn't in a position to trust readily, though.

So why had he picked a woman so reluctant to talk about her past? One who, clearly, was reluctant in her own way to trust?

Because they fit. Or at least, he thought they fit. Not an explanation he'd have voiced aloud, but the best he could do right now.

He finished the beer, but never did turn on the ball game.

CHAPTER SEVEN

"How did the first day go?" Lucy asked as she spooned rice onto her plate. Labor Day weekend had come and gone, which meant Sierra had started school. She'd been holed up in her bedroom when Lucy got home, and this was the first chance they'd had to talk.

Sierra, who had already dished up, watched as Lucy added stir-fry to her plate. "I wish I already had my license."

Startled, Lucy looked up. "Really? You haven't said anything."

Sierra rarely did the typical teenage sullen thing, but for once she was looking sulky. Her shoulders jerked. "Why would I? I can't afford a car anyway."

Lucy blinked. "Sierra, we've never even talked about this."

"And you probably wouldn't let me drive anywhere even if I had a car."

"Okay, stop this right there. I've offered you every opportunity to drive when we're out, and most of the time you didn't want to.

Don't blame me because you don't have a driver's license yet."

Sierra's hair shielded her face as she poked at her dinner. She had redyed her hair in preparation for the start of school. It was still blue, an even more vivid hue if that was possible.

When her foster daughter didn't say anything, Lucy prodded more gently, "What brought this on?"

"Some of my friends are doing Running Start," she finally mumbled.

Lucy knew vaguely about the program, which allowed high-school juniors and seniors in Washington State to take classes at the community college free of charge. Most substituted one or two college classes each semester for those at their high school, but in theory a student could complete requirements for a high-school diploma and an associate of arts degree at the college simultaneously, saving their parents a bundle on college tuition. Sierra had never mentioned Running Start before.

"Who?" Lucy asked, not surprised that Sierra's circle of friends would be the ones doing Running Start.

"Ava." Sierra's best friend. "And Kiernan and Emily. Some others, too, but Emily is going full-time. I knew she was, but... It was weird, not having her there today. And Ava left after lunch. They were both really excited about it. And Chad. He made a big deal to everyone about how he was too smart for high-school math."

Sierra was too smart for high-school math, too. Lucy knew she was. She'd been worrying about this, afraid Sierra would get bored. Running Start would have been perfect for her, but it was true there was no way Lucy could chauffeur her. The community college was in Willis, a twenty-minute drive each way.

"I suppose your friends are all driving themselves," she said thoughtfully. Even if she'd been willing to let Sierra ride with one of them, state law didn't allow new teenage drivers to have other minors as passengers.

Sierra rolled her eyes. "Like, duh. Mommy doesn't usually drive her kid to college."

"Don't be snotty," Lucy snapped. "It's not my fault you weren't motivated to get your license." The minute the words were out, she felt mean. They both knew that Sierra's reluctance was rooted in her mother's death in a traffic accident. "I'm sorry," she said hastily. "But I don't understand why you're mad at me."

Sierra shot to her feet. "I'm not mad at you.

I'm just mad, okay? Forget it! I don't even know why I said anything." She grabbed her plate and stomped to the sink. After scraping her nearly untouched meal into the garbage, she rinsed off the plate and put it in the dishwasher, then started out of the kitchen. In the doorway, her back to Lucy, she stopped and said, "Why can't things ever stay the same?" She didn't wait for an answer. The quiet click of her bedroom door closing came a moment later.

Lucy thought her heart might break.

She looked at her own plate. She should have lost her appetite after the sad little scene, but of course she hadn't. Rather gloomily, she reflected on the fact that nothing dented her appetite. After a minute she picked up her fork and resumed eating.

Maybe, she finally decided, Sierra's outburst was a healthy sign. So far she'd been unnaturally well-behaved for a teenager. She had been cheerfully willing to do chores and to accommodate Lucy's schedule, Lucy's choice of TV programs, Lucy's menu. They hadn't had one single argument, unless you counted their skirmish over Sierra's surprise announcement that she'd tracked down her biological father via the internet and intended to introduce herself in person. And

Lucy couldn't, in all honesty, count that, since Sierra had been hopeful rather than confrontational. It really wasn't normal for a kid her age not to take out some of her roiling emotions on her parent. So maybe this meant she was finally trusting that, in every way that mattered, Lucy *was* a parent. That she wouldn't ditch Sierra if she wasn't 100 percent, unfailingly perfect.

Great theory. But maybe she really was upset about something else altogether, and the driver's license and Running Start and her friends' defection didn't have anything to do with her sulky mood tonight.

Lucy sighed and opened the freezer door to stare at the carton of mint-chocolate-chip ice cream. She could have a small helping….

No. She slammed the door shut. If she was strong, it wouldn't take that long to lose five pounds. Just in case kissing Jon led to more. Given how irresistible his kisses were.

Last week they'd had lunch together twice. Once he'd brought take-out sandwiches and soup again, once a pizza. The second time he'd caught her at a particularly busy time, and he'd willingly hauled bags of food and litter to customers' cars, snatching bites in between. He hadn't seemed disgruntled at all when he kissed her goodbye before going.

He'd taken her and Sierra on a hike to a waterfall, and Lucy to dinner one night. The good-night kiss had been even more shattering than the last one. Her whole body tingled when she remembered. His mouth had both coaxed and devoured hers. He'd held her head so that he could angle it to please him. And one big hand had weighed and kneaded her breast, which had her hips pushing against his. If Sierra hadn't been on the other side of the door, Lucy wasn't sure either of them could have stopped.

They were supposed to go out again this Friday night. Lucy kept watching Sierra for signs that she was starting to resent the time he spent with her. So far, Sierra didn't seem to. She seemed…content with the time and attention he was giving her.

But that contentment didn't mean Lucy could ignore this recent outburst. With another sigh, Lucy went down the hall and knocked on Sierra's door.

"Come in."

Despite Lucy's encouragement to decorate the room to suit herself, Sierra hadn't done anything but hang some posters and placards. She sat now on the bed, her back against a heap of pillows, her computer on yet another pillow on her lap. Music spilled from it. Lucy didn't recognize the band—Sierra was into alternative rock.

"Hey."

Sierra grimaced. "I was bitchy. I'm sorry."

"No, that's okay." Lucy sat at the foot of the bed. "I can see why you felt…left behind."

"Yeah." Sierra grabbed a lock of hair and tugged on it, brushing the ends against her cheek. "We were, like, a *unit,* you know? I knew they'd all signed up for Running Start, but somehow I didn't think about the fact that meant they wouldn't be at school with me."

Lucy wondered if they should talk about what Sierra had said at the end, instead of about Running Start. None of this was really at the heart of her grief.

But maybe that wasn't true. The fact that her friends had moved on without her had put a crack in the sense of security she'd been trying so hard to build. And typical teenage preoccupations like getting a driver's license and friends could maybe, somehow, be controlled. Whereas nothing would bring her mother back.

"You must have friends who aren't doing Running Start."

Sierra lifted one shoulder unhappily. "Oh… sure. Chris and Abby and Rachel."

She didn't have to tell Lucy those weren't

her best friends. On a sigh, Lucy said, "Once you have your license, I don't see why you can't join the Running Start program spring quarter."

Sierra mumbled, "There's no way I can save enough money to buy a car. And I know you can't drive me. That's why I didn't say anything about it in the first place."

"By the time you get your license, we'll manage a car. I promise." She smiled. "It'll probably be a clunker, but we'll find something."

Sierra's face brightened. "Really? You mean that?" Her voice sounded choked, as though she was struggling with emotion.

"Of course I mean it."

"I thought about asking, um, my dad. But…"

"It feels too soon, doesn't it? Although I'm betting he'll be glad to help. And maybe we can ask him to take you shopping for it. I don't know anything about cars. I'd hate to end up with a piece of junk."

"Nobody would dare sell a crap car to the sheriff," Sierra said with satisfaction.

Lucy had to laugh. "I suspect you're right. We'll definitely get him involved. In the meantime, why don't you find out more about

Running Start? Do they have info sessions for parents?"

"Yeah. I didn't say anything because I knew I couldn't do it anyway."

"You can. Once you finish driver's ed and get your license."

"Okay." Sierra tumbled forward, knocking her laptop askew, and gave Lucy a hug. "Thank you."

Lucy's eyes prickled as she returned the hug. It was foolish and probably dangerous to her well-being to let herself love a kid who was only temporarily hers, but she couldn't seem to help herself.

"About what you said about why things have to keep changing—"

"They just do." Sierra sniffed, then pulled back. "I know that."

"Well… There's something I need to tell you." Lucy rubbed her hands on her thighs as she battled a rising case of nerves.

I don't have to do this yet. I could put it off.

But if they were really family, then Sierra needed to know about the decisions Lucy made that would affect her.

Sierra closed her laptop and set it aside, then sat cross-legged, her gaze inquiring. "What?"

"I haven't talked much about my mother."

"I figured you didn't like her."

"No, it's not that." What a thought. Would it be possible to like the woman her mother could be if she stayed straight? "It's…" She hesitated. "She's in prison. Over at Purdy." The Washington Corrections Center for Women, commonly known as Purdy, was in Gig Harbor, on the other side of Puget Sound. Very aware that Sierra was now gaping, Lucy continued, "She's been in there for eight years now. For armed robbery this time."

Sierra's eyes were saucer round. *"This time?"*

"She's been in and out of prison or alcohol and drug treatment programs my whole life. The thing is, she's about to get out."

"Oh, wow."

"I think she's going to move here, to Kanaskat. To be near me. And so I can, sort of, be her sponsor. Help her get a job. Things like that."

"Is she going to be staying here with us?" Sierra's expression changed. "Do you need this room for her? I guess you probably do. I could see if Ava's mom would let me live with them."

"Don't be silly." Lucy squeezed her knee. "I told you, this is your home as long as you need me. No, Mom won't be living with us. I'm actually relieved that I don't have room."

Comprehension showed on the teenager's face. "You don't want her coming here."

Lucy found herself shifting uncomfortably. "I wouldn't say that." She realized she was lying. "No," she admitted. "I kept wishing Mom would say, 'I'm going to a halfway house in Seattle.' But she didn't. And…she's my mother."

Sierra nodded. "So… When's she going to be here?"

"October first. I have to go pick her up."

"That's still three weeks away."

"Yes, but I wanted you to know."

"Okay."

"And…I'd rather you don't tell Jon. I will eventually. He might not like the idea of Mom being around you."

"Just because she's, um—"

"An ex-con?" Lucy nodded. "Because of that."

"That's kind of dumb. I mean, what is she going to do? Corrupt me?"

"I don't suppose he thinks much of people who commit crimes."

"She actually had a gun?" Sierra asked,

sounding fascinated. "And, like, held up a store or something?"

"I don't think she was the one who had the gun, but she was with the man who did. Mom's an addict. She's a different person when she's straight, but she can't seem to stay straight."

"Wow," Sierra said again. "That's…" She couldn't seem to find the right words to finish.

"Yeah," Lucy said. "It pretty much sucked. My mom the addict." She sighed and made herself stand. "Okay. I wanted you to know."

"That's almost worse than having your mom die."

Shocked, Lucy looked down at Sierra. She opened her mouth to utter an automatic *Of course it's not,* but realized suddenly that maybe it was. And she felt like an awful human being for even thinking that.

Some sort of inarticulate sound escaped her, and she left without admitting what she felt. Without saying *I wish my mom was dead.* Horror almost brought her to her knees. She was barely able to stumble into her bedroom. How could she wish anything so awful? She didn't. She couldn't.

Was this the person she'd let her anger and sense of betrayal form her into?

Lucy sank onto the small rocking chair in her room and set it to moving in the most comforting of motions.

Who am I?

"You said you didn't know your father." Jon leaned his elbows on the table and contemplated Lucy.

Tonight they'd gone out for pizza, promising to bring some home to Sierra. He'd planned something fancier, but he'd been tired and it had showed. Lucy had suggested this, and he was relieved. A beer and pizza sounded about right.

She was having a cola. "I don't drink much," she'd told him, sounding almost defiant, as if she'd had to justify her attitude before.

He had only nodded and ordered a glass rather than a pitcher. Better to call a halt at one, as beat as he was.

She traced a pattern on the dampness on her glass before meeting his eyes. "I don't even know who he was."

She looked...stoic. As if not wanting to admit to any particular feelings about the parent whose picture would forever be absent from her photo albums.

"That must have been rough," Jon said quietly.

She shrugged. "You don't miss what you never had."

He didn't buy that, and he was pretty damn sure she didn't, either. "But you see what the other kids have."

She opened her mouth, then closed it again. His eyes narrowed. What was it she didn't want to say?

But she stayed clammed up. He waited a minute, then asked, "What did your mother tell you about him?"

"He was Hispanic. His name was Eduardo. She wouldn't tell me his last name. If she knew it."

That last sounded careless rather than bitter. Jon didn't buy that, either.

After a minute she went on, not looking at him. "I don't think Mom knew he was my father until I was born. She had a brown baby, and I guess he was the only brown-skinned guy she'd slept with."

Shocked despite himself, Jon absorbed the sadness and grief of the little girl she'd been. "You're not all that brown skinned."

She held out her hand and then gave a small

shrug at the obvious fact that his tanned skin was darker than hers. "Still, I look more Hispanic than I do Caucasian. I mark Hispanic on surveys."

"Do you?" he said softly. "Even though you're fifty-fifty and you grew up with a white mother."

"People assume."

"Do you mind?"

Her lashes fluttered several times. He saw her swallow. "No," she said finally, defiant again. "Why would I?"

Because she hated to acknowledge a legacy from a father who hadn't been interested in his child. Maybe that was a simplistic answer, but Jon had a strong suspicion it was accurate.

"Did your mother ever tell him she was pregnant?"

"I don't know. She said he was gone and she didn't know how to get in touch with him, but—" Lucy ran her finger around the rim of her glass "—she might have only said that."

"That's why you were hostile when we first met, isn't it?" he asked, realizing it was true. "You saw me as being like him."

"Don't be ridiculous." But she wouldn't meet his eyes.

"Come on, be honest. You saw us both as equally careless."

"Yes." Her face wore an impassioned, almost angry expression. "Yes, I did. And it's *not* ridiculous. Except…" She faltered and all her indignation disappeared, as if it had never been. "It is. I know that. What you were doing was meant to help women who wanted to be pregnant. It's not the same thing at all as a guy who can't be bothered to use protection."

"A condom might have failed. Or he might have thought your mother was taking care of it." He felt compelled to be the voice of reason. She could be right in her assessment of the man who fathered her, but life was rarely that simple.

"Maybe. Probably she did and it failed. I'm an only kid, so I guess she must have been careful most of the time."

"Did you have a stepfather?"

Lucy shook her head. Dark hair slipped over her shoulder, and she pushed it back. "Mom never married. I didn't have the most stable childhood in the world."

"I'm sorry." He frowned. "That's why you were glad I told you about mine."

"Yes."

"What, you thought we came from two different worlds?"

"We did." There was a trace of that fierceness again.

Or was it fear? he wondered. No, that wasn't right, either. Shame. He was afraid that's what she felt.

"If there's one thing I've learned as a cop, it's that domestic violence, broken homes, child abuse, they cross all economic strata. My parents owned a nice home, that's true. Maybe your mother didn't—"

"We were always in rentals. Even shelters a few times."

That shocked him, too. It also explained some things about her.

He only nodded. "There were probably things you were ashamed of at home. I know there sure as hell were things I was."

They stared at each other. Her lips were slightly parted, her eyes dark and intense. She made his heart pound hard in his chest. He hoped he'd said the right thing. He hoped she couldn't tell he was relieved. She'd had a tough childhood that had left memories that haunted her.

Her secrets weren't ones he had to worry about.

"I think that's our number."

Jolted, he said, "What?"

"Our number. I think they're calling our number."

He shook his head to clear it. "I'll go get the pizza."

When he returned, she gave him a wry smile. "I've caught up with you now. That was my profound thing."

And this was her way of saying *Subject closed*. He could understand why she didn't want to talk about it anymore.

"Okay," he said. "My turn, but I'll save it for next time."

"Probably just as well," Lucy agreed.

"One thing, though."

She'd been reaching for a piece of pizza, but went very still.

"I like the color of your skin. And I think Lucia is a beautiful name."

Dusky color swept across her cheeks. "That's…" She pressed her lips together, then gave a shaky smile. "Nice. It's nice of you."

"No." He returned her smile. "Honest." Then, taking pity on her, he said, "Was I imagining things, or did Sierra sound less than excited about school?"

Lucy seemed relieved at the change of subject. She told him that his daughter was wishing she'd been able to participate in the

Running Start program, but that there was no way she could do it without being able to drive herself.

"Maybe sometime in January you'll help her find a car."

"A car might be a good Christmas present."

Her eyes widened. "A *car*?" She sounded shocked, as if he'd suggested buying the kid her very own rocket ship. "That's kind of extravagant, don't you think?"

"A lot of kids get cars for their sixteenth birthday."

"Did you?"

"Yeah." He grinned. "A month later, I wrecked it. My dad was pissed off. He told me I had to earn the next one. Looking back, I think it's one of the few times he did the right thing where I was concerned."

"How long did it take you to earn the money for one?"

"Close to a year. And then it wasn't anywhere near as nice as the car my parents had bought me. They refused to pay for my insurance after that, either. I can tell you that I drove one hell of a lot more carefully after that. My friends gave me a hard time about driving like an old lady."

Lucy chuckled. "You're right. That was

smart of your parents. So maybe it would be a good thing if Sierra has to save at least part of the cost of her car."

"Maybe." Thoughtfully he asked, "Didn't her mother leave any kind of an estate?"

"Yes, but for now the plan is to use it to pay for college. I expect Sierra will want to go to grad school, too. She should have enough to support herself until she's out in the working world."

"She's together enough to come up with that kind of plan? I didn't think any kid that age understood deferred gratification."

"She and I talked about it. It was my suggestion, but she agreed."

That unfamiliar emotion brimming in his chest was pride, Jon realized. "She's quite a kid."

"Yes, she is."

"Thank you, Lucy." He reached across the table and took her hand. "For what you've done for Sierra."

"You don't have to thank me. I did it for my own reasons."

She made no move to reclaim her hand, though. Jon was glad. He liked the way their fingers linked, like a dovetail joint, and knowing she felt the same. He reached for his pizza with his left hand, which was a little awkward, but he didn't want to let go of Lucy. And so they ate, and talked, and kept holding hands, maybe both a little shy about it.

He wanted to make love to her. Thinking about it was keeping him awake nights. But this—talking, sharing past hurts, flirting gently and savoring a connection as simple as clasped hands—was almost enough. Even without sex, it was better than any relationship he'd had with a woman since Cassia.

It suddenly struck him that he was sitting here in a pizza joint where anyone could see him, holding hands with a woman, and he hadn't given a thought as to whether he might be recognized.

To hell with it. Maybe it would be better if his relationship with Sierra didn't come out until after the election, but there was no reason to make a secret of the fact that he was dating a woman.

A niggling thought crept into his mind. Lucy was a good smoke screen. It wouldn't occur to anyone that he was spending time with Sierra because she was his daughter. People would assume he was seeing both of them because he was interested in Lucy.

He was immediately ashamed that he'd think anything of the kind. He *was* interested in Lucy. She wasn't a smoke screen. The situation where he'd have to decide whether to use her as one hadn't arisen.

Aware that Lucy was watching him with surprise, Jon wondered whether, once a man started thinking like a politician, he could ever quit.

CHAPTER EIGHT

SOMEHOW THE NEXT COUPLE of weeks passed with no more deep sharing. Jon was relieved. He hungered to know all about Lucy, but talking about himself was something else again. He wasn't looking forward to telling her about Cassia, and he'd have to one of these days.

Sexual frustration kept him from brooding too much about any secrets Lucy might be keeping. He was used to moving faster when he wanted a woman, but Lucy was different. The fact that she was Sierra's foster mom complicated things, of course, but it was also that he felt so much more than desire.

That was what kept him awake nights, though. He'd kiss her good-night and go home with his body at a full boil. Jon didn't know how long he could go on this way.

Edie hadn't become any happier with him. She wanted Lucy's life to be an open book. No, what she wanted was for him to open the book.

She accompanied him to the more important public appearances. He'd teased her about her insistence on coming whenever he did TV interviews. That particular morning, she was practically rubbing her hands together in delight because she'd gotten him an interview on a popular morning show. Amused, he thought if she hadn't been wearing the seat belt, her chunky self might have floated up until her head bumped the car roof.

Hiding his smile, he said, "You afraid I'll show up wearing a tie that's too loud?"

Sounding a little pompous, she retorted, "My job is to keep you on message."

Jon sobered. "I haven't lost my focus yet."

"Haven't you?"

He didn't even try to hide his irritation. "You're talking about Lucy again. Let it go."

"You hired me to steer you around land mines. She could be one."

"She isn't."

Like the pit bull she was, Edie asked, "How do you know?"

"She's talked to me. She had a lousy childhood. That's not newsworthy."

"How much has she talked to you?"

Not enough. "I'm satisfied" was all he said, tersely.

Since he was pulling into the studio parking lot, she did let it go. For now. He knew damn well she still had her teeth clenched tight on the whole concept of him dating a woman who wasn't as transparent as a glass of city water.

Well, tough. He was enjoying Lucy. Enjoying Sierra. He could spend time with them, do his job and campaign, too. He was proving that it was possible, wasn't he?

He took Lucy to a Tim McGraw concert, and Sierra dragged them to hear a favorite alternative band at the Showbox in Seattle. He had dinner twice a week at Lucy's, eating produce from her garden and sampling Sierra's desserts. He took Sierra to his mother's one Sunday, a visit Lucy bowed out of, to his disappointment.

On the campaign front Jon spoke to community groups until he suspected he was mumbling the variants of his speech in his sleep. The outgoing sheriff had him involved in union negotiations, and he spent hours at the table talking about overtime and working conditions with representatives of the police union. He plotted the changes he'd make in the department once it was his.

All the while, his opponent had staffers combing through Jon's past looking for anything in his record that could be cast in a suspicious light. He was enraged when Rinnert was quoted as saying Jon's role in a shooting six years ago had been whitewashed.

His first clue about the aspersions was a phone call from a *Seattle Times* reporter.

Unclenching the teeth he'd ground together at the initial question, he said, "The board of inquiry's report is public record. They concluded that I was fully justified in pulling the trigger."

"Randy Rinnert points out that one member of the board was apparently a close personal friend of yours."

Jon actually laughed. "You're kidding, right? As it happens, I went to high school with Ryan Lowell. We recognized each other and determined that I graduated a year behind him. We not only weren't friends, we never even had a class together. I'm assuming Lowell is the guy who Rinnert thinks is my best buddy?"

Papers rustled. "I understand questions were raised about whether you should have waited for backup before confronting the man you shot."

The implication that he'd been itching

to gun a man down in cold blood enraged him. He'd had nightmares for a long time afterward about killing Joseph Brinton. Jon had asked himself so many times whether he could have done anything different. Eventually he had come to peace with himself. These questions—instigated as they were by dirty politicking—challenged that peace. He had to pause a moment to quell his anger before he could respond levelly.

"I'm sure you're well aware those questions are always asked. I made the decision not to wait when I saw him starting toward a car that had just pulled to the curb. The car had two women in it and a toddler in a safety seat in the back. Brinton's behavior had been wildly erratic. It was apparent to me—and was later confirmed with toxicology screening—that he was high on drugs. I could not give him an opportunity to grab a hostage."

"Were you concerned about pulling the trigger with two women and a child so close by?"

For God's sake! What kind of idiotic question was that?

"Yes," he said, with what he considered remarkable civility, "naturally I was. Their safety was paramount in my mind. But they had not yet exited their vehicle and were not in my line of fire. I had been attempting to talk Brinton down. I closed the distance between us and regained his attention to distract him from the women. Once he rushed me with the knife, I acted in the only way I could."

The reporter finally disconnected after mentioning that he would be calling one of the two women for comment.

"You do that," Jon said. The women had considered him a hero.

He was still far enough ahead in the polls that he resisted any temptation to sling mud himself. He happened to know that there had been two domestic disturbance calls to Rinnert's house within a matter of weeks three years ago. Jon wanted to keep his message to the public focused on what he could bring to the job. On what was strong about the department and what could be better. Not on Randy Rinnert's personal problems. But he also knew that, if the race became tighter, Edie would be pushing him to turn the spotlight on Rinnert's character. Jon found the idea distasteful. This was one of those moments—and there were too many of them—when he couldn't help wondering if the price for political office was too high.

Another one of those moments had come when Edie suggested he run a background check on Lucy. He'd almost taken her head off.

"Just to be on the safe side," she said mildly.

"You want me to abuse my authority to run a check on someone for a personal reason. That would look great if it came out. Are you aware we fired a deputy for running background checks on all the guys his daughters dated?"

"Ah…no. I didn't know that," she admitted.

"I wouldn't do it anyway," he said, his voice hard. "I know everything I have to about Lucy. Give me some credit."

"You pay me to foresee problems. I understand why you don't want to hear this, but becoming involved in a romantic relationship at this point is dangerous, Jon. You haven't known this woman very long. And the risks are especially high given that we're trying to keep your daughter's existence quiet."

"Back off." He'd hung up the phone, his gut churning.

Sitting at his desk, his chair swiveled so he could gaze out the window, he couldn't help remembering the time he'd told Lucy he wanted to know her. He'd asked her to let him. What she'd said was, haltingly, "It's… hard for me. But I'll try."

What had she meant by that? Was it the stuff she'd started to tell him about? The mother who apparently had a lot of boyfriends and didn't provide an economically stable home for her daughter? The fact that Lucy's birth seemed to have been an accident?

Or was there more? Things she hadn't said yet? He wished he knew. It wasn't only Edie's suggestion that had him reaching for the antacids he kept in a desk drawer. It was the fact that he was so damned tempted to follow it. To cheat, and learn everything he could about Lucia Malone without waiting for her to trust him enough to share her secrets.

But even if Edie was right and Lucy was a threat to his campaign, this was one temptation he refused to give in to. How would he feel if their positions were reversed? If she was asking questions about him behind his back?

He'd feel betrayed, and he knew damn well she'd feel the same. He also knew it wasn't something he would have considered for even a minute if it weren't for the upcoming election.

Falling for somebody was always a risk.

One he hadn't taken in sixteen years. Not since he had loved Cassia and lost her in such a painful way.

Lucy was nothing like Cassia. Jon supposed he wasn't much like the young man he'd been then, either. Cassia had been sunny. Completely without guile, capable of uncomplicated happiness. He'd loved that about her. She smiled in the morning before her eyes were open. She wanted to be a teacher, and she loved kindergarten-level humor. She'd call him out of the blue with a knock-knock joke, and have him laughing over something so dumb he wouldn't dare to try to explain to anyone else. Cassia's parents had been hippies who'd successfully run a health-food store in Ashland, Oregon. Her dad had long, graying hair he wore in a ponytail, and her mom had a braid of fading blond hair long enough to sit on. Compared to his parents, they'd been a revelation: accepting, warm, philosophical.

They'd called him several times after Cassia's funeral. He hadn't returned the calls. He'd managed to hug them and stand beside them as the urn containing her ashes was laid to rest, but he didn't want to know what the loss of their only child had done to them.

No, admit it—he hadn't been thinking of them at all. He'd been too consumed by an unholy combination of rage and guilt to spare much thought for anyone else.

Cassia was like water so clear, you knew looking that there were no undercurrents. No deep pools. You could see all the wonders swimming within.

Lucy was more like a deep spot at a crook of the White River. Not turbulent; the white water rushed past. You could lie on a rock and gaze into the green depths, catching occasional glimpses of a shadow shifting toward the bottom, but you wouldn't be able to quite make out the shape. This seemingly quiet water held mysteries and possibilities, but no simple answers.

Why that appealed to him so much when he'd spent the past fifteen years trying to see the world in black and white, Jon couldn't have said. He had two columns: right and wrong. Voters, he was learning, liked that about him. He generally tried not to listen to the inner doubting voice that whispered *It's not that easy.*

Cassia would be alive if the wrong decision hadn't been made. He had to hold to the rigid backbone of his beliefs. He'd become a cop for her; he'd become the kind of man he was because of her.

And yet there was an irony in knowing

how much he'd changed. That now he was drawn to a woman full of complexity, shadows, compassion. No, Lucy was nothing like Cassia. Instinct told him that for Lucy, happiness didn't come easily.

Jon worried about what his need for her said about him.

Would I still love Cassia if she'd lived?

The question was unanswerable. He wasn't the same man he would have been if Cassia hadn't been murdered.

Suddenly restless, Jon pushed back his chair and paced to the window.

Could Lucy Malone be dangerous for him?

Maybe.

But he was going to take the risk.

He picked up his cell phone, dialing her store number from memory.

"Barks and Purrs—may I help you?" she said.

"Are you free for lunch?"

LUCY STOOD ALONE in the middle of the empty apartment, hugging herself as if she were cold, and realized how much she hated the idea of bringing her mom here.

Which was dumb. Her mother would be living on public assistance initially, and Lucy couldn't afford to help much. This place wasn't that bad.

An old house had been carved into apartments in the fifties or sixties, at a guess, and not much had been remodeled since. This apartment was down a flight of concrete steps to the daylight basement. The high half window in the bedroom looked out to a weedy backyard, while the view from the main room was to a cement walkway, so her mom would see people's feet going by. The refrigerator was an antique with a freezer that Lucy would have to defrost. The bathroom sink had rust stains. The linoleum was cracking. Woodwork had been painted so many times without being stripped that it was lumpy.

But it was clean, and it was cheap. The door was solid and had a good lock. The building was close enough to downtown that her mother could walk once she found a job. A bus stopped only a couple of blocks away, and the bus system offered excellent service throughout the county. There hadn't been that many places listed for rent right now, not in Lucy's price range. The apartment would do, if only temporarily.

After she'd paid the deposit, the landlord had left her alone. She'd intended to make a list of the absolute basic furnishings she'd need to find at garage sales before her mom got here. But so far she wasn't doing anything but standing stock-still dealing with feelings she hated to examine.

She forced herself to anyway.

It didn't take much self-analysis to realize that she didn't like the apartment because she'd lived in too many places like it. No, worse places than this. There had been one basement apartment like this when Lucy was…she didn't remember. Seven or eight, maybe. For a while it had been only Lucy and her mom living in it, but then a man joined them. She could see his face, but couldn't remember his name. Looking back, she guessed he'd been selling drugs. Strangers came and went at all hours. The curtains were kept drawn no matter how nice the day outside. Her mother pretended everything was great, but Lucy had mostly been scared. She'd tried to be invisible.

Lucy ate whatever she could find in the morning and at school always insisted she'd forgotten her lunch money. After the first few times, the cafeteria ladies gave her a peanut-butter sandwich and that was all. She hated going home at the end of the day. For some reason, she had a vivid memory of walking down a cracked sidewalk scuffing her feet, going as slowly as she possibly could.

She remembered the night when the police came and bundled her mother into the back of a squad car along with the man. It had happened other times, outside other apartments and houses, but that one stood out in her memory. As they led Lucy to another car, her mom was struggling and sobbing, "My baby! Who'll take care of my baby?" Lucy had strained to look over her shoulder, and tears had streamed down her face, and yet somewhere inside she was…relieved.

She thought she remembered it so well because she'd secretly *wished* it would happen. Before that, she'd wanted so desperately to be with her mommy, social workers or police had had to rip her away and she'd screamed and screamed and she'd thrown temper tantrums the first weeks in whatever foster homes she was sent to.

Bad memories always faded, and she would be so excited when her mom got out again. For a long time she trusted in every fresh start. Sometimes they had six months— once a whole year—before something went wrong and her mom would be so upset or stressed she used just a little. Then a little more. And once again eviction notices would appear and the police would show up. After a while, even when things were good, Lucy stopped believing that it would last. Of course, she was right.

She shivered, looking around the perfectly clean but still somehow dank and depressing apartment, and knew it wouldn't last this time, either. Even though her mom had seemed different these past few years when Lucy visited her. She seemed to hold herself straighter. She claimed the craving was gone, but she'd said that before. What was definitely different was that she didn't make excuses for her behavior anymore. Her regret for the way she'd failed Lucy seemed genuine. Lucy knew she was desperate for forgiveness. What she didn't know yet was whether she could even pretend to give it. She didn't let herself acknowledge it very often, but deep inside she was still angry. So angry.

Angry enough to wish that, like Sierra's mom, her own was dead?

Appalled anew at the wistful ghost of a thought that whispered in her head, Lucy shuddered. Was that who she wanted to be?

No. Chilled, she knew that for her own sake she had to give her mom another chance. She'd been so young every other time her mother had gotten out. Needy. Asking, not giving. This time she could give. Okay, genuine forgiveness might be beyond her, but she had to know that she could be unselfish, that her love meant something. How could she give it again, to Sierra or Jon or anyone else, if she didn't prove to herself that she was capable of sticking with someone through the worst?

No, she wouldn't enable her mother's worst behavior. Lucy had learned enough about the pitfalls. But her mom did seem different this time. And maybe Lucy could tip the balance one way or the other.

Cold inside and out, she faced the risk she was taking. She could lose Jon. Her heart tightened in fear, but she knew that she had to go through with this anyway.

Or she wouldn't be able to live with herself.

She locked the apartment and walked around the building to the street, where she had left her car at the curb. The smell of food cooking and a woman's voice calling something in Spanish came from the open window of one of the other apartments. A couple of young men were working on a car in the small parking lot. The hood was propped open and one was bent over the engine while the other man peered over his shoulder. Lucy carefully didn't look at them.

She had to tell Jon, and soon. Right or wrong, she'd made her decision. Eleven days from now, she would be picking up her mother and bringing her to this apartment. She'd invite her to dinner that night, introduce her to Sierra.

The idea of telling him made her feel sick to her stomach. No, he'd never been anything but understanding to her. She'd dropped enough hints about her childhood that he couldn't be totally surprised when he heard the rest.

Sitting in her car, not starting it, she tried to reconcile the seemingly tolerant man she'd gotten to know with the candidate for sheriff who didn't sound tolerant at all. She'd looked at his campaign literature. His entire stance was about being tough on crime, holding people responsible for their misdeeds. He didn't believe in third and fourth and fifth chances. Growing up poor was no excuse, he said; drug addiction was no excuse.

Lucy had no idea which chance this would be for her mother. Seventh? Eighth? Ninth? An addiction as powerful as her mom's *wasn't* an excuse, not for hurting other people. But it was an explanation, and Lucy worried Jon didn't care about explanations.

Criminal behavior deserves swift, inevitable and harsh consequences.

She shuddered. If only he talked about forgiveness, too, or about fresh starts.

I'm in love with him. But what if her mother was more than he could stomach?

A few more days. Surely that won't matter.

JON WAS SAVORING the apple pie Sierra had made when she suddenly jumped up from the table, announcing, "I've got homework."

With a surprised look at Sierra's barely touched dessert, Lucy said, "I was going to put on some coffee. I can boil water for tea if you'd rather."

Already scooping up her dishes, Sierra shook her head. "I don't want anything." She looked at Jon. "Will you come say goodbye before you go?"

"Sure." He smiled at her. "This is great pie. I think I've put on five pounds in the past month from eating here."

His daughter made a rude noise. "Like you'd ever get fat." But he could see from the color in her cheeks that she was pleased.

He watched, bemused, as she deposited her dishes in the dishwasher and vanished with remarkable haste. He looked at Lucy. "What's going on with her? Did I do something? Or is she dying to closet herself in her bedroom so she can spend the next two hours talking on the phone to her boyfriend?"

"No boyfriend yet." Lucy wrinkled her nose. "I think she's trying to give us time alone."

Jon scraped a hand over his chin. "Huh."

The signs had been there. Apparently he was oblivious. He *had* noticed that whenever he suggested an outing, Sierra wanted to invite Lucy, too. Nor was this the first time she'd made an excuse to leave them alone for a while after dinner.

While he mulled over the realization, Lucy stood to pour the coffee. Watching her, he wondered if she was embarrassed that Sierra was plotting to create a family for herself. Or was she embarrassed only because he'd failed to notice?

He was still debating whether they should talk about it when she set the mug in front of him, then sat with her own. "How goes the campaign?" she asked in a breezy voice, letting him know she didn't want to talk about Sierra's hopes.

"On the surface, good. But I've got to tell you, it's getting ugly more often than I'd like," he admitted. He told her about the *Seattle Times* reporter's questions.

She frowned at him. "Did this happen recently? They haven't done an article. Or else I missed it."

"He called on Monday. You're right, there's been no article, which tells me he confirmed everything I told him and determined that there was nothing newsworthy in the incident."

"Is that how you think about it?" Her brown eyes were somber. "As an *incident?*"

The discussion they were on the verge of having was inevitable. Cops lived with the potential for violence every time they reported for a shift. In his experience, civilians were either ghoulishly fascinated or repelled. There was rarely a middle ground. He was strangely reluctant to find out where Lucy fell on the spectrum.

"No. I killed a man. I have to live with the knowledge, and it's not something I ever took lightly."

"What happened?"

He related the events. He didn't try to paint himself as the hero the two women in that car had wanted to make him. "I was working homicide, so I wasn't in uniform. I'd been knocking on doors looking for someone. The irony is, I just happened to be there when he went off his rocker." He shrugged. "I could have been off duty."

"But you wouldn't have been armed if you were, would you?" she asked.

He gave her a wary glance. "I usually am."

Her eyes widened. After a moment she nodded. He carried discreetly now, sometimes in a shoulder holster, sometimes at his right hip. The badge clipped to his belt in front, but he didn't try to advertise the fact that he was armed.

Her gaze slipped lower, as if she was searching for the telltale lump. "I guess I'm not very observant, am I?"

"I don't have a weapon on me right now," he said to reassure her. "I usually lock it in the glove compartment when I'm here."

"Oh." She looked into her coffee cup. "Is that the only time you've had to shoot someone?"

"No. I was shot myself during a traffic stop when I'd been a deputy only a couple of years. I fired back as the car accelerated away. Punctured a tire, shattered the rear and front windshields and wounded the guy. But he didn't die. It's different when you kill someone." He was silent for a moment. "Worse when you see his face as he dies."

He didn't even know why he'd said that. It wasn't the kind of thing he usually told anyone. He'd talked about it with the police psychologist he'd been required to meet with after the shooting, but not to anyone since. He guessed, once again, it came down to his need to be sure Lucy knew who he really was. He had dark places inside, ones he'd made the decision to keep hidden years ago. But what he wanted to have with Lucy wasn't possible if he didn't make a leap of faith.

She gave his hand a quick squeeze, withdrawing her own before he could grab on and hold tight. "I can imagine," she said quietly. "I suppose it's one of the reasons you have to keep a lock on that file cabinet you have in your head, isn't it?"

He was momentarily startled, having forgotten that he'd shared his mental imagery. "Yeah." His voice came out hoarse. "It took a long while before I could lock that one away, though. I had to satisfy myself first that I couldn't have done something different. Something that would have led to a better outcome."

"Usually we're our own worst critic. Did you ever come to peace with yourself over it?"

"Yeah." He felt himself relax. Not physically, but inside, where he'd been braced for an unwelcome reaction from Lucy. He should have known better. "Yeah, I did."

She kept ignoring her cooling cup of coffee, just as he was his own. Her teeth worried her lip, and he waited to find out what was troubling her.

Finally it came out. "I've been wondering. Is it your experiences as a police officer that have made you so…harsh when you talk about people who commit crimes? I mean, everyone makes mistakes. The way I grew up, I saw kids who never had a chance."

"Didn't they? From what you've said, you had it pretty rough yourself. Did you steal cars? Burglarize your neighbors to support a drug habit?" His voice was hard. "Sell yourself?"

Too late, he thought, *Shit*. What if she had? Was that what she was trying to tell him? That she'd done time in juvie? That her past wasn't as pure as the driven snow? Had he made her *afraid* to tell him?

He felt her retreat, although as far as he could tell she didn't move a muscle. It was far more subtle than any obvious flinch. He was stung to realize that, however inadvertently, he'd hurt her.

It seemed like a long time before she said quietly, "No. But I wasn't physically abused, for example."

Still harsh, he said, "I was."

She nodded. Light shimmered on her glossy dark hair. "But you weren't also poor. Nobody was selling drugs in the hallway outside your apartment." She had started softly, but her voice gained strength. Anger resonated in it. "Your mother wasn't turning tricks. You didn't go to school knowing other kids would shun you because you smelled. You didn't go hungry every day because there wasn't any food in the house and nobody had money to give you for lunch."

He swore. "Was that you, Lucy? Did your mother—"

"No." She clamped her mouth shut. Eventually, she relented enough to say, "But we lived in some pretty crummy places. I told you that. I saw what was going on around me."

Jon felt sick. "You think I'm a son of a bitch."

"No." Her expression softened. "Mostly, I wonder what happened to make you so unwilling to see that when a crime's committed, the victim isn't the only human involved."

"Most cops end up pretty hard-assed. It's natural, when you arrest the same scum over and over again, when you see their victims." He let out a huff of air. "But you're right. I've never been sympathetic. I was on a..." He rarely fumbled for words, but he did now. This wasn't something he'd been ready to share yet. But he could see that he had to. "A sort of quest, you might say, when I decided to go into law enforcement. To put away bad guys, and keep them put away where they belonged." Jon grimaced. "Law enforcement was a sharp left turn for me. In college I majored in philosophy, believe it or not. Probably mostly to piss my father off. Then I got practical. Started work on an MBA."

"Really?"

He grinned briefly at her astonishment. "Oh, yeah. At twenty-four, I was about halfway through, telling myself I was doing the right thing." He paused. "I was engaged— Cassia and I were living together."

Lucy waited, her expression apprehensive.

"I loved her." He swallowed, composing himself. "My father didn't. No surprise there. He told me she was a lightweight. He was wrong. Cassia was…happy. She always thought the best of everyone."

He struggled to continue, to tell the rest of the story when the very thought of what had happened to all that goodness almost brought him to his knees.

"She had just graduated herself. She was doing her student teaching—first grade. She was going for elementary-school certification. She had a part-time job as a barista at a place down by Lake Union."

Lucy nodded, recognizing that had some significance.

"She had to close one night a week. It wasn't a great neighborhood. Rougher than it is now. Sometimes I picked her up. I knew it made her nervous, waiting for the bus." This was another story he hadn't told in so many years that putting it in words now cast him back. Made him relive that night. "Some guys wanted me to play poker. I got pretty drunk. It was three in the morning before I made it to the apartment and discovered Cassia wasn't there. No sign she'd ever gotten home. She didn't carry a cell phone—not everyone did fifteen years ago."

"Oh, Jon," she whispered.

"I hammered on a couple of the neighbors' doors. Nobody had seen her or heard her. I got one of the neighbors to drive me down to her espresso stand. It was closed up. Then I saw some flashing lights, right at the head of an alley a block and a half away. Not far from the bus stop."

He told the rest of the story. Running over there. Hands grabbing at him to stop him, but not succeeding. He'd made it far enough to see her sprawled beside a Dumpster, looking like a carelessly discarded doll, not at all like the vital, happy young woman she was. He didn't tell Lucy the details. The way Cassia's skirt had been shoved up to her waist, leaving her naked below it, her legs parted. Or her face. Dear God, her face. He later learned she'd been strangled after she was raped. The physical manifestations of strangulation were hideous.

He'd begun to bellow, fighting those hands that pulled him away. He'd fallen to his knees eventually, hands braced on the rough sidewalk as he puked. Finally he had hammered a fist into a concrete wall until his hand was bloody.

"She was murdered by a man who'd walked out of prison the day before. He'd been convicted of two rapes. He had started to strangle the second victim, but she was saved by some passersby who saw what was happening.

He was a good boy in prison, though, and claimed to have been sexually abused by a stepfather when he was a kid. God knows how many women he'd raped before he was actually caught. Got parole the first time he came up for it. He had been out of prison for exactly thirty-six hours when he saw Cassia waiting at the bus stop. Alone."

Pain and empathy brimmed in Lucy's big brown eyes. She groped for his hand on the table, and he let her take it although he felt physically unable to turn his over and return her grip. "You've never forgiven yourself, have you?"

CHAPTER NINE

A SHOCK WENT THROUGH JON. Lucy had read him without any trouble, understood the guilt he'd carried ever since. "You think I should have shrugged and figured it was bad luck I picked the wrong night to get drunk?"

"What if Cassia hadn't been living with you? Wouldn't she have been at that bus stop anyway?"

"I don't know!" he shouted.

Lucy looked at him with such compassion, he could hardly bear it. "Do you really think it's so unforgivable that you didn't go pick her up that one night?"

"Yes." The word scraped his throat. His face contorted. "Yes!" Then he took a deep, shuddering breath and shook his head. "No. I know better. I don't think about it—about her—for months at a time. When I do... I'd give anything to go back and do it over."

"Of course you would." Her thumb caressed the back of his hand. "And you've been trying ever since, haven't you?"

"That's simplistic," he argued. Damn, he felt raw inside and out. Exposed, and he didn't like it.

Her eyes were unbelievably soft, so tender he couldn't have looked away if he'd tried.

"Yes, I know it is. But that doesn't mean it isn't true."

"Yeah." He was still hoarse. "Hell. I can't deny it."

He tugged at her hand, pulling her out of her seat. Lucy came around the corner of the table. Jon let go of her hand so that he could wrap his arms around her waist and bury his face between her breasts. He closed his eyes and lost himself in her heartbeat, the rise and fall of her chest as she breathed. Her scent. He felt her stroke his hair and neck. Not since he was a little boy had anyone comforted him like this. He couldn't have accepted it from anyone else.

He almost had himself pulled together when he heard the patter of footsteps and Sierra saying, "Did Dad forget to say goodbye?"

Jon straightened with a jerk, his hands falling from Lucy. She had turned as if to shield him by the time Sierra bounced into the kitchen.

Voice calm, Lucy said, "No, he was just thinking about going. We got to talking."

Jon stood. "I had better be on my way."

He sensed Lucy's quick, worried look, but didn't meet her eyes. The feeling of being stripped bare hadn't left him. Did he regret telling her? No. He didn't even think that was why he was so shaken. It was Lucy's embrace that had rattled him so badly. Or maybe discovering how pathetically grateful he was to have her of all people want to hold him when he hurt.

He managed the goodbyes, and the drive home. It wasn't until he was turning into his own driveway that Jon pulled back from his own emotions enough to think about Lucy's and start wondering. Why the passion when she'd cried, *You didn't go to school knowing other kids would shun you because you smelled. You didn't go hungry every day because there wasn't any food in the house and nobody had money to give you for lunch.*

Frowning, he waited for his garage door to rise. How had she put it?

Everyone makes mistakes.

Something told him she wasn't really talking about *everyone*. She was talking about *someone*.

But who? Herself? Or someone else?

OH, WOW. Lucy gripped the seat belt crossing her chest as though it were a climbing rope and she was dangling on a rock face. She was *really* close to chickening out. What had made her think she was ready for this?

Almost at random, she blurted, "You've never said where you lived."

Driving with his usual casual competence, Jon glanced at her. "Willis. It's not exciting. I have a town house. Almost no outside maintenance. It's not someplace I'd want to raise a family, but…" His big shoulders moved. "I work long hours."

"Gardening isn't *maintenance*."

"My mother would say the same thing. Me, I've never had time to catch the gardening bug."

"I guess most men don't."

"After tasting vegetables right from your backyard, I might be inspired to wield a hoe." Accelerating when a light turned green, he glanced at her again. "You're a better cook than I am."

She laughed, despite her attack of nerves. "Is that a warning?"

The curve of his mouth was irresistible. "Afraid so."

She'd known she was agreeing to more than dinner when he suggested he cook for her this time. Or at least…she assumed she was agreeing to more. And she *was* ready.

Except she was scared, too, because she shouldn't be preparing to make love with a man she couldn't trust. And she didn't, or she would have been able to bring herself to tell him about her mother.

She should, before they got naked, but… she wasn't going to. She wanted this. *Him.* Even if it was only this once.

In one of those peculiar moments of clarity, Lucy understood that she trusted him with her body, but not with the wounded part of her that had never healed.

The turn signal went on, and he announced, "My neighborhood."

He sounded so relaxed, it made Lucy mad. His tone suggested that first-time sex with a woman he was dating wasn't that earth-shaking an event for him. In the fifteen years since his fiancée had died, he'd probably had *dozens* of relationships. Of course he wasn't nervous.

Knowing she was being irrational, Lucy peered ahead at the street of town houses. They were new, designed in the currently popular Craftsman style, distinguishable from each other mainly by individual paint colors. He made another turn, and she discovered that an alley ran behind the homes and the garages were accessed via the alley.

He reached up and pushed a button, then drove right into an almost completely bare double garage. A rolling tool chest was positioned against the rear wall, but there was no workbench, no lawn mower, no rack to hold rakes and shovels and hoes. No clutter.

"You really *don't* garden."

"I pay a yard service for what little has to be done." He turned off the engine and closed the double door. "Have I disillusioned you?"

"No. I just…hadn't thought." Couldn't imagine was what she meant.

They both got out and he held open a door, gesturing her through. Landscaped with an elegantly shaped Japanese maple and a few shrubs, the backyard was tiny, separated from the neighboring ones by a cedar-slat fence. A deck with built-in benches held a couple of big tubs filled with fall-blooming flowers.

"I do water them on the days no one from the service comes," Jon murmured.

"They're beautiful," she admitted. "I never fertilize my hanging baskets enough."

Unlocking one of the French doors, he shot her a wicked smile. "I *never* fertilize mine."

Lucy laughed. "Then you have elves who sneak around when you aren't here and do it."

She admired the beautifully cared for yard. "They prune, too. And bark."

"I put out bowls of milk for them." He ushered her inside.

The interior was beautiful, but not really personal any more than the yard was, she discovered. Partly because there was no clutter. Either he was really tidy or he had a martinet of a housekeeper.

Most of the first story was a single open space, with generous windows front and back. The floor was gleaming hardwood except for the kitchen area, which was ceramic tiled. Lucy trailed her fingers over the leather sofa to discover it was buttery soft. She wondered how often anyone sat on it. The big recliner facing the large-screen TV looked more used. A cordless phone, the TV guide section from the newspaper and a couple of remote controls covered an end table next to it. Bookcases flanked a fireplace that was so clean she wondered if Jon had ever sullied it with a fire. Books filled the shelves that weren't occupied by a state-of-the-art stereo system.

Aware that Jon was watching her, Lucy went to examine the spines of books to see what he read. Science fiction, biographies, history and—maybe not surprisingly—philosophy.

"No mysteries?"

He grunted. "I find myself critiquing them."

"I suppose so."

She followed him toward the kitchen. The space flowed into a dining area with a long table she thought was cherry and six matching chairs. The kitchen was separated from it only by a breakfast bar, tiled in rust. The cabinets were cherry, too, she thought—nice, but probably not custom. She suspected he'd added very little to the house—furniture, books and a few pieces of artwork. While he began opening cupboards and getting things out, she wandered to look more closely at the paintings that hung on white walls. They were interesting, Lucy decided. Jon must have chosen them himself.

One, she was intrigued to see, was an oil or acrylic of a garden scene in fall. The colors and textures were glorious, although it was plain that leaves were rotting on the ground and flowers fading. The artist had captured a moment of peaceful decay, and yet there was also a hint of something more melancholic. After frowning at the painting, Lucy turned her head to see that Jon stood watching her, a frying pan in his hand.

"Does your garden ever look sad?" he asked unexpectedly.

"I don't think of it that way. I would have

been cutting these plants back, starting to mulch. Putting it to rest. This garden looks… neglected." That was it, she realized. It was as if there was no human hand around to touch it.

"Pretty doesn't always appeal to me."

No, she could see that. The other paintings weren't conventionally pretty, either. She wandered from one to the next, pausing longest at a watercolor of a couple scarcely visible in dense fog on a beach. There was something terribly lonely about these two people, even though they were together. Maybe, she reflected, it was because they weren't holding hands or touching in any way. They were together, but…not.

Eventually she pulled out a stool at the breakfast bar and perched on it. "Can I do anything?"

"Nope. I marinated steaks, made a salad earlier and I'm sautéing baby potatoes. Nothing complicated." His crooked grin was rueful. "Which is all I'm capable of."

"Oh, I think you're plenty complicated," Lucy teased.

He lifted one dark eyebrow. "I'm not the only one who is."

"Maybe not," she admitted. She didn't think of herself as complicated, but she also knew that what people saw on her surface wasn't quite what they'd get.

They chatted easily enough while Jon cooked. He poured them both glasses of wine, and finally consented to let her set the table while he removed sizzling steaks from the broiler.

Over dinner they talked about movies and books and music. Lucy firmly steered him away from the subject of family, even though she would have liked to know more about his. His relationship with his mother had seemed cordial, but not without underlying strain. He maintained an indefinable distance, and Lucy had seen the flicker of hurt on his mother's face a couple of times. Did he still harbor anger that she hadn't protected him better, or was something else wrong between them? Or maybe, Lucy thought, she was misreading them altogether. But she couldn't ask, because then he would have wanted to know about her mother, and she didn't want to talk about her mom.

Not yet.

She kept losing track of what he was saying. She'd find herself watching his lips move, and remembering the last time he'd kissed her. Or she would be captivated by his hand, wrapped around his wineglass. His hands were as large and graceful as the rest of him. He was long fingered, and yet his palms were broad, his wrists twice the thickness of hers. The backs of his fingers were lightly dusted with hair, as were his forearms and wrists. He wasn't a particularly hairy man, but she'd seen brown curls on his chest when he undid several buttons on his shirt.

He obviously wasn't wearing a holster or weapon right now. He had on jeans and an oxford cloth shirt with the sleeves rolled up a couple of times. Athletic shoes, she'd noticed earlier, that looked well-worn. She recalled him saying that he ran for exercise.

Oh, Lord, she thought in renewed panic. He was so beautifully fit, and she wasn't. Well, she wouldn't say she was in terrible shape. Goodness knows, she was on her feet most of the day and worked hard at her store and in her garden. But she'd never exercised for the sake of exercise. And…she was curvy, not sleek. She hated to imagine what she'd look like in spandex.

She contributed to the conversation, although a minute later she couldn't remember what she'd said. She was looking at his hands again, imagining him gripping a pistol.

Imagining him cupping her breast.

Her cheeks heated at the thought. She came

back to herself to realize that Jon's eyes had narrowed slightly and he was doing nothing but looking at her. His expression was razor sharp, intent. Embarrassed, she wondered if he could read her mind.

"This was great," she told him enthusiastically. "You lied. You can cook."

"My repertoire is limited." He cleared his throat. "I should have offered you something to drink besides wine."

"I'm fine." She'd sipped at a truly excellent merlot, but she hadn't wanted to get blurry. She had been glad to see that Jon hadn't refilled his glass, either.

"I should offer you coffee." His gaze was locked with hers. "But…coffee isn't quite what I have on my mind."

"I…don't have it on mine, either," she admitted. Her voice had squeaked a little at the end.

Jon didn't seem to mind. He pushed his chair back and rose. "Lucy. Maybe I'm making a big assumption…."

She shook her head.

"Thank God," he said roughly, and held out a hand to her.

For a moment she stared at it, her belly cramping as she thought about the way he touched her. Then she laid her hand in his, and let him pull her to her feet.

The next moment, he'd gathered her close and was kissing her.

HE LOVED HER TASTE. And the lush feel of her body against his.

Jon should have started more tenderly, but he hadn't. He'd fitted his mouth to hers and claimed it, his tongue sliding right past her teeth and stroking hers. If she minded, he couldn't tell. She whimpered, rose on tiptoe and wrapped her arms around his neck. He kept kissing her until his lungs screamed for oxygen, then pulled back only to press more openmouthed kisses to her softly rounded cheek. He sucked on her earlobe, then nipped it while she trembled and gasped.

"Let's take this upstairs before I can't walk," he said huskily.

"Yes. Please."

Impulse overcame him. Before her hands could leave his neck, he gripped her buttocks and lifted her. With a squeak, she wrapped her legs around his waist. Of course that meant he had to kiss her again while he squeezed her butt and moved her against him in a way that half crazed him.

Eventually he got his feet moving, but it

was lucky the place didn't have many walls, because he might have walked into one. Jon took his mouth from hers long enough to climb the stairs, time she used to her advantage to nibble and lick on his neck. He was groaning by the time he reached the second story and started down the short hall to his bedroom.

He didn't set her down; he let her fall and went with her, landing right where he wanted to be, on top of her with his erection cradled between her thighs. Looking at him, her eyes were huge and startled, the brown so warm he thought of gooey chocolate-chip cookies or hot cocoa on a cold day. He loved her eyes, too, he realized.

And her hair. It was fanned out around her on the duvet in dark waves. He tangled his fingers in it, savoring the texture of heavy, coarse silk. He imagined her astride him, that hair cloaking her naked body and tickling his if she bent forward.

"Since the first time I saw you, I've imagined you here," he murmured. He sounded drunk with pleasure already. "You're beautiful. Perfect."

Her nose crinkled. "I'm short. And plump."

"Perfect," he repeated. "Not all men like bony women."

Lucy smiled and stroked his face with one hand. "I'm glad you don't. I've…been thinking about this since the first time I saw you, too."

"Sierra says you don't date."

"She hasn't known me that long." She seemed fascinated by the rough texture of his jaw. "I date. Just, um, not very often."

He bent to nuzzle her face. "How often?"

Breathless, she managed to say, "Not… very."

He sank into her for a deep, hungry kiss. His hips rocked against hers, and his hand found her breast under her shirt. Damn. He had to get her out of that bra. With a groan he rolled to his side and began peeling the shirt over her head.

In the act of reaching around her for the clasp, he stopped simply to look at Lucy. The bra, satin and lace, was a dark rose that matched her cheeks with the soft flush. Beautiful skin the delicious color of milk darkened with a dollop of coffee.

"So pretty," he said in a thick voice, finally unhooking the bra then slipping a finger under it to pull it away from her gorgeous, generous breasts.

Her nipples were already taut with arousal. Perfect. He licked the broad, dark aureoles and kissed creamy skin and the tight nubbins of her nipples and finally suckled while she arched toward his mouth, gripped the back of his head and let tiny gasps and moans escape.

At one point he realized she was unbuttoning his shirt and he helped by shrugging out of it. It damn near killed him to pull away eventually to untie and kick off his shoes and tug off first his jeans then hers, but the reward was the sight of her delectable body, small but perfectly proportioned. Tiny waist, breasts that filled his large hands, hips that curved the way a woman's should and legs long for her height. Her belly was soft instead of firm with muscle. He liked that. He liked it so much, he had to slide down and lay his cheek against it before going lower yet, to the nest of midnight-dark curls with the same texture as the hair spilling over his bed.

He saw her head rise from the pillow. "Jon?" She sounded shocked. "Wait. What are you—"

Hadn't any man ever tasted her here? he wondered, bemused. She bucked at the initial stroke of his tongue. He muttered words of praise, telling her that she was spicy and sexy and how desperately he wanted to be inside her.

She was panting, her hips rising and falling rhythmically when he finally crawled up her length. He was at her damp entrance when common sense slammed into him.

"Damn. I almost forgot." Swearing, he rolled away from her and groped in the drawer of his bedside table.

"Oh, no," she said. "I'm not on birth control."

"Don't worry." He tore open the packet and rolled it on. He hated wearing a condom. If he asked, would she start on birth-control pills or a patch?

When he came back to her, she whispered, "I'm not very experienced."

What did *that* mean? He made himself stop again, although he was already nudging at her entrance. "You're not a virgin?"

"No. I just…haven't done this in a long time." She sounded embarrassed. "I hope you didn't expect—"

"Sweetheart, all I expect is *you*." He lifted himself to look down at her, his weight resting on his elbows, and cupped her face in his hands. "All I want is you."

"Oh." Her eyes searched his for a moment. Her teeth bit into her lower lip. "Okay," she finally whispered. "I want you, too."

"Good." He grinned at her, vaguely aware

that he probably looked more savage than reassuring, but he didn't think he could wait another minute. Another second. He began pushing forward, trying to go slowly, but oh, *damn,* she felt good. Tight, but slick, too. Her eyes were unfocused and her fingers were clenching his biceps, tiny bites of pain from her nails that somehow heightened all the other sensations.

Once he was seated as deep as he could go, he unclenched his jaw to ask, "Are you all right?" When she nodded, he began moving. He couldn't go slowly, not this time, and she didn't seem to want him to. Her hips rocked to meet his every thrust, and it seemed to him she was demanding that he lunge deeper, harder, faster. He didn't know if he was going to be able to draw this out long enough for her, but he'd barely framed the fear in his mind when she convulsed. Gritting his teeth against the staggering pleasure, he let himself go and had the distant thought that he'd never felt anything like this.

He sagged on top of her, a part of him knowing he was too heavy to sprawl on her this way, but the will to roll away was missing. Her arms closed around him tightly, almost fiercely. He felt her kissing his shoulder, and thought, *well, hell, where else could her mouth go?*

With a groan that came from deep in his chest, he levered himself up and came down on his side, pulling her with him so that their bodies stayed pressed together.

"I think I've died and gone to heaven," he murmured against hair that seemed to have taken on a life of its own, heavy locks lying across his chest and throat and chin.

"Mmm." She snuggled closer, although he didn't know how that was possible.

Lucy was so relaxed he wondered if she was going to sleep. He felt sated, but energized, too. He realized he was smiling. Exhilaration buzzed in him until he could almost hear the sound, nearly forgotten but familiar. He had to think to nail it down. The hum was like contented bumblebees working his mother's garden on a hot day.

He could close his eyes and be there again, sprawling on the lawn he'd just mowed, the sharp scent of freshly cut grass in his nostrils, listening to the hum. Being happy.

Was that the last time he'd been this happy?

No. His smile died. Of course not. He had been happy with Cassia. It was…a different kind of happiness.

Jon searched himself for any feeling of guilt, and was grateful not to find it. He couldn't even quite see Cassia's face, although he tried to summon it. As it should be after making love to a gorgeous woman. He was a little shocked at how good he felt, how peaceful, but not in any way ready to surrender it.

With that same, faint shock, he thought, *I'm in love with Lucy.*

Sierra was a hell of a smart kid. She just might get her wish after all.

The three of them as a family was sounding really good right now.

CHAPTER TEN

THEY MADE LOVE AGAIN before Jon took Lucy home. She hated to leave, and she could tell he didn't want to let her. It was hard not to notice. He kissed her one more time on her doorstep, said, "Good night," then growled, "Damn it," kissed her again before all but shoving her inside. "Lock up."

She did, glad to have a moment to collect herself prior to seeing Sierra. It wasn't that late. The living room was dark, but her foster daughter had left the hall light on and her bedroom door stood open. Apparently she wasn't taking any chance that Lucy would sneak to bed without stopping to talk.

Would she be able to tell anything was different? Lucy touched her cheek that she suspected was whisker burned, and her lips that felt swollen. She blushed at the mere memory of what they'd done. Oh, heavens, she probably smelled like sex.

But Sierra was innocent—at least Lucy was

reasonably sure she was—so she probably wouldn't notice.

Right. Uh-huh. Sierra noticed *everything*.

Lucy sighed and went to the teenager's bedroom. "I'm home."

Sierra was on her bed, as always, laptop open on her stomach, her head propped up with pillows enough for her to see the screen. The position looked uncomfortable but never seemed to bother her.

"I heard you." Her interested gaze—so disconcertingly like her father's—swept over Lucy. "Have fun?"

"I did." Mistress of nonchalance, Lucy smiled. "He can cook."

"Cool. What'd he make?"

Lucy told her. "No dessert, though."

"He said he doesn't bake. That he eats, like, store-bought cookies." Sierra closed the computer and scooched higher against the headboard. "What's his house like?"

Did Sierra mind that he'd taken Lucy there and not her? Lucy couldn't tell. She did her best to describe it. "It's a lot nicer than this," she finished ruefully. "Although he says he doesn't spend that much time there."

"I think he's here whenever he isn't out doing his running-for-office thing," Sierra observed.

"That's probably true."

"It's weird that, like, six weeks ago we didn't know him." Sierra's forehead puckered. "You were freaked when I said I wanted to meet him."

Shoulder against the door frame, Lucy gave a soft laugh. "I was."

"But I was right. You were wrong." The teenager grinned, looking mischievous. "Say it. I was right."

"It could have turned out differently."

"I was right," she prompted. "And who was wrong?"

Laughing, rolling her eyes, Lucy said, "I was wrong. You were right. Lucky, too, but right. I think…he really wants to be your dad."

Sierra's smile faded. "I wish…"

Lucy straightened in the doorway. "What?"

Her foster daughter gave a jerky shrug. "I guess that Mom could know."

Gentling her voice, Lucy said, "Maybe she can."

"She never took me to church. I don't think she believed in an afterlife."

Very softly, Lucy quoted, "'There are more things in heaven and earth, Horatio, than are dreamt of in your philosophy.'"

Sierra frowned. "What's that from?"

"Shakespeare. *Hamlet,* I'm pretty sure. I don't know why I remember it."

"'There are more things in heaven and earth…'" Sierra murmured, the lost look on her face tugging at Lucy's heart. "Why Horatio?"

"Uh…I don't remember. Hamlet must have been talking to somebody named Horatio."

"That's an awful name."

"Maybe it wasn't in 1600. It might have been the equivalent of Chad, or Evan."

"Horatio." Sierra grinned.

"How come you haven't read *Hamlet?*" Lucy asked. "Don't they educate kids anymore?"

"The only Shakespeare we've ever read was *Romeo and Juliet* in eighth grade. Out loud. It didn't sound that great, the way some of the kids read it."

Lucy laughed. "I'll bet. Read *Hamlet.* In fact, read *something,* instead of spending all your time on the computer."

"Dad said that the other day."

It struck Lucy how much more naturally Sierra was saying *Dad.* She felt a pang. No, worse than that—a brief but painful cramp in her chest. Sierra had a dad now. They were getting really comfortable with each other.

Father-daughter. Once the election was over, wouldn't it occur to Jon that there was no reason Sierra couldn't live with him?

Or…was that part of Lucy's attraction to him? The notion of them as a family? She examined the idea and knew how seductive it was.

But family included the in-laws, and he hadn't met *her* family yet. She could just imagine introducing her. "Have I mentioned my mother? Terry Malone. She's an ex-con and former drug addict, but she'd be the perfect grandmother to your kids."

Feeling sick, Lucy thought, *I should have told him.*

She would. Soon. Sometime before next Thursday, when she was picking up her mom and bringing her home.

JON SAT AT HIS DESK flipping through a pile of memos, most of which were only FYI—no action on his part required. He skimmed with only half his attention while he ate a deli sandwich. Staffing changes, new protocols, complaints about the state that conference rooms were being left in—put another way, throw out your own goddamn coffee cups. A list of recent parolees who would be taking up residence in the county. His interest was no more than idle in that one; individual units would take note of particular names depending on their areas of interest. He ran his gaze down the list nonetheless, his eyes stopping briefly at a child sex offender, a drug trafficker, an SOB who'd beaten the crap out of his wife, who was nonetheless apparently taking him back. Jon recognized one name, someone he'd put away for second-degree murder. Good to know Finch was already out, Jon thought cynically.

He had already flipped to the next memo—something about a recruitment drive—when his brain processed one of the last names he'd seen. A woman.

Terry Malone. It was the coincidence of the last name that had caught his eye. Had to be chance… But he stared in shock at the address she had given for her residence.

Lucy's.

This Terry Malone been convicted of first-degree robbery and her sentence indicated it was committed with a firearm. She had a lengthy rap sheet. These days, the third-strike law would have gotten her prison for life with no possibility of parole. She'd been lucky, sentenced a few months before the law took effect.

This was Lucy's mother?

The bits and pieces Lucy had told him wove together, for the first time forming a whole cloth. She hadn't hidden her anxiety about her mother or the fact that she'd had a crappy childhood. But plenty of people had that without a parent who'd been in and out of prison during the years when said parent should have been attending parent-teacher conferences and driving her kid to soccer practice.

Later he might care who'd done those things for Lucy. Right now anger roared through him, a white-hot sheet of it. This was why she'd talked about people making mistakes, why she'd been groping for extenuating circumstances. Why she'd plainly been worried about his lack of sympathy for criminals.

Jon tried to rein himself in. Maybe it wasn't her mother. Maybe this was an aunt or even a sister…. No, she'd said she was an only child, and from the list of priors this woman was too old to be Lucy's sibling anyway.

This had to be her mother, then. The one who had raised her daughter in places where drug deals were happening in the hall outside their door. Who had sent her to school without a lunch and maybe without break-fast. Who hadn't seen to it that she had clean clothes. Who'd…turned tricks? God, had she done that?

He felt sick as well as angry. Why in *hell* was Lucy even thinking about taking this woman in? Did she not have the courage to say no?

A guttural sound escaped him. *Did she really think for a minute that he'd let her expose* his daughter *to this piece of scum?*

He reached for the phone, but didn't dial. No. He had to talk to her in person.

How could she not tell him about this? Had she intended to introduce *mom* with some lame story about how she'd decided to move to town to be near her daughter? The idea that Lucy would deceive him like that fanned the flames of his rage. His skin hurt, so much fury was moving through him. Not only fury, but a sense of betrayal. He'd convinced him-self he was in love with her and that she must be falling for him, too. He'd felt something he hadn't in fifteen years…. Longer. Admit it. He'd never felt anything like this. The emo-tions welling up had tied him in knots inside, but in a good way.

He bowed his head and dug his fingers into

his hair. Eyes closed, he remembered how he had felt after making love with Lucy. Holding her in his arms. The glory and the peace.

Oh, shit. I'll have to tell Edie.

Asset or detriment?

He'd trusted Lucy.

This wasn't just about Sierra. It was also about what a scandal involving Lucy would do to his chances of winning the election.

Apparently she didn't care.

He wouldn't call Edie until tomorrow. He'd give Lucy a chance first. Maybe her mother had given her address without Lucy's knowledge. Lucy might not be aware her mother thought they were going to have an affecting reconciliation and that, oh, surely she had a spare bed. Maybe Lucy had a plan that *didn't* involve introducing Terry Malone to an innocent sixteen-year-old.

He'd have given anything not to be obligated to give a talk to a veterans' group this evening, but there was no getting out of it. At least they were likely to provide a sympathetic audience. He'd get through it, and then he would go to Lucy's.

JON'S PHONE CALL that afternoon was beyond terse.

"I need to talk to you."

"Really?" The door shut behind Mr. Hendricks and his grossly overweight, elderly pug, Sebastian. Closing the cash-register drawer, Lucy said in surprise, "Well, I don't have any customers right now—"

"No." Jon's voice was completely expressionless. "I want to come over tonight. Say, nine o'clock?"

"I… Yes, I guess that's okay," she faltered.

With barely an "I'll see you then," he ended the call.

Lucy was on tenterhooks for the rest of the day. Could he have found out about her mother? But how on earth…? Her worries raced and collided in her head like bumper cars.

He'd called and talked to Sierra last night. She'd taken the phone in her room. Without being able to make out words, Lucy had heard her artlessly chattering. Had she slipped? Asking her to keep a secret hadn't been fair, Lucy silently acknowledged. But… Sierra was honest enough to have admitted she'd opened her mouth and said something she hadn't meant to.

Maybe this wasn't about her mom at all. Had Jon's opponent found out about Sierra? Maybe he was planning to make some kind of statement and force Jon's hand. If so, the timing couldn't be worse.

I could still call Mom and say, I'm sorry, but you can't come here.

No. Steadier now, she accepted that she'd made the only decision she could. Accepted the risks. She was in love with Jon. Loved Sierra. Had come to love Sierra so quickly and easily in part because Lucy, too, had been the child who lost her mother. But unlike Sierra, Lucy had another chance, and she had to take it.

If Jon loved her, he'd understand. He'd look past his own prejudices and help. If he didn't… Pain squeezed her chest. If he didn't, well, what would she really have lost?

Sierra looked surprised when Lucy told her over dinner that Jon was coming over.

"He said he wants to talk to me. He sounded serious."

The teenager frowned. "Like, mad serious?"

"I don't know." No matter how many times she'd turned their brief phone conversation over in her mind, she still couldn't read his emotional state.

When he showed up finally, at almost nine-thirty, Sierra let him in. Lucy, trying to look casual, was curled on one end of the sofa with a book. Even as he spoke to his daughter, his gaze found Lucy.

The uncomfortable thump in her chest wasn't close to a regular beat.

He looked…haggard. And hard, too. No, worse than that. Blank, the way he had when Sierra first told him she thought she was his daughter. Absolutely no emotion was allowed to leach out. She wasn't sure she wanted to know what was going through his head.

He'd wrenched his tie loose and it hung askew. The suit coat had been left in the car. The white shirt was wrinkled, the sleeves rolled up. His hair was as rumpled as hair that short could get. Lucy would have sworn new lines bracketed his eyes and mouth. And—most shocking—he wore a big black pistol in a holster at his waist. Had he forgotten to take it off and lock it in his glove compartment? Or was he making some kind of point? Asserting authority in a horribly visual way.

She wrenched her gaze from the gun and started to get up. "You look tired. Would you like a cup of coffee? Or we have leftover lasagna if you haven't eaten."

"No." His expression didn't soften. He looked at his daughter and said, "Sierra,

I have things I need to discuss with Lucy. Would you mind?"

"I guess I should go to bed anyway. I mean, I have school tomorrow." Nervous glances flicking between the two adults, Sierra backed toward the short hall. "Night, Lucy. And, um, Dad."

"Good night," he said. He didn't move until they heard her bedroom door shut. Then he walked over and sat on the easy chair a few feet from Lucy, whose fingernails were biting into her palms.

"Tell me about your mother."

All the oxygen in her lungs escaped in a rush. Dots swam before her eyes. She had to remind herself how to breathe. Finally, around an enormous lump in her throat, she said, "How did you find out?"

His mouth thinned. "Tell me."

Lucy looked down at her hands. "You know she's being released from prison."

He said nothing.

"She's been in for eight years this time. That's the longest ever. I've lost track of how many times she's been in. I was a baby the first time. I mostly grew up in foster homes and haven't lived with her for more than eighteen months at a stretch." Lucy paused. "She's, um, an addict."

"Heroin?"

She shook her head. "Opiates. Downers of any kind. She drinks if she can't get anything else." She bit her lip until it hurt. "She tries. Really she does. She's been through every kind of drug treatment program there is. But…wow. Once she'd been out scarcely two hours when she'd conned a doctor into giving her a prescription for painkillers."

"Did she prostitute herself?"

Lucy had to look up at that. "No. Where did you get that idea?" She thought over their conversations and the details of her early life she'd shared, wondering what she might have said that would give him that impression. "Oh. It was what I said when we talked about people in desperate situations. No, that wasn't Mom. I told you, we lived in some really awful places. Once we lived for three or four months in one of those motels where you can rent rooms by the week. It was near Sea-Tac Airport, on the Pacific Highway."

She knew she didn't have to tell him what a problem prostitution was there. The Green River killer had picked up many of his victims on that strip.

"Mostly the motel was where women—and some teenage girls, too—took their johns. I was—" she struggled for enough air to fill her lungs "—like, eleven or twelve. I could tell those girls weren't that much older than I was." She shivered and discovered she'd wrapped her arms tightly around herself, a bandage on a wound she rarely let herself acknowledge. She wished Jon was holding her instead, but he hadn't moved. Lucy risked a glance at his face, and regretted doing so.

He stared at her incredulously, his eyes so cold they looked like shards of ice. "Mom? You still call her *Mom?*"

Lucy's spine stiffened. "She *is* my mother. For better or worse."

"Obviously it's for worse." He uttered an obscenity that shouldn't have shocked her but did. "Tell me you're not opening your door to her."

"I— Not exactly."

"She listed your home—this address—as the residence where her parole officer could contact her."

"I've found her another place to live."

"Where?"

"An apartment. It's a few blocks away."

"A few blocks away."

"Yes. I can help her get a job and…" She'd begun to rock slightly. Not enough for him to notice. Please. Only enough to help her contain the painful swell of emotions that wanted to burst out of her. "Just help her."

He stood suddenly, but not to come to her. Instead he swung away and began to pace. "Lucy, why?" Two strides to one end of her tiny living room, two strides back, each turn jerky. "This is so unbelievably stupid, I told myself you didn't know anything about it. That your mother was trying to take advantage of you. So make me understand why you would do this."

"She's my mother!" The cry came from her heart. "She's all I've got. Why can't you understand that?"

He laughed, but without humor it sounded more like a snarl. "Because she forfeited any right to your loyalty or love the first time she used drugs when she had a baby who needed her. Did she use when she was pregnant with you?"

She knew her rocking had become more pronounced; she couldn't help herself. Her mom swore she had stayed straight throughout the pregnancy. Lucy had never known for sure. But she didn't seem to be too damaged, so she *wanted* to believe.

"I know she loves me. She was so scared for me when they took her away. I can still see her struggling, crying. And then…and then she'd write me every day, and cry when I came to see her. I really, truly believe she couldn't help herself."

His gaze burned into hers. "We all make decisions. Every minute, every hour, every day. Brave ones or cowardly ones. Strong or weak. Smart or stupid. Those decisions aren't easy, not for any of us." His voice rose to a roar. "What possible excuse is there for someone who makes the wrong ones, over and over? For someone who will do anything for her next fix? Anything at all?"

"When she was straight, she was a good mother. We laughed. She loved to garden. Wherever we lived, she had tubs of flowers even if there wasn't a yard. That awful hotel, she had African violets. I still remember a row of them on the windowsill. I got that from her." Lucy talked fast, the words spilling out. "And animals. I remember this time we saw a dog get hit by a car. It was going too fast and the driver didn't stop. You could tell the dog was a stray. It was really skinny and mangy. It was a big dog. Mom hurt her back getting it into the car and we took it to a vet. We didn't have very much money, but she told the vet she'd pay for him to treat it."

The dog had died. Lucy remembered her distraught mother pleading with the veterinarian to take care of the dog, and Lucy, who had been standing there watching the brown eyes film over, had known it was too late.

"What did she do, hold up a liquor store to get the money?" Jon asked in that voice as hard and jagged as gravel.

Lucy stared at him in outrage. "No. She's not like that. She's not!"

He paused long enough to stare down at her, contempt twisting his mouth. "Who are you kidding? She was convicted of armed robbery."

"She held jobs. They weren't very good ones, because once you have a record, no one wants to hire you. Mostly she was a waitress. But once she started using…" This was so hard to talk about. She'd never imagined telling him in the face of an expression so cold and forbidding. "She always found a man. She'd get, I don't know, mixed up in what they were doing. Mostly selling drugs. The last one…she was with him when he held up a store. She didn't know he was going to do it. But she was there, and she didn't stop it, and she got in the car with him when they left."

"Just hanging with him, was she?"

"She's not excusing herself. I'm not excusing her."

"Where were you when she and her boyfriend were holding up this store?"

Lucy was vaguely shocked to realize that she had drawn her knees up to her chest. She was all but in a fetal position, holding herself as tightly as she could. "I didn't live with her anymore. Not once I graduated from high school. I was in school to become a veterinary technician." She didn't cry. She didn't. She'd used up all her tears years ago. But her vision blurred anyway. In a whisper, she said, "Mom was at my graduation. She was so proud."

She thought his face contorted, although she couldn't be sure. But if it had, he scrubbed away the emotion with a rough swipe of his hand.

"Lucy…" His voice had become gentler, too, but maybe that was in her imagination, as well. "You must see that this is a mistake. Did you really intend to let Sierra get to know this woman? What if she starts using?"

"I'll know if she does."

"Are you going to welcome your mother's next boyfriend to your home, too?" His tone hardened again the way his expression had. "Introduce *him* to my daughter?"

"I think Mom desperately needs me. She's changed, Jon. I really believe that. This is her chance. Her last real chance. It's the first time she's ever looked honestly at herself. When I've been to visit her, she hasn't made excuses. She has so many regrets, it hurts to listen to her."

He was shaking his head, but Lucy plowed on.

"I can tell she believes she can mend everything that's ever been wrong between us. And she can't, but I don't know how to say that."

"Finally, a grain of common sense."

"Don't disparage me!" Lucy lifted her head, and her arms loosened from their clasp around her knees. "Mom won't make it if the hurt between us is still festering. Can't you see that? I have to give her that, even if—" She couldn't finish. Didn't let herself say, *Even if I don't want to. Even if I sometimes wish she was dead like Sierra's mother is.*

Jon *would* understand that, and Lucy couldn't bear it. She hated the part of her that would even think such a thing, and she couldn't love a man who would say coldly, "You're right. Too bad your mother isn't dead." She didn't want confirmation he was that man.

"You know what Rinnert will do with this wonderful gem you've handed him? Can't you imagine the editorials? Captain Brenner admits his lover's mother was just released from Washington Corrections Center for Women after serving eight years for armed robbery."

"We're not—"

"We are." His voice roughened. "We were."

Lucy went utterly still. She couldn't have looked at him to save her life.

She should have told him before she made love to him. It would have been bad, but not like this. Not agonizing.

"You need to go," she said, proud of herself for speaking almost levelly. "I knew—" Oh, damn. *Now* her voice had to break. "I was afraid to tell you, but I had myself convinced you were someone you aren't. We both made a mistake."

"I'm going." His hands were curled into fists at his sides. His knuckles showed white. "But I'll be back, Lucy. I can't forget my daughter is here, right down the hall."

She said nothing. After a moment he went to the front door and let himself out without saying another word.

Had he ever left without a reminder to lock up?

Lucy rested her forehead on her knees and let the tears soak into her jeans. *Please,* she thought. Begged. *Please, Sierra, be in bed. Don't come out to see what your father wanted.*

CHAPTER ELEVEN

"ALL RIGHT." Edie pushed aside the remnants of her lunch. "We need to think damage control."

Jon knew she'd rather be pacing, but they'd chosen to meet in a restaurant. A pancake house, safely anonymous, where they'd be unlikely to be noticed in a back booth.

Damage control.

He was almost numb today. Almost, yet not quite. When he relaxed his guard, pain sneaked in like a stiletto between his ribs. That sharp, that deadly. Most of the time, he kept himself in the altered state that allowed cops to see horrific things and keep working, heads clear and thoughts sharp. He wished he could find black humor in any of this to release some of the tension, but had failed so far. There was nothing funny in the fact that Lucy had let him walk into this completely unprepared.

Almost kindly, Edie said, "You can't let Sierra stay with Ms. Malone."

"No," he agreed. He had to clear his throat. "I've already cleared my schedule so I can meet her when she gets home from school."

"Will Ms. Malone be there?"

"No, but I can get Sierra packed up and then she and I can stop by the store. I can't take Sierra without letting Lucy know."

"Of course not. Is the social worker supervising your daughter's foster home aware of you?"

"I don't know," Jon admitted. "I didn't think to ask."

Edie made a note in front of her, as though they were putting together a plan of attack like any other. "You'll need to get in touch."

"Yes."

"Will you be taking Sierra to stay with your mother?"

At least she hadn't said *your daughter* in that clinical way. She'd acknowledged that Sierra was someone. An individual. Jon hadn't realized that he'd been bristling all this time.

"I don't see why she can't stay with me," Jon said slowly. "She wouldn't have to change schools. If she were younger, it would be different, but she turns seventeen *next year.* She can make herself dinner evenings I can't be home. There's no issue with her being unsupervised. Sierra's a good kid. She and I have developed a solid relationship." That was the only thing he had to hold on to, to feel good about. "She's close to Lucy. My mother is still a virtual stranger."

He could see Edie ticking off one point on her mental checklist.

"All right. We may still be able to slide out of this. Is Ms. Malone likely to go to the media?"

He violently rejected the idea. "No. For God's sake."

Edie scrutinized him with shrewd eyes in which, surprisingly, he read sympathy. "Is she aware you're planning to remove your daughter from her home?"

Did she know how much she sounded like an attorney questioning a defendant on the stand? Or perhaps he was a witness. She was chipping away at his resistance, trying to focus him on the central point. For her, that was doing whatever necessary to get him elected.

That's what he'd hired her for. The anger bubbling in him wasn't fair. Jon knew that. He also suspected Edie knew he was feeling it. Did she have any idea that he had loved Lucy? That he was bleeding internally?

He gave his head a shake. It didn't matter.

Lucy had lied to him, if only by omission. She had to have known she was putting at risk something that mattered hugely to him. Worse yet, she'd been willing to put Sierra at risk. That was the part he really couldn't grapple with. She'd rescued a teenager left alone in the world, taken her into her home and arms and heart. How did she reconcile that with exposing Sierra to a woman who'd walked out of a drug treatment center and scored herself an illegal prescription within hours? A woman who *always found a man*. How had Lucy put it? *She'd get, I don't know, mixed up in what they were doing*. Yeah, as if Mommy had stumbled into a situation in her innocence. *Happened* to be at his side when the latest boyfriend pulled a .38 on an eighteen-year-old clerk at a Gas N Shop.

He had trouble believing Lucy could be that delusional. Yet he had to believe it, because he didn't have any choice.

"If Sierra is living with me, I may have to introduce her. Our press packet says I don't have any children."

"And it wouldn't look good if you suddenly have a teenage girl living with you," Edie agreed. "But we probably have a few days to pick our time and place."

"All right." He looked at the lunch he'd

barely touched. His stomach did a slow roll and he pushed the plate away before pulling his wallet out. "Anything else?"

"No. We're covered." Edie slid out of the booth. She hesitated as he peeled a couple of bills off and dropped them on the small tray with the check. "Jon…"

He glanced up, taken aback to hear anything tentative from a woman so confident and bracing that no candidate *she* was shepherding into office was ever allowed to have a doubt.

"Yeah?"

"I'm sorry." She gave one brisk nod, turned and walked away, leaving him staring after her in surprise.

WOULDN'T YOU KNOW that, on a day when Lucy would have given anything to be nonstop busy, the store would be dead? Downtown generally was slow. There was scarcely any traffic passing in front of her windows. She had no appointments with food or supply reps. No need for an inventory. No ordering waiting for her attention.

Lucy dusted. She rearranged the back room. Straightened canned food on shelves until the stacks were as perfectly aligned and impressive as an architectural model.

She ached for the sound of the bell over the door. Almost wept when one of her regulars came in with her dumb-as-a-box silver-tip Persian, who was on a harness and leash but actually rode around clutched to Olive Parson's shoulder. Lucy had never actually seen the cat stand on her own four feet. Mrs. Parsons had laughingly admitted that Tabitha's favorite occupation at home was sitting in front of the floor-length mirror in the bedroom gazing at herself.

Gratefully Lucy chatted with her as she rang up a sale of the same food and litter Mrs. Parsons always bought. As always, the Persian declined to even sniff the proffered goody. Given her squished face and nonexistent nose, she probably *couldn't* smell.

Mrs. Parsons chuckled and said, "My, what a picky eater."

Left alone again, Lucy wondered bleakly whether this day would ever end.

She hadn't had to make any explanations to Sierra last night, thank goodness. Either she'd genuinely been asleep, or she'd known by osmosis that Lucy was desperate not to talk.

When Lucy stumbled out of her bedroom this morning, eyes half-swollen shut, Sierra had said hurriedly, "Forgot to tell you I have to go early today. I'm talking to Ms. Abrams about being a TA." She eyed Lucy warily. "Did something happen with Dad?"

Lucy nodded. "He found out about my mother being released from prison. He's... not happy."

Book bag slung over her shoulder, Sierra didn't move. "Oh."

"How are you getting to school early?"

"Carlos Gomez. He's a senior, and yes, Mama Lucy, he's had his license long enough to be allowed to drive me."

Lucy nodded. Carlos was a nice kid, half a head shorter than Sierra and therefore unlikely to be a romantic interest. He was part of Sierra's crowd of computer nerds and geniuses. After he'd earned a perfect score on the math side of the SAT, a teacher had encouraged him to apply to MIT as well as his local choices. "Okay," she said. "See you this afternoon."

Sierra surprised her by rushing forward and giving her a brief, hard hug before dashing out the door.

As the day wore on, Lucy's depression morphed into anger. She was a good, law-abiding person who was not responsible for her mother's crimes. And her mom, who *was* responsible for them, had served her time.

She'd accepted her punishment, and now she had a right to be treated like a human being. Apparently Jon Brenner thought every kid who shoplifted should be locked away for life in the special offenders' unit at the correctional institute. Didn't he believe anyone ever learned from a mistake? Was rehabilitated? Kicked a drug habit?

Dumb question. No, he didn't.

She'd brought a book but couldn't concentrate enough to read. Come late afternoon, she was perched on her stool behind the old-fashioned wooden counter brooding when the door opened and Jon and Sierra walked in.

Lucy's gaze flew first to Jon's face, as blank and hard as it had been last night, then to Sierra's distraught one. Her heart clenched.

"Lucy!" Sierra flew to her.

Lucy was still on the stool when the teenager flung herself at her, almost knocking her off. Lucy's arms closed hard around Sierra. For one minute she let herself press her cheek to her foster daughter's bright blue head, close her eyes and fiercely hug this girl she loved so much. Then she let one arm drop and straightened, looking past Sierra to her father.

"Sierra's coming home with me," he said with no apparent emotion at all.

"Because I'm so incapable of keeping her safe."

"Because you're using bad judgment."

She kept her chin high. "You mean I value family, and I believe people are capable of redemption."

His expression never changed; there was no flicker of compassion in his eyes. "Your mother's had more than enough chances at redemption. She's flunked every one."

Sierra shivered in Lucy's embrace. Despite the tsunami of anguish rising in her, Lucy knew they couldn't keep arguing in front of her. And maybe he was even right. Maybe she was using bad judgment; maybe her mom didn't deserve even the pathetic remnants of love Lucy still felt. In this single instant, under his stony gaze, Lucy shriveled inside. She was a child again, living with the humiliation of having a parent in prison, of having a home only because the state paid someone to provide it. She was the little girl who knew she wasn't important enough to her own mommy to change anything, who knew she didn't have a daddy because he didn't even want to know she existed. She felt incredibly small, meaningless, useless, and she hated Jon for stripping her of all her hard-gained self-esteem.

She had to get them out of there before she fell apart.

She tilted her head so that she didn't have to see him. "Honey," she whispered, for Sierra alone. "It's okay. He's your dad."

Sierra pulled back to look at her with damp eyes.

Lucy cupped her face. "You have to give him a chance. I'll always be here if you need me. I promise."

Tears overflowed and trickled down Sierra's cheeks. Her mascara ran. Lucy knew she'd crack any minute. "Please," she whispered. "Right now it's the best thing to do."

The teenager bobbed her head. She gave Lucy a last, fervent hug then fled the store.

"I'm sorry it came to this," Jon said quietly.

Lucy glared at him. "Don't say that. Don't you dare. What you've done is hateful. You're no better than my father. You got—what?— a couple hundred bucks for the sperm that created Sierra? You never gave a thought to her. You weren't there when she really needed you. And you have the gall to be sanctimonious with me? I want you to leave. Now. Before I call 911 and have you arrested for custodial interference. Because we both know who has legal custody, and *it isn't you*."

Their gazes held for an excruciating moment, then he walked out.

Lucy sat very still for a minute. Two minutes. When a sob racked her, she slid from the stool and rushed to the front door, where she flipped the sign from Open to Closed and turned the deadbolt lock. She barely made it to her back room before the first tears fell. Her fingers gripped the back of the desk chair, but it didn't hold her up. She crumpled to the floor, buried her face in her arms and cried.

"You said you'd found me an apartment?" her mother asked.

They were driving across the Tacoma Narrows Bridge, which soared so high over Puget Sound, it always scared Lucy. The lanes felt too narrow, her hands sweaty on the steering wheel. Going and coming, this had always been her most dreaded part of the trip to visit her mother. Even worse than having to be searched.

"I haven't told you, but Sierra isn't living with me anymore," she said. "She's gone to stay with her dad."

Her mother was watching her anxiously. "Not because of me?"

Lucy's first thought was bitter. *Yes. Yes!*

Entirely because of you. All the anger of her childhood hurled words she wanted to say so badly that holding them back was a battle she barely won.

But then she had a strange and surprising realization. She didn't even know where it came from. It *wasn't* because of her mom that Jon had snatched Sierra away. He'd done it because of his own narrow-minded, intolerant views. Perhaps because of his own, unhealed wounds.

But that, Lucy thought, still bitterly, was an excuse, and he didn't believe in those.

The most painful part was her awareness that in taking Sierra away he'd shown that he hadn't felt anything very important for her, Lucy. Not even trust. Not even enough liking to motivate him to *listen* to her. To talk about compromises.

After a long, throat-aching moment, aware of her mother waiting, Lucy admitted, "He didn't like it that you'd be around, but that wasn't the whole story. He and Sierra were getting along so well, sooner or later it made sense for her to live with him. She didn't need a foster home anymore."

Out of the corner of her eye Lucy saw her mother's face contort before she averted it.

"I don't want to make trouble, and I already am."

Thank God they were leaving the bridge behind. Lucy wriggled her shoulders to relax them, but it didn't work. Too much of her tension had to do with her passenger.

"I've promised Sierra I'd be available if she needs me," she said. "In the meantime, there's no reason you can't have my spare bedroom. I assume that eventually you'll want your own place, but you can save money by staying with me for now, at least until you find a job."

"If you're sure." Lucy felt the weight of her mother's troubled gaze.

Mom had aged terribly these past eight years. It wasn't as though Lucy hadn't seen her; most months she'd visited. But somehow seeing her now, outside the prison gates, changed Lucy's perspective. Her mom's light brown hair was graying. Her skin looked older than it should for her years. Once a pretty woman, now she was thin and brittle. She was—Lucy calculated quickly—almost fifty. Her birthday was coming up in November, right before Thanksgiving.

That meant she'd been twenty-one when she got pregnant with Lucy. Twenty-two when she had her. Not very old at all.

In fact, the same age Jon had been when he'd thought selling his sperm was a fine and dandy idea. Lucy wished she could point that out to him.

She looked away from the road briefly to her mother's hands, wringing together in her lap. The knuckles looked knobbier than they should.

She frowned. "You're getting arthritis."

"I'm afraid so." Her mom's hands stilled, and she looked ruefully at them. "My mother got arthritis early, too. Did I ever tell you that?"

"I don't think so."

Lucy didn't know much at all about her grandparents, whom she'd never met. They had cut their daughter off before Lucy was born, and not relented even for the sake of their granddaughter. Her grandmother had been forty when Mom was born, Lucy did know that, her grandfather four years older. Terry had talked about how rigid and stern they'd been compared to her friends' parents. Even if they'd been willing, Lucy could see that taking in a baby when they were in their sixties wouldn't have been ideal. Not that it mattered, since they weren't willing. She knew they'd been contacted several times when she was cast on the state as a dependent of the court. She'd always wondered, secretly, whether they'd rejected her because she was half-Hispanic and looked it. Had they despised the part of her that was her mother... or the part that was her father?

Automatically blocking off old hurts, Lucy said, "You'll have to tell me more about them. If nothing else, I ought to know health issues. That kind of thing."

"I don't know what kind of health problems they had later on. They were healthy the last time I saw them." Terry was quiet for a moment. "I tried calling them about ten or eleven years ago. Papa answered. All he said was, 'Your mother has passed away,' and then he hung up on me."

"Oh, Mom."

"It wasn't exactly a shock. Your grandmother would have been eighty. Imagine that." She shook her head. "I just felt the need to try. Hearing she'd died and I'd never even had a chance to say I was sorry..." Her mouth worked. "That hurt."

"I can imagine," Lucy said quietly. Too well. Wasn't she in the same boat, needing closure that might not be possible? Except *she* was the one who was supposed to forgive, not the other way around.

For all practical purposes, she had realized

long ago, she was the parent, not the daughter. She ought to be empathizing with her grandparents rather than with her mother.

Terry hadn't rebelled until she was seventeen and started dating a boy who introduced her to alcohol and parties. By the time she was twenty, her parents had ordered her from the house. Lucy couldn't help wondering whether her mother's life would have been different if they'd fought a little harder for her.

It was part of the reason Lucy hadn't yet been able to say *enough*. And maybe that made her foolish, but she'd rather be a soft touch than as icy and unforgiving inside as Jon.

She wasn't the only tense one in the car. Her mom's fingers writhed, betraying her growing anxiety. This must be terribly frightening. All the times she'd failed before had to be on her mind. Lucy guessed her own mixed feelings must be obvious. The chance of successfully reintegrating into society would have to be higher for someone being released from prison into a stable family offering a real welcome and love. Lucy, racked with ambivalence, wasn't a very solid foundation to build on.

I'm better than nothing, she reminded herself.

"Did you check into NA and AA meetings?" her mother asked suddenly, and Lucy realized their thoughts had paralleled.

"Yes. You can attend one or the other every day, if you want." Narcotics Anonymous meetings were held in the back room of a local coffee shop, Alcoholics Anonymous meetings at a grange hall. "All within walking distance." Lucy turned onto her own street. "Here we are," she said brightly.

"Oh." Terry leaned forward. She'd seen photos of Lucy's small house and garden. Now her face lit up at the sight of it. "Oh, honey. It's beautiful."

A rush of emotion tightened Lucy's throat. "I knew you'd like the garden. I wish you'd seen it earlier, when it was at its height. Next year—" But she couldn't finish, because who knew about next year?

After she parked, they set her mom's bag on the front porch and Lucy gave her a tour of the garden. A few roses still bloomed, and some late perennials were only now starting to fade. Foliage had turned to gold and scarlet and orange. The garden smelled richer than at any other time of the year, as if the sweet scent of flowers had masked something deeper. The earth itself.

"I'm glad you like to garden," her mother said softly.

"I got it from you."

They looked at each other and smiled, really smiled, for the first time, as if this one thing mother had passed to daughter gave them enough connection to offer hope.

Please God, Lucy thought, wishing she could trust that hope.

CHAPTER TWELVE

APPROACHING SIERRA'S BEDROOM, Jon was surprised to hear his daughter's voice coming beneath the door. Did she have a friend over?

But then, as though she'd heard his footsteps, she said a hasty "Bye, Lucy."

Two words, two kicks to his chest. The boot delivering the kicks was steel toed.

Jon went still, his knuckles an inch from the paneled door. He fought a silent battle with himself, trying to believe it was the grief in Sierra's voice that hurt, but knowing he was lying to himself.

He wanted to talk to Lucy, to say, *I think I might have screwed up.* But the more rational side of him didn't think he had, and he couldn't talk to her when he was at war with himself. Assuming she was even willing to talk to *him.* And why would she be? He'd hurt her, and badly. He knew he had.

After a moment, Jon knocked.

"Come in."

He opened the door and found Sierra where she seemed to spend most of her time, on her bed with her laptop. Separating her from the damn thing had become his personal challenge.

"Dinner's ready," he said, then nodded at the computer. "Homework?"

"Not really." She didn't move.

Jon waited.

"I'm not that hungry."

She said the same thing every night. He knew she snacked when she got home from school and that she wasn't a big eater, but he'd also seen her come joyously flying when Lucy called, "Dinner's ready."

"Come and eat anyway. Tell me about your day."

After a moment long enough to qualify as insolent, Sierra shrugged and closed her laptop, sliding it onto the bed. He turned away, assuming she'd follow. She wasn't quite willing to be deliberately disobedient, thank God, and he was trying not to push her into a corner where she felt she had to be.

All the former ease in their relationship had vanished. His fault, he acknowledged. She'd seen his brutality to Lucy, the one person in the world Sierra loved, and she didn't understand his explanations.

Maybe, he thought, that's because Lucy was right. He'd never been there when Sierra needed him. He hadn't known, hadn't wanted to know, that he had a daughter somewhere who did need him. In one way, he wasn't at fault. In another way, he was terribly so.

Feeling weary, he got plates for the pizza he'd picked up on the way home. He should have made a salad, too, but had salved his conscience by buying the veggie special.

Lucy would have made a salad. Or provided a real, home-cooked meal to start with.

Now he was not only tired—he was swamped by a sense of inadequacy.

Sierra pulled out a chair and curled her lip at the sight of the pizza. "I don't like mushrooms."

"Pick them off."

"Or pineapple."

"Pick that off, too."

She sighed heavily.

Irritation began to rise in him. How would Lucy handle this? Ignore the snotty attitude? Confront it directly? Jon had no idea.

On the job, he believed in directness. *Okay, then,* he thought.

He popped the top off a bottle of dark imported beer. "Sierra, you came looking for me. Not the other way around."

She flashed a startled, wary look at him.

"We talked about your expectations. You claimed not to have many."

"I didn't. I *liked* living with Lucy."

Jon nodded. "I understand that. And I understand why. But once you found me, there were only a couple of directions for us to go."

She was listening, if not happily.

With a sense of unreality, he thought, *I'm sitting here, at my own dining-room table, trying to talk sense to a sixteen-year-old girl with neon-bright blue hair and a goddamn barbell through her eyebrow. A girl who is my child, whether at this moment either of us likes it or not.*

"One was that I said, 'So?'"

She flinched.

"Alternatively, we could have the kind of relationship we probably both envisioned initially. I'd be like a divorced father. See you every couple of weeks. We'd do something fun, converse awkwardly. If you needed money, you'd ask me and I'd hand it over, relieved I could do something meaningful and easy."

She bowed her head.

"Or I could become a real parent."

More silence.

"I'm betting your mother sometimes made decisions you didn't like."

Her shoulders jerked and she mumbled something.

"What was that?"

She lifted her head and her blazing eyes pierced his. "She *was* really my mom! Lucy was right. I'm the one who had to find you, and you didn't even want me." When he opened his mouth, she shook her head fiercely. "Don't lie. You know you didn't. But Lucy—" Sierra choked. "After Mom died and Lucy found out no one else wanted me, she didn't even go home and think about it for the night. *She* wanted me." Voice dying, she finished, "She loves me."

Reeling from her pain and contempt, Jon would have said, *I love you, too,* but he knew damn well she wouldn't believe him. What stunned him was realizing how true it was. He'd have given anything to go back and be the father she'd needed, when she needed him. But he couldn't.

"I have to do what I think is right," he said tiredly. "You have to understand, Sierra, I've dedicated my career to putting people like Lucy's mother behind bars, and then doing it all over again when they get out and reoffend. Lucy doesn't want to give up on her own parent. I get that." Did he? With no hope Sierra was really hearing him, he forged on, telling her what he'd learned after looking up the details of Terry Malone's record, including police reports on the last crime. "This woman has been a drug addict all of Lucy's life. She's been convicted of possessing drugs, of selling them, of theft. Last time, she was part of an armed robbery. The clerk at the store was eighteen years old." He paused to let that sink in. "A kid. Lucy's mother and her partner held a gun on her. They made her lie down on the floor with her hands behind her head. She thought they were going to execute her, and she peed her pants while they rifled through the cash register and talked about how to get the safe open." He knew his voice had been rising. Discovered that in his intense frustration he'd planted both hands on the table and risen to his feet as if she were a subordinate he had to dominate. He drew a ragged breath and finished quietly, "That's Lucy's mother."

Sierra burst into tears, flung away from the table and raced for the stairs.

Jon slammed his fist into the palm of his other hand. What he wanted was to throw his beer bottle and watch it smash against the wall. He wanted to kick over chairs, punch his fist through a wall. Instead he squeezed the bridge of his nose and struggled for calm.

He never doubted himself. He'd gotten where he was for a lot of reasons. Because he was smart, decisive, a natural leader. He knew right from wrong and didn't muddy the waters with sociological hogwash. His absolute, complete certainty was his greatest strength, and Jon knew it.

All it had taken was one beautiful, loving, tormented woman to fracture his certainty.

Eyes closed, he thought, *Lucy's weakening me.*

Maybe he should count his blessings that things had happened this way. Loving Lucy wasn't compatible with being the man he'd made of himself, the crusader who needed to save as many innocents as he could to atone for Cassia.

His fingers tightened on the bridge of his nose until he could have sworn cartilage creaked, but he didn't feel the pain. All he knew was if he backed down on this—if he said, *Sure, fine, it's okay that my daughter hangs out with a convicted armed robber*— he'd violate his deepest beliefs.

He would lose the election, and he'd deserve to.

He'd already lost Lucy, and he was in danger of losing Sierra, too.

"YOU'RE GOING to the NA meeting?" Lucy asked.

Her mother was clearing the table. "Yes. It starts at seven."

Terry had gone every evening since she'd arrived almost a week ago. Or so she said. It was pathetic, but every night Lucy wondered if that's where she was really going. When Terry returned home, Lucy found herself watching for any unsteadiness of gait, any slur in her voice, any redness in her eyes.

Dumb. I'd never know if Mom was out scoring drugs all day while I'm at the store.

"Are you making friends at the meetings?" she asked, so casually her mom turned to look at her.

"No," she said after a moment. "There's support, but most of the people who come are more your age than mine." She gave an odd laugh. "Maybe the ones who would be my age are dead."

Lucy couldn't imagine what to say to that.

"The NA crowd is younger," Terry said.

"AA has more older people at meetings, but mostly men."

Lucy felt herself tense. Her mother always, always hooked up with a man. Lucy couldn't remember whether that signaled the beginning of the end, or if she added the men to help her support a drug habit after she'd started using again.

"Did you apply for any jobs today?" she asked.

"A couple of waitress positions." Her mother closed the dishwasher. She gave a small, discouraged shrug. "Neither were encouraging."

"Remember that I can use you tomorrow. I think I can assume Sierra won't be showing up."

"Only if you really need me, and it's not make-work."

"I really need you," Lucy said honestly. "Saturday is my busy day. Plus Sierra stocked shelves for me. I got in a good-size order today."

"You know I'll be glad to work for you. And you don't have to pay me. You'll have to spend half the day telling me what to do."

"I have to train any new employee and I pay them anyway."

"I didn't buy any groceries this week. No,

don't argue with me, Lucy." For a moment she sounded astonishingly momlike. "It's all in the family, after all."

"Yes." Lucy found herself smiling. "I guess it is."

"Honey…" Her mother sat at the table again. "You know one of these days we have to really talk."

Dear God, she didn't want to. They were getting along. Doing well. Lucy was managing because they hadn't ripped the bandage off old wounds.

The new ones Jon had dealt her were painful enough.

"What is there to say, Mom? It's pointless."

"No." Terry's eyes were so sad. "I'd really like to know what you feel, Lucy. I need us to quit pretending it's all right."

The storm rose inside Lucy. She ground the heel of her hand against her breastbone, trying to quell it. "What good will it do for me to get angry? To tell you how many times and ways you hurt me? Tell me that." God. Anguish rose to burn her esophagus. "What good will it do?"

"We should start with honesty."

"No." Lucy rose. "That's the last thing we need, Mom. Trust me."

"I don't even know for sure what happened to you when we weren't together. Whether people were good to you, or—"

"Go to your meeting." Lucy walked away, went into her bedroom and shut the door. She stood there shaking, thinking, *I can't do this*.

I have to do this.

She wished with all her heart that she could call Jon. That she hadn't made the choice she had. The one she couldn't unmake, that she still knew was the right one, however much it hurt.

THE SURPRISE WAS that Terry turned out to be an excellent employee. She already knew how to work a cash register, she had a good eye for layout and she enjoyed the pets customers brought into the store. She seemed truly happy to chat with people and didn't even mind cleaning the cage that held a litter of kittens and the young mother cat from the animal shelter.

Once, in the middle of the day, Lucy heard a laugh of such delight, everything inside her went absolutely still, rapt. Her mom used to laugh like that. Memories tumbled from hidden places. Lucy on a merry-go-round at a playground, thrilled and clinging tightly to the bars as she spun faster and faster until her mom, who was running around and around, fell down and laughed. Mom reading her stories from the library at bedtime, her voice gruff or high and silly or whatever tone was required by the dialogue until they were both giggling. Her mother trying to make animal-shaped pancakes and chortling at the ludicrous results.

Lucy turned to see that her mom was playing with two of the kittens that hadn't yet been adopted. Hadn't they had a kitten once? Lucy thought so. She hated knowing it had likely been abandoned when her mom went wherever it was that time, and Lucy went back into foster care. But…her mom had tried. It was easy to forget how hard she'd tried, and what a truly wonderful mother she'd been.

In between.

That's how Lucy had always thought of it. *In between* the last foster home and the bad times. She'd wanted so much for the in-between time to stretch, to become forever.

The fact that it never did had embittered her. She supposed that's why she'd suppressed the happy memories. There were so many of them. She stood there in the middle of the store, utterly captivated by her mother's laughter, and had trouble breathing as she remembered.

For a moment her chest ached. Why were the good times so fragile?

Her mom carefully closed the cage door, then turned to her, still smiling. "Oh, I hope someone adopts the mommy cat. Did you see her playing, too?"

"She's barely a year old herself. Really still a kitten. She'll get a home. I won't take any more kittens until she's been adopted, too."

"That's good." Her mom nodded, seemingly pleased. "I'm glad you do this."

"Did we have a kitten once?" Lucy heard the strangeness in her voice. "I remember a gray and white one."

The joy dimmed on her mother's face. "No. I wanted to. But I was always afraid—" She cleared her throat. "No, that kitten belonged to a neighbor."

"Oh. I just suddenly remembered...."

Her mom's smile was tentative but beautiful. "You loved playing with it. It was one of those times I wished so much I could give you everything you deserved."

Lucy's mouth trembled. The best she could do was nod. She wished, too. She'd wished then, wished now. But she was suddenly glad to have remembered the happiness.

The bell over the door rang and a couple she didn't know came in. Their dog was developing hot spots and they wondered if the problem was food related. A few minutes later, counseling the people on the difference between grocery-store brands and the high-quality nutrition offered by the foods she sold, Lucy glanced over and saw her mother ringing up a sale as if she was a pro.

She could afford to hire her for more hours than just Saturdays. This might work out.

Maybe if locals got to know her here at the store, someone would consider hiring her for their own business. There it was again: that tiny kernel of hope Lucy could never quite let go. Her mother had been going to NA and AA meetings, and that was good, wasn't it? She hadn't used in eight years.

Lucy smiled at the couple she was helping and, once they'd made up their minds, said, "That's a good choice." As the man hefted a big bag of kibble, Lucy gestured toward the counter. "My mother will ring you up while I help these other people."

Lucy didn't move immediately after they walked away. She hated the emotions churning in her. Most of all, the hope.

Who was she kidding? This was an in-between time, that's all. She wished she could treasure it for what it was, for what she could give and later feel good about, but she'd never guessed that, in giving, she would lose so much.

She loved her mother, but...she loved Sierra, too. And Jon. She wanted to think that she didn't really, that he wasn't the man she'd believed him to be. But she knew that was a lie. Jon *was* a good man. Too bad he had scars that were still as tender as her own.

I'm the one who lied to him, Lucy thought dully. *From the very beginning, I knew what he'd think once he heard about Mom.*

If she'd told him up front, maybe nothing ever would have developed between them. She might still have lost Sierra, but she would never have had him to lose.

Nothing like hindsight.

Lucy addressed the new customers. "How can I help you?"

HE MUST BE CRAZY, but...damn it, he was here. Jon sat in his unmarked official vehicle and gazed at the facade of Lucy's store.

She'd made it inviting. The big wooden sign that read Barks and Purrs also had a painted cat batting a toy mouse and a dog with his leash—the *S* at the end of *Purrs*—dangling hopefully from his mouth. The display in the two plate-glass windows was appealing, combining the wonderful textures and colors of beds and toys and sisal scratchers with some gift items, such as wind chimes with dancing metal cats, a tall raku glazed greyhound and some bright puppets for children.

Get your ass out of the car and walk in there.

He only wished he had the slightest idea what to say once he was face-to-face with Lucy. That was provided she didn't throw him out before he had a chance to reason with her.

All he had to do was close his eyes to see her that last time. Passionate, fiery, her hair all but crackling with her rage, her eyes snapping with it—and glazed with tears.

Jon made a ragged sound, got out, locked the car and crossed the sidewalk to the door of her store.

Once inside he saw no one, although he heard a voice in the back room. Movement caught his eye—a cat in the cage near the door, not quite a kitten but not really an adult either, he realized. A pretty little tabby who, at the sight of him, rose to her feet and bumped her head against the mesh.

"Hi, little one," he murmured, and held out his fingers to her inquiring nose.

She purred.

From the back room, Lucy called, "I'll be with you in a moment."

Crap. He'd rather be kicking in the door to arrest a violent fugitive. And yet he ached to see her.

He approached the counter and waited stoically.

She appeared with a bright smile for a potential customer, her hair captured in a thick braid that bounced over her shoulder. With jeans, she wore a red sweater that hugged her lush curves and flattered the warm tone of her skin. She was…beautiful.

"Lucy."

Her smile vanished as if it had never been. She stopped where she was, a good fifteen feet away from him. "Let me guess." She didn't sound friendly. "You don't think I'm decent enough to operate a business in your jurisdiction. Maybe I'm selling drugs out of the storeroom. Do you have a search warrant?"

"You know better than that," he said stiffly. "I came hoping we could talk."

She crossed her arms in front of her. "About?"

"Sierra." He paused. Admitted the truth. "Us."

Her eyes were darker than usual, bitter chocolate. "How can there possibly *be* an *us?*"

"Please," he said. "Let me take you to lunch."

They stared at each other for a long moment. He was scarcely aware of someone else exiting the back room, some woman. Jon knew Lucy had a couple of part-time employees. Sierra had been one, he remembered belatedly. He hadn't thought of it, but by yanking her away, he'd left Lucy in the lurch in more ways than one.

"Go, Lucy," the other woman said, and Jon flicked a grateful glance at her.

He knew immediately who this was, and shock punched him. He didn't know what he'd expected, but not this sweet-faced, middle-aged woman. Their coloring was quite different, but without any trouble he could see Lucy in her features. She, too, was small, with the same round chin and gentle mouth. She looked ten years older than he knew she was. Drug use took a toll. Damn it, he shouldn't be taken aback by the fact that she looked as if she should be a grandmother taking her grandkids for the day. He knew better; crooks looked like everyone else. They didn't all have tattoos wrapping their arms and sneers twisting their lips. They came in grandmotherly packages, too.

Yet for some reason, experience didn't keep him from being unsettled.

He and she gazed at each other, and he saw that she knew who he was. She wouldn't have heard anything good.

"I'm Lucy's mother," she said quietly, and came forward to her daughter's side.

Jon bent his head. "Ms. Malone."

Lucy's gaze challenged him. "Mom's working part-time for me."

"I forgot that Sierra did. I'm sorry."

She gave a sharp laugh. "That's actually funny. Of all things to be sorry for."

He was sorry for more than that, but he clamped his mouth shut.

"Fine," she said at last. "Mom, you sure you can hold down the fort for half an hour or so?"

Her mother smiled at her. "You know I can."

"Yeah." Lucy's face softened for an instant. She gave her mother a quick hug that was far more awkward than the ones she'd so often given Sierra, then stalked toward the front of the store.

Jon reached the door before her and held it open. "The Country Table?"

She sailed past him. "Sure."

The small diner was only half a block away. They'd eaten there several times before, or he'd gotten lunch from there and brought it to her store. Without even looking at him, she headed for a booth and slipped in. Jon sat down opposite her.

Neither said anything until the waitress brought ice water and menus.

Lucy pushed hers aside. "Sierra has been calling me."

"I know."

"I'm surprised you haven't forbidden it."

Despite everything, her hostility stung. "I'm not that big an SOB."

"You gave a pretty good imitation of one."

Jon sighed. "I know I did. I…damaged what we had going."

Lucy stared him down. "You think?"

"Why didn't you tell me, Lucy?"

She studied the uninspiring art hanging on the opposite wall. "I would have before Mom's release day. I was working my way up to it."

He wanted her small hand nestled in his, but knew better than to reach for it. "Telling me was that hard?"

A spark of hurt in her eyes, she finally

looked at him again. "It went so well when I did."

"I was blindsided. You shouldn't have kept something like that from me. You knew damn well how I'd feel about it."

"And that," she said, "was exactly why I didn't feel like I could talk to you. I never had the slightest doubt how you'd react. But as long as we didn't have the conversation, I could—" She shrugged, as if to express the hopelessness.

"You could what?"

"Pretend." Lucy's twisted smile didn't look like any he'd seen on her face before. "Apparently I'm good at that."

"What's that supposed to—"

The waitress's arrival disrupted his question. They gave their orders without having looked at menus. He had no appetite, and suspected Lucy didn't either, but they had to go through the motions.

"What do you mean?" he asked when they were alone again.

She shook her head, her expression closed. "Never mind. Jon, why are you here?"

"I was angry."

"I noticed."

"I miss you. Sierra misses you."

She shifted on the bench seat as if to hide

the way she'd flinched. "So you're saying you were wrong?"

Taking a chance, he reached for her hand. She moved it before he could touch her, tucking her hands out of sight beneath the table.

After an uncomfortable moment, Jon admitted, "I was hoping you might have realized I was right."

Lucy made a soft sound that could have been a laugh. "Then you're out of luck. My mother let me down on a pretty regular basis when I was a kid. But she was also a really good mother a lot of the time. She's the only person who ever truly loved me." Her face spasmed. Her voice hitched. "And right now she needs me."

"Lucy…"

Despite the brief display of emotion, she managed to look nearly expressionless. "She may not make it. And if she doesn't, it won't be because I failed her. Do you understand? I'm her only hope. Not even for Sierra—" again her voice wobbled "—can I turn my back on Mom."

Jon leaned against the booth feeling… Hell. So much that he couldn't have articulated it. He hurt, he knew that. And he knew she did, too.

"Sierra loves you." The rest was hard to

say. He hadn't been sure he ever wanted to make himself this vulnerable. But he had to say it. "I'm in love with you, Lucy. Your mother's *not* the only person who has ever loved you."

Her eyes were bright with hurt as profound as anything he felt. "Sierra loved me because I'm all she had. And you..." She swallowed. "If you were really in love with me, you would have listened to what I was trying to tell you. You'd have helped me find a way to do what I have to do for Mom, instead of charging in and snatching Sierra away as if I'm too dirty to associate with her. I thought maybe there was the smallest chance you were here to say 'I was wrong.' But I should have known better. I did know better." She slid off the seat, even though the waitress was bearing down on them with their food.

In desperation, he said, "Don't do this, Lucy."

The waitress came to a stop at their table and began unloading the tray. Probably assuming Lucy was on her way to the restroom, she beamed and said, "Enjoy your lunches," before leaving.

Lucy looked at him. "You know what? I actually *wish* I thought this was all about Sierra. You going all noble and paternal.

I'd still think you were wrong, but at least I could understand that. But I don't think that's what it's about at all. It's the election, isn't it? How it would look to the public that you're seeing a woman whose mother was convicted of armed robbery. That you're trusting your daughter to that woman." She mimed an expression of shock, clapping her hands to her cheeks. "Dear God, what does that say about your judgment?" She dropped her hands and her voice hardened. "You don't really believe that nice woman you just met is going to corrupt your daughter. Nope. It's all about public perception." Her gaze moved over him one last time, scathing. "Do you do a self-check every evening? 'Did I come across looking good today?' Here's a clue. In my eyes, you didn't."

She grabbed the sandwich off the plate, then marched out. The door settled softly closed behind her. He saw her through the window, and then she was gone. Jon was left frozen in place, bludgeoned by her contempt.

Did he deserve every word?

CHAPTER THIRTEEN

IN THE NEXT COUPLE OF WEEKS, Lucy saw Sierra several times. She came by the store after school, and Lucy drove her home after closing. For each of those visits she'd told Sierra in advance that her mother wouldn't be there so she could, in turn, assure Jon that she'd remain uncorrupted.

Lucy and Sierra talked at least briefly every day. Sierra told her Jon was trying, but he wasn't home that much.

"He's...different. He hides it, but I can tell he's mad or...something. I don't know. He never smiles. He tries to get me to talk, but he's all fakey."

Aching inside, Lucy reminded her, "You know, you might want to cut him a break. He doesn't have a whole lot of experience at being a parent. It's not surprising that knowing what to say to you doesn't come naturally for him."

"Why do you make excuses for him?" Sierra asked. "You should hate him."

Yes. She should. Why didn't she?

Because I love him. Duh.

"Because I understand why he did what he did," Lucy said softly. "I don't like it, but I understand."

"Well, I don't." Sierra choked up. "It was stupid. And you know what else? It showed that he doesn't trust me."

Lucy supposed it did. "Remember that he hasn't known you that long," she said, somewhat weakly.

Sierra's response was a rude noise.

In fact, Lucy reflected later, Sierra was quite frequently sounding more like a *teenager* than she ever had. Lucy's vengeful side took a certain pleasure in Jon's discovery that his daughter wasn't the bright, cheerful, startlingly mature young woman she'd seemed. That in fact she could be sullen, rude and uncooperative. He deserved everything she could throw at him.

Only, Lucy didn't like knowing Sierra was miserably unhappy.

So am I, Lucy admitted to herself. And it sounded as though maybe Jon was, too. He certainly hadn't looked very happy that day he came to see her.

The only positive in all this was Lucy's relationship with her mother. So far they'd avoided the talk Terry had suggested, the one where she wept and expressed all her regret and repentance and Lucy exploded and vented her rage and hurt. The odd part was, it didn't seem as if they needed to.

They did talk. Mostly about little things. Lucy about her garden and Sierra and the few guys she'd dated. Friends and the several cooking classes she'd taken through the local food co-op. Her mom about the other women she'd called friends at Purdy, the various jobs she'd held there, books she'd read, tidbits about her parents.

They worked in Lucy's garden, doing a final weeding, cutting back dried stalks and mulching. Terry happily took on the task of painting the bathroom once they settled on a cheerful shade of peach. Despite a light rain one day, Lucy got up on a ladder and cleaned the gutters while her mom followed along below scraping up the sodden leaves and putting them in the wheelbarrow to add to the compost pile. Her mom worked at the store three days a week now and proved herself a natural at retail.

What Lucy kept discovering was how much she'd gotten from her mother. Maybe it was hereditary, maybe learned, but the truth was they had a lot in common.

And eventually they started talking about the bigger things. Why Lucy had wanted to go into business for herself, why creating a real home mattered so much. Why she couldn't have imagined not taking in Sierra. Terry did talk about regrets, but they were personal ones. Never learning to rely on herself. The fatal flaw of needing a man around, even if she didn't love him, even if he was a creep. Her stupidity in starting to take drugs in the first place, in not seeing where she was going until it was too late, in convincing herself over and over that she didn't need help quitting or that no one would help her anyway.

"And really," she admitted, "that wasn't it. I was lying to myself. It was addiction. Going to an AA meeting and saying 'Please help me' would have meant *not* taking that drink, and I wanted it so much. Do you know, every single time it started with me telling myself I could use today, have a drink today, but tomorrow I'd be straight again? Today was just a little stressful—I deserved it. I can't even say I knew I was lying. I was all about the lies. I *had* to believe them. If I didn't…" She grimaced. "I'd have to despise myself. And that wasn't acceptable."

So in the end, Lucy realized that they were

talking about regret and hurt, but in a way
that was gentler than she'd expected. The
emotions felt muted.

She was beginning to think she could forgive her mother after all. Which convinced
her she had made the right decision. This
was what mattered. If her relationship with
her mother could be mended, maybe *Lucy*
wouldn't feel so broken.

She should be happier than she'd ever been
in her life instead of desolate.

All her misery was Jon's fault. She hoped
Sierra made *him* miserable. She hoped he
lost the damn election. She hoped he came
begging some day, giving her the chance to
curl her lip and say, *You wish*.

And then she laughed at herself, if ruefully,
because she wasn't acting any more mature
than Sierra, but that was okay.

He didn't *deserve* mature.

JON STOOD at his mother's kitchen window
and watched Sierra out in the yard with the
older of her two cousins, Reese. His mother's
dog raced in circles around them, yapping
away.

Patrick, only ten, was fascinated by Sierra
and eager to have her show him the cool
things she could do on the computer. Reese,

on the other hand, at twelve had become self-conscious with girls. He wasn't quite as beanpole skinny and therefore homely as Jon had been at that age—he'd gotten a somewhat more compact build as well as brown eyes from his father—but having just started middle school he didn't have a lot of finesse with girls, either. Earlier, when Sierra had smiled at him and said, "Hey, will you push me on the tire swing?" poor Reese had turned beet-red and barely managed to mumble, "Um, sure. I mean, if you want. I mean, yeah, okay."

She hadn't smiled at her father that way in weeks. Not since she'd found him waiting in front of Lucy's house and heard that he expected her to pack her things and come with him.

Today's visit to his mother's house was the first outing of any kind she'd agreed to with even a semblance of good humor. Even so, he'd done all the talking on the way here. Her relief at escaping him once they arrived was blatant.

In her eyes, he sure wasn't Father of the Year. He watched her sail high on the tire swing attached to a sturdy branch on the maple tree. He felt old when he realized the maple hadn't been big enough to support a swing when he was her age.

"She's a sweetheart," his mother said behind him. "You must be counting your blessings."

Jon gave a grunt that was half laugh. *You betcha. I've got so many blessings right now, how can I count them?*

He turned away from the window to face his mother, who sat at the round oak table nursing a cup of tea and looking serene. She did that well. He'd never been able to understand it.

He hadn't even known the question was brewing until it came out of his mouth, the edges ground ragged with anger. "Why did you put up with Dad?"

Her flinch was tiny but visible. "Were our lives really so bad?"

Jon shoved his hands into his pockets and leaned against the kitchen counter. "He was a bastard, and you know it."

"He loved us."

"Maybe you. And Lily. I don't think love was one of the things he felt for me."

Guilt should have chilled his anger when he saw the distress on her face, but it didn't. He'd been burying his resentment for too long.

"That's not true," she insisted. "He didn't know how to express it—"

"Beating the shit out of me seemed to work for him."

"If you just hadn't been so defiant—"

"So it was my fault?" His shoulders and neck were rigid. He maintained the casual pose, though.

"No," his mother cried. Tears glazed her eyes. "Of course it wasn't. I think he simply didn't know how to relate to you. His father hit him, you know. That's all he grew up knowing."

He looked at her in disbelief. "How could you love a man like that?"

She bent her head and seemed to gaze into the teacup. "I didn't know he had it in him. With me, he was…impatient, sometimes gruff, but I could make excuses for it. He had a lot of fine qualities, too, you know. He was a good provider, and faithful. I always believed he loved me. And Lily." When she lifted her head again and met Jon's eyes anguish had transformed her face into someone he hardly knew. "Maybe if he hadn't had a son… If we'd only had girls… I used to wonder. I did leave him the once, you know. But what would have happened to us? I couldn't have gone home again, and I had next to no job skills. What kind of life would we have had?" It was a cry from the heart.

Jon couldn't do anything *but* ponder her question and his deep, bitter belief that she should have left his father for his sake.

Lily had been the apple of Dad's eye. His little flower, he'd called her. Jon knew his sister had been distressed by the different treatment their father doled out. But he couldn't, in all honesty, argue that she would have been better off if Mom had left Dad.

Mom? She probably wouldn't have fared better, either. Jon loved his mother, but she wasn't a career woman. Maybe she would have remarried. But what were the odds a stepfather would have done more than merely tolerate his two stepchildren? Jon knew a few people who'd gotten lucky and had great stepparents, but he knew others who hadn't.

He'd survived his childhood. As brutal as his father had sometimes been, Jon suspected he'd pulled his punches out of fear his wife would leave him again if he didn't. She *had* protected Jon, although not the way he'd wanted her to.

"I don't know," he said slowly. "I haven't thought about any of this for years. I suppose it's suddenly having a daughter that got me started."

And Lucy. Lucy, whose childhood made his seem like a trip to Disneyland. Lucy, who was struggling with complicated feelings toward the only parent she had. The mother who was the only person who'd ever loved her.

He clenched his teeth against the pain. *Damn it, no.* He knew she hadn't believed him when he said it, but he loved her, too. He'd even been entertaining thoughts about forever when her mother exploded between them. He suspected he would have asked Lucy to marry him by now, if she hadn't chosen Terry over him and Sierra.

But she had.

"Is it only Sierra?" his mother asked softly. "I thought that maybe for the first time since Cassia…"

"I thought so, too," he admitted. "But there were too many complications. We couldn't make it work."

"Oh, Jon."

He couldn't handle the pity in her eyes. Straightening, he said, "Did I tell you the *Dispatch* is going to endorse me? Don't know about the *Times* yet. It's early, but every little bit helps."

She brightened, made appropriate exclamations, and then remembered she needed to get the baked beans in to heat. Subject changed successfully.

Nothing resolved in his head.

PUSHING ASIDE his empty bowl, Jon opened the *Seattle Times* to the local section. This was Friday, so he set aside the sports page along with the advertising inserts. Once upon a time he'd followed UW football as well as the Seahawks more closely. Lately he had time only to skim postgame articles in case the subject came up when he was at one of his political events.

"What in the hell was the coaching staff thinking, sending in that junior quarterback instead of Hensel?" someone would say.

He could say knowledgeably, "The kid didn't do that badly, considering. Face it, the season's lost anyway. Why not give him some seasoning?"

Like he gave a damn.

He reached for his coffee as Sierra plunked down a bowl of cereal on the dining-room table and pulled out her chair.

"Good morning," he said, glancing up to see that she wore cartoon-printed flannel pajama bottoms that hung low on her hips and a thin tank top that clung to her small breasts. Jon averted his gaze uncomfortably.

He didn't like even noticing his daughter had breasts. This was the kind of thing a father usually grew into. Or maybe they were all uneasy with any awareness of a daughter's sexuality. How was he supposed to know?

He took a long swallow of coffee. Forget the *Times*. He had to be out the door in twenty-five minutes, and he still had a couple of calls to return. He groped at his belt and realized he'd left his BlackBerry upstairs by his bed. He started to stand as she flopped herself into her chair.

"I asked Lucy if I could have dinner at her house tonight."

Jon's attention snapped to his daughter, who was staring defiantly at him across the table. "What?"

"I thought I could go over there after school and stay for dinner."

"What did she say?"

Her lower lip protruded. "No. Of course. She knows *you'd* say no."

"Because her mother will be there."

Sierra glared at him.

He hated that pout. It irritated him and made him feel guilty all at once. "She's right."

"Why?" she cried. "Why do you even want

me living with you if you don't know me at
all?"

Jon struggled for patience. "How does my
saying I don't want you sitting down to dinner
with a woman who's been a drug addict for
thirty years mean I don't know you?"

"Because you should know *I'm* not going
to become a druggy just because I meet one."
The way she looked at him was damned near
as scathing as Lucy's last stare had been. "Do
you know how many kids at the high school
use? Everybody goes to parties. I know two
girls who are pregnant and another one who
had an abortion this summer. Somehow *I*
haven't gotten pregnant yet."

Not an announcement he wanted to hear.
Okay, he knew sixteen-year-old girls got
pregnant. Ones a lot younger than that did.
Thirteen-, fourteen-year-old runaways were
picked up for hooking all the time. But this
was his daughter. Jon gritted his teeth.

"I'm well aware that Lucy's mother doesn't
have a contagious virus. That doesn't mean
I think it's okay for you to spend time with a
woman like that." Even he knew he sounded
like a prig. He didn't need Sierra's incredu-
lous stare to tell him.

She pushed her cereal bowl away. Milk

slopped onto the quilted place mat and pooled on the wood surface. "I love Lucy."

"I know," Jon said quietly. "And I know you don't understand."

"I thought I wanted a real dad, but I wish I'd never looked for you. Lucy is my family," she spat, and jumped to her feet. "Not you!"

He closed his eyes briefly and groped for self-control. And, maybe, a touch of insight about what Sierra needed from him.

Lucy, tell me how to handle this. Tell me what to say.

She'd know. He had no doubt she would.

The irony didn't escape him. He needed her. And yet here he was, telling his teenage daughter Lucy was forbidden to her. That Lucy was someone who made lousy decisions, who couldn't be trusted. And he knew better, but damn it, *damn it,* she'd pushed him too far. Why couldn't she see that? Why wasn't she willing to relent enough to allow him to back off from his ultimatum, too? How could he, if she wouldn't?

And yeah, she was right. This *was* partly about the election. What was he supposed to do, throw it away for love?

"Sierra…"

"Oh, what's the use?" The teenager raced for the stairs. The thunder of her footsteps sounded as if she was a 250-pound line-backer, not a slight and airy girl.

Jon winced in advance of the door slamming up above.

He scrubbed a hand over his face. *That went well.* His life had turned into a melodrama. To top it off, he hadn't made a single phone call, and now if he made any he'd be late. He stared balefully at the mess on the table and realized he had to clean it up before he left.

Swearing, he grabbed Sierra's cereal bowl and his coffee cup and carried both to the kitchen sink.

LUCY HADN'T ENJOYED the short drive home from work so much in ages. Not, she thought with a pang, since she'd had Sierra chattering beside her.

She and her mother were both excited. Her mom had worked a half day today for Harry Tullis, who owned the used bookstore half a block from Barks and Purrs. A help-wanted sign had gone up in his window Wednesday.

"Will it make things awkward for you if I apply and he doesn't hire me?" her mom had asked.

Lucy had hastened to assure her that she

knew Harry only casually, mostly from the downtown merchants association meetings.

Terry had disappeared down the street and returned triumphant. "It's only eight hours a week right now. Two half days, but he thinks he might lose his other part-time employee and that would mean more hours."

Lucy had hugged her mother with genuine pleasure. "It's just what you wanted—books."

Seeing her mother's pleasure made Lucy's day. Apparently business had been slow this afternoon—no surprise given that it was for Lucy, too. But the absence of customers had given her mom time to browse shelves and get familiar with the stock. Lucy already knew that Harry carried an exceptional local history section as well as an enormous fantasy and science-fiction section. Her mom was delighted by both.

Lucy unlocked her front door and stepped back to let her mother go in first. When she started to follow, she ran right into her mom, who had come to an abrupt stop. "What—"

"It smells like someone's cooking dinner."

It did. Like…spaghetti. Which so happened to be Sierra's specialty. Lucy pushed past her mother and hurried to the kitchen.

Sure enough, Sierra wore Lucy's voluminous white chef's apron and was stirring sauce in a saucepan on the stove. She grinned, although her cheeks were suspiciously pink. "Hey. I thought I'd surprise you."

Lucy crossed her arms and said sternly, "Sierra Lind. What are you doing here?"

Her chin jutted out. "I wanted to come." She looked past Lucy. "Is this your mom?"

Jon was going to be furious. For once, Lucy couldn't blame him. "Yes. Mom, meet Sierra, who should *not* be here. Sierra, meet my mother, Terry."

"Pleased to meet you," her mother murmured.

Sierra waved the spoon. Spatters of red sauce flew. "Oops," she said sheepishly. "Hi."

"Answer my question."

Sierra's chin came up. "I got mad and came anyway."

"Does your father know?"

Sierra looked down at her toes, painted as blue as her hair. "I sort of left him a phone message."

Dear God. "*Sort of?*"

Defiance flashed in her eyes when she lifted her head again. "I did leave him a message, but I left it on his home phone. I didn't want to call his cell."

"Because he answers that."

Mouth mulish, she shrugged.

Lucy reached for her own phone.

"Don't call him," Sierra cried.

"Of course I have to call him. He has a right to know where you are."

"He'll find out when he gets home."

"Which will be when?"

"Who knows? Probably late. He's, like, *never* home. He probably won't even notice I'm not there until tomorrow. If then."

Whoa. Wait. *Tomorrow?* Sierra thought she was here to *stay?*

Lucy cleared her throat. "Leaving aside the whole issue of whether you're a dinner guest or imagine you're moving back in, I don't buy it that your father is that indifferent." Tempting though it was to think the worst of him. "You're seriously telling me he won't stop by your bedroom to check on you, even if he comes in late?"

Sierra resumed studying her toes.

"You don't see him at breakfast?"

"Sometimes," she mumbled.

"Is he going to blame me because you're here?"

She looked up at that. "No! I told him you said no. Okay?"

Her mom, Lucy realized, had discreetly absented herself. Suddenly tired, Lucy asked, "Then why are you here?" even though she knew.

"Because I want to live with you, not him," Sierra cried passionately. "I brought clothes and everything. I won't go back."

Oh, man. All Lucy wanted to do was gather this child into her arms and hug her. But how could she? With her agreement, Jon now had temporary custody. She couldn't imagine what would happen if she tried to defend Sierra's right to choose where she was going to live.

"Sierra...you have to go back. He's your father."

Sierra looked her right in the eye and said, "If you make me, I'll run away. He's being stupid and irrational and he has no *right*. You know he doesn't."

"Legally—"

"I don't care about legally. I'm sixteen. I want to live with you." She suddenly looked stricken. "Unless you don't want me."

Emotion rushed through Lucy like a tsunami hitting the shoreline. Overpowering, inescapable. "You know I do," she whispered. "You know I love you."

Sierra burst into noisy sobs, dropped the spoon and flung herself into Lucy's arms.

Lucy was lost.

CHAPTER FOURTEEN

Jon got home early to find the house empty. No sign Sierra had ever made it home from school. Her book bag wasn't flung in its usual spot on her desk, her laptop didn't repose on her bed. In fact, her bed was made. He stood in the bedroom doorway staring at it. Had she made it even once since coming to live with him?

Feeling a chill, he stepped into the room. No dirty clothes dangled over the rim of the mesh hamper he'd bought for her. No shoes lay wherever she'd kicked them off. The desk was tidy, drawers all closed.

Maybe she'd felt guilty for her outburst this morning and cleaned her bedroom. Put in a load of laundry before she left for school.

Swearing, he slid open her closet door and saw with relief that her clothes still hung in there. Shoes tangled haphazardly on the carpeted floor.

Okay. She'd had some after-school thing

and simply wasn't home yet. She should have called to let him know, but—

As if on cue, his cell phone vibrated at his waist and he glanced down. He tensed at the number displayed on the screen.

Lucy's.

Flipping the phone open, he said, "Lucy?"

"Jon." She sounded calm. "I thought I'd better let you know that Sierra is here."

The headache he'd been fighting all day clamped tighter. "What the hell?"

"I think you'd better come over."

"To pick her up? Damn straight."

"She says she won't go with you."

He swore.

"She made spaghetti. Will you come to dinner and let us all talk about this?"

"You mean let her get her spoiled way?"

"Spoiled?" Her tone bristled. "My fault?"

"If the shoe fits." He was too furious to care if he sounded less than mature.

"Fine," she said tersely. "One way or the other, we'll see you when we see you." The next second, she was gone.

He slammed his cell phone closed and wondered if she'd done the same. The string of obscenities he let loose didn't make him feel any better. Lucy thought she was going to win, did she? Jon couldn't believe she didn't know him better than that by now.

He detoured by the bathroom and downed enough ibuprofen to kill any pain that was merely physical, then left the house.

The drive wasn't long enough to allow him get a grip on his turbulent emotions or for his headache to let up. He stalked to the front door and hammered on it.

Lucy opened it and cocked her head. "Are we going to have a scene?"

He hated the way it took only the sight of her to knock him back. Her feet were bare and she wore faded jeans and a bright yellow T-shirt. Her wealth of dark hair cascaded over her shoulders and breasts. He wanted to plunge his hands into it and kiss her until neither of them remembered why he was there.

"Yes," he said in a hard voice. "Unless Sierra has her things together and is ready to go."

"We just started to eat."

"*We.*"

Color stained her cheeks. "Yes, my mother is here. She's probably in the kitchen right now jotting down the phone numbers of all the drug dealers she knows. She always made sure I knew where to buy. She was an open kind of mom." She swung around and stalked away.

Jon had no trouble catching up to her and reached the kitchen on her heels.

Sierra had squeezed in on the far side of the table, wedged where he couldn't grab her even if he'd been inclined. She met his eyes, her expression mutinous.

He ignored Lucy's mother, who also sat at the table, his attention all on his daughter. "You couldn't even leave me a note?"

"I left a phone message."

He removed his phone from his belt and made a point of staring at it. No messages.

"On your home phone." Which she knew he scarcely used.

"Sierra, this isn't an option."

"Don't I have any say in my life?"

"Not about where you live."

"I could go to court and ask to be emancipated."

A sharp, humorless laugh broke from him. "Claiming I'm abusive?"

Her eyes glittered with anger. "Claiming you're a stranger who thinks he can take over my life. Your sperm got Mom pregnant. So what? That doesn't make you my father."

Beside him, Lucy said, "She's right. It

doesn't. I'm sorry I ever encouraged this relationship."

That hurt more than he wanted to admit even to himself. "It's you two who came to me, not the other way around. None of us can undo it. I take my responsibilities seriously."

Lucy's lip curled. "Every girl's dream. To be one of Daddy's responsibilities."

"It damn well beats the alternative," he snarled, then remembered too late how close to home he'd struck.

Lucy's face paled.

"Enough!"

Startled, they all stared at Lucy's mother.

"There is a child here," she said sharply. "If you're going to yell at each other, go somewhere else. Otherwise, sit and discuss this like two reasonable adults."

Jon looked at Lucy's stricken expression, then at his daughter, whose eyes were glittering with tears. A huge wave of helplessness overcame him. Now what?

Terry raised her eyebrows at him. "Have you eaten?" she asked in a much softer tone.

"No."

"Then take a seat. Everyone. Eat."

He focused on the table and realized it was

set for four. Stiffly Jon moved to the chair adjacent to Sierra's. She didn't look at him when he sat.

"Would you like something to drink?" Lucy asked him, as cordial as a waitress at the end of a twelve-hour shift from hell.

The county sheriff's department was over 750 employees strong. How did he expect to be able to handle the job if he couldn't handle one petite, fiery woman and one defiant teenage girl?

"Milk is fine."

She poured him a glass and set it at his place without comment, then took her own seat. After a minute, she handed him a bowl of spaghetti.

Jon added sauce, took a slice of garlic bread and some salad. This felt surreal.

Sierra's hair hid her face from him. She didn't so much as pick up her fork.

Terry studied him, then said, "I can only apologize for my part in all this. If I'd known how much disruption I was going to be causing, I would have made other arrangements when I was released."

"I wouldn't have let you," Lucy snapped.

Terry didn't even glance at her daughter. Her eyes held his, and he couldn't help seeing she meant what she'd said. Her regret looked genuine.

He dipped his head in acknowledgment.

She laid a hand on Sierra's. "You're a good cook. Thank you."

"You're welcome," his daughter mumbled.

"I started a new job today."

When no one else said anything, Jon felt compelled to be polite, for reasons mysterious to him. "I thought you were working for Lucy."

"I am, three days a week. And I love it." She smiled at Lucy. "I'm a huge reader, though, and I worked in the library at the correctional institute. I was hoping to find something in a library or bookstore, and I did. Only a few hours a week, but I can't think of anything more wonderful than being able to talk about books with customers." She chatted about the used bookstore that Jon knew was on the same block as Lucy's store, how she'd be working only two half days a week but it was a foot in the door.

He realized he was eating, and that Terry was right—the spaghetti was good. If his schedule wasn't so unpredictable, it might have occurred to him to ask if Sierra would take on some cooking chores at home. Would that have helped? He wished it had occurred to him.

"You must have come here right after school," he said.

He saw a flash of pale eyes from beneath her hair. She shrugged.

"It was nice of her to make dinner as a surprise." Lucy narrowed her eyes at him, but her voice was even. "Mom and I were both tired. We were going to flip a coin to see who had to cook."

Nice? Sierra had cooked dinner to make a statement. *See? I'm comfortable even in the kitchen. I belong here.* She was trying to make it as hard as possible for Lucy to bundle her into the car and take her back to him.

Jon kept eating. Conversation flowed around him, all conducted by Terry and Lucy, although Sierra was coaxed into an occasional response. His headache was easing, he realized. The food helped. Throttling back on the rage probably did, too.

Now what?

He had no more idea than he'd had when he sat down. You could grab a toddler, buckle her into her car seat even if she was in the middle of a screaming tantrum and haul her ass home. You couldn't do the same to a teenager, as much as he wished he could. He detested feeling so helpless.

"Coffee?" Lucy's mother asked him.

"Yeah, thanks." He looked down to realize his plate was empty. Lucy had eaten too, and even Sierra had polished off part of her dinner.

"I'll leave you three to talk," Terry said, and smiled at him. "Thank you for eating with us, Captain Brenner."

Now he felt like an ass. "I appreciate you calming us all down. You missed your calling. You should have been a hostage negotiator."

She chuckled and left the kitchen. Jon sighed and looked first at Sierra—head down again, hair swinging in place to hide her face—and then Lucy, who stared back at him. He almost smiled. Terry might have a talent for mediation, but her daughter didn't. She was still mad, and didn't mind him knowing.

"All right, Sierra," he said finally. "Has living with me really been that terrible?"

"Yes," she cried, then hunched her shoulders and mumbled, "No. I mean, it's not terrible. But it's lonely, and I miss the cats, and you don't talk to me. You never listen."

Guilty, he thought bleakly. Aloud, he said,

"In fairness, I don't think you've been listening to me very well, either."

She didn't say anything.

He sighed and turned his attention to Lucy. "Tell me how unreasonable I'm being."

"I think if you'd taken Sierra to live with you because it was time, that would have been different. What you did was snatch her away from the only person she trusted, implying that I *wasn't* trustworthy. You hurt me, but that isn't the point."

Yeah, it was. He lay awake nights knowing how much he had hurt her and longing for a redo. But he knew what she was saying. Sierra was the issue here. He nodded.

More tentatively, Lucy said, "Maybe I shouldn't be speaking for you, Sierra…"

"It's okay."

Lucy's eyes, dark with emotion, met his. "Losing a parent would have to be horrible for any kid. But losing your only parent…" As if she couldn't help herself, she reached across the table and touched Sierra's hand, which turned to grip hers.

It was a sight that twisted Jon up inside. This was where they'd begun—him moved more than he wanted to admit to see the flow of trust and love between this woman and this girl.

"Sierra found me. Or I found her. And yes, she found you, too. You *do* matter to her, Jon. Don't think you don't."

He risked a glance at his daughter and met her teary, entreating gaze. His heart did an uncomfortable bump.

"But when you took her the way you did, what you were doing was undermining the all-too-precarious stability she'd found. You were saying, 'Lucy isn't trustworthy,' and maybe even, 'Your judgment is faulty.' Can't you see that?"

He swallowed. Yeah. He could. That *was* what he'd been saying, despite all the times he'd commented to Lucy on what an extraordinary young woman Sierra was, for all that he'd admired and even envied the bond between them.

Had he been *jealous?* he wondered, appalled, then shook his head. No. He'd felt included. They'd let him become part of their family, and nothing had ever meant more to him in his life.

"I do understand you have a problem because of the election. And…that I let you down, not telling you about Mom." Lucy sounded unhappy. "I'm sorry, Jon."

"No." He heard his own gruffness. "I'm sorry that I didn't talk about this with you.

It's— Hell. I don't know what the answer is now. Do you really want me to throw the election?"

Her eyes, like Sierra's, beseeched him. "Of course not. But nobody has found out about us. Have they?"

"I think it's safe to assume Rinnert knows I'm dating you. He simply hasn't learned anything about you yet that he thinks he can use." Jon paused. "But he's looking, Lucy. Don't kid yourself. And yeah, that sounds paranoid, but—what's the saying?—even paranoids have enemies?

"Sierra." Jon looked at his daughter. "Come home with me. The election is only a few weeks away. Give me that long."

"And then what?" Sierra's eyes flashed. "You'll let me live with Lucy? What will people think then?"

His head had begun to ache again. What *would* people think? Did it matter? He couldn't seem to make his brain function.

Lucy stood. "It's time for me to leave you two to talk. This isn't about me."

"No." He pushed back his chair. "You're wrong. It's about you, too."

Her expression was remote, neither warm nor angry. She shook her head. "It's really not," she said with a finality that scared him.

She smiled gently at Sierra. "Let me know what you decide, honey." Then she left the kitchen.

Jon had no trouble hearing what she didn't say. This was about Sierra because Lucy and he were done. He'd blown it; there was no going back.

He'd loved two women in his life. He'd held himself accountable for Cassia's death, and he knew he was, but only in part. This loss, however, was on him. One hundred percent.

Sierra turned a stricken gaze on Jon, and he saw that she'd heard the unspoken, too. They stared at each other for what had to be a minute.

Then he reached out and took her hand, grateful that she let him. "Okay, honey," he said. "Tell me what you want. I'll listen this time."

JON WAS IN A MEETING regarding budget overruns when his phone rang. With the intention of muting the ring and letting the call go to voice mail, he glanced at the screen. Lieutenant Stevens, head of SWAT.

He excused himself, stepped out in the hall and answered.

"You like to know when we're going to be on the evening news, right?" Stevens said.

He had to laugh. That was one way of putting it. "I do like a heads-up," he agreed. "What's happening?"

"Guy got out of prison maybe a month ago for attempting to kill his wife. Now he's holding her, their kids and a neighbor woman hostage. He's waving around some serious weaponry. We've evacuated the block."

Jon opened the conference-room door, signaled that the meeting was over and started walking rapidly to his office. "Names?"

He swore when he heard the man's. Leonard Ullman had been released the same week as Terry Malone. Jon remembered noticing the name above hers and shaking his head because Ullman's wife was apparently—and inexplicably—taking the guy back.

"All right," he said. "Anybody succeeded in talking to him yet?"

"Bettinger's trying."

"Good." Ronnie Bettinger was one of the best negotiators they had. "How old are the kids?" They, of course, were the newsworthy part of this scenario.

"Neighbor's husband says four and—" A siren temporarily drowned him out. Jon next heard, "—thinks the youngest is four. That one's a little girl. Jessica." His voice was tight. Stevens had two daughters himself, one about that age. "Older one's a boy, just started first grade."

Their worst nightmare. Young, frightened children held hostage. "Keep me informed."

Jon considered driving over there. Being there to make the major calls. Maybe he should. But if he won the election in two weeks' time, he intended to promote Curt Stevens to his current job. This was a trial by fire, he thought.

Instead of sitting down behind his desk, he went to stare out the window, although he didn't see a thing. Damn it, damn it. *This* was why he shouldn't have left Sierra at Lucy's.

Groaning, he rolled his shoulders in a futile attempt to relieve tension. Frustration gripped him. He'd known when he saw Ullman's name that he would be hurting his wife again. It was a given.

The same way it was a given that, sooner or later, Terry would take that first drink or pop the first pill. Then the part-time job at the bookstore wouldn't be enough to pay for her habit. She'd start conning money out of Lucy. Then stealing from the till at Lucy's store and the bookstore. But that wouldn't be enough. She'd have to escalate somehow, and it would be ugly.

Jon squeezed his tense neck muscles. He had to be fair. Terry wasn't going to hurt Sierra. Despite her having been involved in the armed robbery, she wasn't a violent criminal. Terry *hadn't* been the one holding the gun. Yeah, she was there. But there was one thing in the police report that Jon hadn't told Sierra because he hadn't wanted to feel any softening at all for Terry. It was in the interview with the eighteen-year-old clerk, who'd talked about being scared to death, about the crazy look in the guy's eyes and the way his hands shook. But what she'd also said was that the woman had pleaded for him not to hurt anyone.

"She was crying," the clerk said. "When they left, he grabbed her hand and yanked her with him. She was looking over her shoulder at me…."

The typed text hadn't interjected expressions. The officer conducting the interview hadn't pursued the subject. He didn't care what expression Terry Malone had had on her face. She'd been a participant in the armed robbery. Her tears might have bought her a plea bargain if her rap sheet hadn't been so lengthy, but it was. Nobody cared.

But Jon found he did now.

He pictured the woman with the gentle face so like Lucy's and tried to reconcile her with someone who could, in any stretch of the imagination, be involved in holding up a convenience store. He couldn't.

Two days ago, after leaving Sierra in Lucy's care despite his better judgment, he had called Terry's parole officer and asked how she was doing. Better than good, he'd been told. She was attending Narcotics Anonymous and Alcoholics Anonymous meetings daily, was working, reporting in, had a positive attitude.

Now that he'd met her he knew: she was doing her best. He remembered the real glow of pleasure on her face when she'd talked about her new job. The sharp reproof in her voice when she said, "There is a child here." *He* had been failing Sierra and Lucy both; still was. She, he suspected, was honestly trying to redeem herself.

So who was the better person?

His cell phone rang.

"We've got the kids safe," Lieutenant Stevens told him. "The boy boosted his little sister out the bathroom window, then followed her."

"Good for him." The kids' escape put the

remaining two adults in greater peril, though. Ullman would be enraged.

"Bettinger has him on the phone. He doesn't know the kids are gone yet. He's threatening to kill the neighbor."

"Has he said what he wants?"

"He doesn't want anything we can give him. The wife was leaving him. Now she says she didn't mean it, but he's not that dumb. Hold on." He muffled the phone, finally came back. "Guess I was wrong. He does want something. We're delivering pizza and beer."

"Good," Jon said again, although the beer was a risk. Alcohol lowered inhibitions, the kind that kept a man from pulling the trigger. It could increase his depression. But it could also make him sleepy, careless.

Two hours later the whole thing was over. Leonard had drunk his six-pack and collapsed weeping. The neighbor woman wrenched the gun out of his hand and fled the house; SWAT members stormed in. His wife, also sobbing, had tried to protect him from the big bad cops.

Hell, she'd probably take him back again when he got out of prison next time.

Jon made a statement to the press lauding the courage of the children and the neighbor woman, praising the professional conduct of his officers and the skill the negotiator had employed in talking Mr. Ullman down. Then he returned to his office and called Sierra.

"I saw stuff on TV," she said. "Were you there?"

"No. I spend most of my time behind a desk these days."

"Were you ever on the SWAT team?"

"Yes. I did a few years." Going in, it had seemed glamorous, but he hadn't liked the job. He wasn't into the adrenaline the way some cops were. Homicide had suited him much better.

"I'm glad you're not doing it anymore," Sierra told him. "It looks scary."

They talked a little. He told her about the intense training and planning, the teamwork, the bulletproof vests, but admitted she was right. Being the first one through the door was risky.

"Leonard Ullman just got out of prison a month ago," he said.

Sierra caught on right away and said indignantly, "And you think because he did something like this that Lucy's mom will."

"No," he admitted. "I don't think that. I didn't say that. This is your turn to listen.

What I'm telling you is that this is the kind of thing that gives me a certain bias."

After a moment his daughter said, "Okay." Just that. One word. Thoughtful. And then, "Are you coming over tonight?"

"No, I'm speaking to—" he couldn't even remember and had to glance at his calendar "—a youth advocates group."

"Oh. Tomorrow night?" she asked hopefully.

"Jaycees." Jon rubbed the back of his neck. "I'm sorry, Sierra. I'll call."

"Okay," she said again, but this time he heard her vulnerability.

A now familiar wave of inadequacy washed over him. "I really am sorry."

"No, Dad, I meant okay," she said more sturdily.

He promised one more time to call tomorrow, then hung up.

He was tied up every night this week until Saturday. Tomorrow was going to be a bitch, but…what if Wednesday he showed up at Lucy's store with lunch in hand? Would she give him the time of day?

There was only one way to find out, wasn't there?

His depression didn't lift.

TUESDAY AFTERNOON, Lucy felt good about
the day when she flipped the sign to Closed.
Receipts were way up from the past couple
of Tuesdays, and she'd adopted out the
young mother cat to a nice family who had
just bought their first house. They'd come
looking for a kitten, but fallen in love with
Ellabelle.

Her mom wasn't working today, and Sierra
would be home from school. One or the other
would have started dinner, thank goodness.
That was the best part of no longer living
alone. Lucy liked to cook, but not when she'd
had a long day at work.

As long as she didn't think about Jon,
everything was fine and she had no excuse
for feeling down. It wasn't as if she and Jon
were serious before the blowup. Maybe they
wouldn't ever have gotten serious. She'd
always known their relationship had developed partly because of good old-fashioned
proximity. He wanted to spend time with his
daughter—ergo he spent time with Lucy, too.
And the idea of the three of them being a
family was seductive.

She was the foolish one, letting herself fall
in love so fast. Live and learn, she thought,
but wasn't sure she'd actually learned a
thing.

She was half a block away from her house when, horrified, she abruptly focused on the TV truck parked in front. No. *Two* TV trucks from competing stations.

Her cell phone rang. She fumbled for it as she continued past her house and turned the corner to circle the block. She managed to get the phone open as she reached the alley.

"Lucy?" Sierra's voice was small and scared. "Are you coming home soon?"

"I'm here. I saw. You haven't talked to them, have you?" Lucy turned into the alley.

"No. I mean, I started to open the door and then freaked and closed it as fast as I could."

"We need to call your dad." She stopped the car behind her back fence. Another car could squeeze by if need be, and this wasn't garbage day. Usually she wouldn't leave her car there, but it would be fine for now.

"I tried, but it kicked right to voice mail."

"Okay." Getting out of her car, she felt dizzy. *Don't hyperventilate.* "I'm sneaking in the back way."

A voice shouted, "Ms. Malone. Are you Ms. Malone?"

An attractive blonde woman with a microphone was racing down the alley, a cameraman lumbering behind. Every instinct urged Lucy to run, but that would look guilty. As if she had something to hide.

She whisked into her yard, closed the gate in the picket fence to give herself a barrier however puny and waited until the breathless reporter reached her. Then she said, "Yes? Can I help you?"

"Ms. Lucia Malone?"

Heart drumming, she said, "That's right." Although she didn't look at it, she could see from the corner of her eye that the camera lens was trained on her.

"Records indicate you have a foster daughter, Sierra Lind."

"I do."

"We understand that Sierra's father is, in fact, in the picture. That he's a regular visitor to your home."

Lying wasn't an option. Jon would now have to come clean, Lucy presumed. But that was up to him. As mad as she was at him, she wouldn't do anything to hurt him—or to damage his chance of being elected.

"I'm sorry," she said. "Sierra is a minor and entitled to privacy. I don't know where you got your information, but I'm not going to confirm or deny it. Please excuse me." She turned and hurried toward the house, spinning around only when she heard the squeak of the gate latch behind her.

The cameraman leaned over the low fence, aiming his enormous camera. The blonde had started into her garden, picking her way gingerly on the stepping stones. "Ms. Malone, please talk to us about—"

"You're trespassing," Lucy said icily. "If you don't get off my property, I'll call 911." She still had her cell phone in her hand and flipped it open.

The blonde hastily retreated.

She was still calling questions after Lucy when she reached the house and let herself in.

"Oh, Lucy!" Sierra flung herself into her arms. "We didn't know what to do."

Terry was hovering behind her. She flinched as the doorbell rang. "They keep trying. Sierra started to open the door the first time the doorbell rang, so they know she's here."

Lucy was determined not to let either her mother or Sierra suspect how shaken she was. "We'll ignore them," she said firmly. "I told the fake blonde back there that if she trespasses, I'll call 911. I'm going to stick my head out in front and tell anyone there the same thing. At least that should get them off the porch."

Before her nerve could give out, she marched straight through the house, flung open the front door and found herself facing a different reporter and cameraman as well as what she guessed was a print reporter, all on her walkway or porch.

"You need to get off my property," she said. "Now. I'll call the police if you don't. I have nothing else to say." She slammed the door and fell against it. She could see her mom and Sierra clinging together in the hall, well away from windows. *We're under assault,* she thought in disbelief.

This was what Jon had feared all along. She hadn't imagined his relationship to Sierra or herself being anywhere near this newsworthy. His opponent must have whipped up this little frenzy with an implication of real scandal.

But they weren't asking about her mom. Which meant they didn't know about her yet. Or didn't know he had dated Lucy? The questions the blonde had called after her all had to do with Sierra.

Her existence alone might be scandalous enough to derail his campaign, though. Captain Black-and-White, Law-and-Order, had been tracked down by an unknown daughter. *Sperm donor* didn't sound good. *Deadbeat Dad* sounded worse.

Hand shaking, she opened her cell phone.

CHAPTER FIFTEEN

JON WAS SHRUGGING ON his suit jacket in preparation for leaving the office when his cell phone rang. He glanced at the number, which was unfamiliar, and thought of not answering, but what was the point? He'd only have to call someone back. He had half an hour to spare; the drive to the restaurant where he was speaking to the Jaycees was a short one.

He lifted the phone. "Brenner."

"Captain Brenner, this is Richard Anderson with KCRN TV News. Would you care to comment on a report that you have a daughter living in foster care rather than in your home?"

His luck had finally run out. Meantime, another call was coming in. Another reporter…? No, Lucy's number, he saw. He couldn't switch over.

With calm he didn't feel, he said, "I had intended to make an announcement when she was ready. Please don't try to speak to her."

"We're outside the home where she lives right now. She did come to the door earlier but wouldn't answer questions."

"Stay away from her," he snapped, and ended the call.

Lucy had given up, or had been switched to voice mail. He hit the lights in his office and hustled for the elevator. *That son of a bitch Rinnert.* So much for feeling grudging respect that Rinnert wasn't going to try to sling this kind of mud.

The elevator was crowded. He wedged his way in anyway, and turned his back on the other occupants. The doors took their time closing; the elevator jerked. He stared at the numbers above the door, willing them to change faster. Impatience prickled like an electric charge, raising the hairs on his body.

Was Lucy with Sierra? *Please don't let her be alone.*

He had to step aside and let people out on two levels of the parking garage before the elevator reached his floor. He kept himself to a walk now, not wanting to draw attention, but not wasting any time, either. Once in his SUV, he had to wait to back out while a pickup across from him inched out from a too-small spot. His tension climbed. His fingers drummed on the steering wheel.

It was one of those drives when every light seemed to turn against him. His phone kept ringing. Numbers he didn't know. Reporters. Somewhere along the way it occurred to him that he would be late to his speaking engagement. In a lull between rings, he called Edie and told her quickly what was happening.

"Have you decided what to say?" she asked.

"No. Yes," he said, realizing he had. "The truth. Can't be worse than the alternatives."

"I was beginning to hope."

"Me, too."

He ended the call blocks from Lucy's house. He'd already seen the TV trucks ahead. Lucy's car wasn't in the driveway. She hadn't phoned again. Was she afraid to go home?

He pulled up in front of the neighbor's house and got out. People were clustered on the sidewalk. He'd half expected to see them on the porch or peering in windows. Were they respecting the fact that Sierra was a kid, or had someone threatened them? If it was Lucy's mother who had, she'd gained his eternal friendship.

He was ten feet away when one of the

reporters spotted him and the whole herd turned and enveloped him. He was used to it, which didn't make him any more relaxed, but he was less intimidated than Lucy or a sixteen-year-old girl would be. He had his game face on, and knew it to be effective. He would look hard and remote and completely professional no matter what was going on inside.

"Captain Brenner, we're told that you have a daughter despite information you gave early in the campaign that you weren't married, never had been and had no children."

"Excuse me," he said politely, and forged through the crowd until he reached the open gate to Lucy's front walkway. Shouting questions, the crowd plunged through after him. He turned to face them. "Were you asked to stay off this property?"

Feet shuffled backward.

"If you'll give me a minute, I'll make a statement. First, I'd like to ensure you haven't scared the daylights out of my daughter."

He turned his back on renewed questions and took the three steps to the porch in two, rapping hard on the door. "Lucy. Sierra. It's Jon."

The door opened and he slipped in. Lucy was right in front of him and he enveloped her in his arms before he could think better of it. For an instant she went stiff, then melted against him.

"Thank God you're here. We didn't know what to do."

"A reporter called me and said they were out front." Over her head he saw Sierra and Terry, holding each other. Sierra started forward and he waved her back. "Don't get near the windows, honey. I'll deal with them." He gently, reluctantly held Lucy away from him. "Have any of you talked to them?"

"Sierra started to answer the door earlier and slammed it quickly when she saw the TV camera. They waylaid me when I got home and I told them I'd call the police if they stepped foot on the property. I said I wasn't going to confirm or deny any information they had."

"Good girl." He kissed her cheek and gently brushed the hair back from her high, curving forehead. "This is my fault. I should have made an announcement sooner. It was stupid to think I could keep any secrets."

"It's my fault," Sierra declared passionately. "I never thought... I didn't mean..."

"I know you didn't." He smiled at her, then at Lucy's mother.

He was conscious, suddenly, of a strange

sensation. One minute he'd been roiling with anger and guilt and a hundred other emotions. Now…all he'd had to do was take Lucy in his arms, rest his cheek for a moment against her head, see that Sierra was being guarded fiercely by both women and he felt… at peace.

The truth shall free you. To hell with the election.

He let himself look into Lucy's eyes, seeing her anxiety and a question he hoped he understood, and then he opened the door again and let himself out onto the porch.

He raised his hand for silence as he went down the steps and walked toward the crowd of reporters. "I'd like to make a statement."

Behind him, he heard the door open again. Lucy, at least, must have stepped out behind him. He glanced back and saw her. She'd left the door partially open, perhaps so that Sierra could hear what he said.

The cameras were rolling. A flash went off. Another.

"I have a sixteen-year-old daughter named Sierra Lind," he said. "Obviously you know that. Sierra's mother was killed ten months ago by a drunk driver in a head-on car accident. I did not at the time know that I had a daughter, nor did she know who her father was." He paused. "I had never met Sierra's mother. She went to a fertility clinic to get pregnant. When I was putting myself through college, I donated sperm."

He waited through the ensuing uproar, astonishingly calm. When he heard an opening, he raised his voice. "I was twenty-one years old." He permitted himself a crooked smile. "Cocky enough to think I was doing women a favor."

There were a few chuckles.

Good.

He kept talking. Told them about seeing the pregnant woman catching a bus by herself. His sudden realization that she could be carrying *his* baby. His decision to earn money another way.

He told them how Sierra had found him. "I am more fortunate than I can tell you. Sierra is an exceptionally bright young woman with a 4.0 grade point average and an expertise in computers we could use in the crime lab."

More laughs.

"Thanks to her mother, she's also mature and good-hearted. I really am lucky. I can take no credit for having a daughter who fills me with pride every time I see her." He glanced over his shoulder. Lucy smiled at him, and he drew encouragement from that.

He needed her forgiveness as he'd never needed anything in his life.

"I would have come forth with her existence sooner, but Sierra is still grieving. She found me, but we've had to work out what that means. However much I want to, I can never be as much to her as the parent she lost was. Sierra had no other family to take her in after her mother's death. However, at the time she worked part-time at Barks and Purrs, the pet-supply store here in town. When the owner, Lucy Malone, learned that Sierra would have to go into foster care, she opened her home and heart to my daughter. She is—" Damned if he didn't have to stop to clear his throat. "Lucy Malone is the most compassionate person I've ever met. I'm going to tell you, if my opponent hasn't already—" he allowed his tone to become momentarily dry "—that I'm grateful to Sierra for finding me for a reason that doesn't have anything to do with our relationship. Ms. Malone and I have been dating."

He should stop there, he thought, but the way Lucy had relaxed trustingly against him had filled him with certainty. Or maybe recklessness. Whatever it was, he continued, "The three of us, along with Ms. Malone's mother, who has recently come to stay, feel like a family. You're rushing me, but I'll admit that I'm hoping we will become one. Now, if you'll excuse me, I'm also hoping Sierra—who so happens to be an excellent cook—has dinner ready. No questions."

They shouted them anyway. He walked toward the house, his eyes on Lucy. Hers on his.

He barely heard the questions, until one brought him to a stop. "How do you reconcile having been a sperm donor with your frequent insistence on taking personal responsibility for all your actions?"

Jon hesitated, then turned to face them once again. Finally, a good question. He lifted a hand for a second time, and was rewarded with quiet.

"I'm not the man I was at twenty-one." He looked from face to face, and chose to let remembered anger and grief leak into his voice. "My life changed—I changed—three years later, when someone I loved was brutally murdered by a man who'd been granted early release from prison for good behavior. He had been out for a day and a half. He had committed violent crimes before. The arresting officer for his last crime traveled to Walla Walla to plead for his parole to be denied. The prison psychologist also recommended keeping him behind bars. I saw my friend's body. That is the moment when I became the man I am now." He paused again. "I hope I was never careless in my decisions. I did, and do, believe that women who can't conceive any other way should have the option of fertility treatments with donated sperm. I can't possibly regret having helped Rebecca Lind become pregnant. She, and now I, gained a remarkable daughter from that choice. When I learned about Sierra and knew that searching for me was no whim on her part, that she needed her father, I immediately took steps to confirm that she was, in fact, my child. Once we knew for sure, I didn't hesitate to build a relationship with her. *That's* taking personal responsibility." Nodding, he once again turned his back on them and walked into the house.

Lucy closed and locked the door behind him. Before he could try to read how she'd reacted to his statement, Sierra tumbled forward, Terry close behind. Jon held out his arms for his daughter, who flung herself at him as if he was her savior.

No, he realized with astonishment. Her dad. An automatic hero.

He didn't think anything in his life had ever felt this good.

LUCY'S EYES FLOODED with tears. She couldn't help it. Sniffling, she swiped at them. Sierra was crying, too. Jon had his cheek pressed to Sierra's bright blue head, and his eyes were squeezed shut so tight, Lucy suspected *he* was battling tears.

On impulse, Lucy reached out to grab her mother's hand. They stood there, fingers intertwined, and waited until Jon's grip on his daughter loosened and he lifted his head.

He smiled first at Sierra and murmured, "You okay, honey?"

She gulped and nodded. "I'm a mess."

He laughed. Arm still around her, he turned to face Lucy and her mother.

"I'm sorrier than I can say that all of you got sucked into this. I handled it badly," he said frankly. "I was never ashamed of Sierra, and I hope she'll forgive me for acting as though I was."

She leaned her head momentarily against him. "I never thought that. I didn't," she insisted when he started to speak. "You were way nicer than I ever thought you would be."

"It's Lucy's forgiveness I need most of all," he said, voice suddenly deeper, rougher. "And Terry's."

"I always understood," Lucy's mother said

quickly. "I was selfish in asking anything at all of Lucy. I told myself that maybe she needed me, but now that I've met Sierra and you, I know she didn't."

That wasn't true, Lucy knew suddenly. She *had* needed her mother. No matter what happened down the line, she would remember the good times, the love. Not only the bewilderment and hurt.

But before she could say anything, her mom went on. "I admire what you said out there. I want you to know that." She visibly gathered her dignity, gently removing her hand from Lucy's. "And I want you to know that I'm planning tomorrow to call my parole officer and let him know that I'll be going elsewhere."

"No," Lucy cried, and was astonished when Jon echoed her.

"No. I was wrong. You and Lucy were right." His regret was obvious when his gaze met Lucy's for a moment before returning to her mother. "Lucy tried to tell me that she did need you. And that you needed her, and how much that meant to her. I wouldn't listen, even though I know how much I'd do for my mother, or my sister or her boys." He hesitated. "Has Lucy told you about Cassia?"

She shook her head. Sierra stared at him.

His voice had that rough timbre again. "We were engaged to be married. I loved her. She was raped and murdered, and I let the tragedy affect me profoundly. I want to believe I've done some good because of the circumstances under which I lost her. But grief also made me rigid, unwilling to forgive. The irony is that, in losing Cassia, I became more like my father than I ever wanted to admit. An angry, intolerant man. The last thing I ever wanted to be."

Lucy couldn't listen to any more. "That's ridiculous," she snapped. "I don't believe for a minute that you're anything like your father. Even when you're mad, you're controlled. You'd never lash out at anyone the way he did. And you *have* done good. You've given meaning to Cassia's death. She'd be proud of you."

He swallowed and struggled for composure. "Lucy," he said. That was all. Just her name. Low and desperate.

Her mom held out a hand to Sierra. Unable to tear her gaze from Jon's, Lucy was barely aware of the other two backing away, disappearing. Leaving them alone.

She stepped forward, less sure of herself than she wanted to be. What he'd said out there—had he really meant it? She prayed it hadn't been just a way for him to garner sympathy. Or, worse yet, gather the three of them under his protection because of his unyielding sense of responsibility.

"I'm so sorry," he said. "So damned sorry. I don't know how you can ever forgive me. But it's been killing me, Lucy. Sticking to a principle when I knew how much I'd hurt you. Being without you."

"Oh, Jon," she whispered.

He lifted a hand. It trembled. She'd never seen him less than steady and sure. He cupped her cheek. His thumb traced over her lips. "I love you, Lucy Malone." When she quivered, he said, "Maybe it's too soon. I shouldn't have told the whole world I wanted you to be my wife before I asked you. I put you on the spot, and that wasn't fair."

Dazed, she said, "You did mean it."

"I don't blame you if you doubt me." He sighed. "I screwed up. All I can ask you right now is to give me a chance to prove you *can* trust me. That I trust you."

"The election…" She had to ask. Tried to formulate how, but he was already shaking his head.

"It doesn't matter."

"That's not true. Of course it matters."

He gave her a smile. Crooked but real.

"You're right. I still want to win. If you'll support me, I'll go back to campaigning tomorrow. But I won't compromise myself again. You've made me understand a lot of things I didn't know about myself. I always believed I was driven solely by Cassia's murder. And yeah, that was part of it, but not all. I don't think I'd acknowledged how angry I still was at my father." He was silent for a moment. "And at my mother. Maybe I didn't want to hear you because if you could forgive yours, why was it that I couldn't forgive mine? And yeah, I changed my career path from business to law enforcement, but I suspect my ambition had as much to do with proving my father wrong as it did with needing to save other innocents. I hated the son of a bitch. He told me often enough I wouldn't amount to anything. I had to be more noble, smarter, more successful than he was. Even after he died, that need never left me." His laugh was gruff. "That's pretty damned pathetic, letting your life be all about Daddy."

Lucy's heart felt lighter than it had in weeks. She smiled at him. "You're asking me? The woman whose life has been all about Mommy?"

"No." Now both his big hands framed her face. "You triumphed over a tough childhood.

You must have felt abandoned, over and over. Unloved. So how did you end up able to take chances like you did giving up one career to start a small business? You had to know how risky that was. And how did you end up a woman who could unhesitatingly give so much to a girl you couldn't have known that well?"

Her eyes burned again. She tilted her face to press a kiss against his broad palm. "You make me sound a lot more special than I am. I *like* my life, but it's not brave, and nothing I do has a lot of impact on anyone else." Making him understand was important. She couldn't let him see her as something she wasn't. "I'm not like you, Jon," she tried to explain. "Opening the store is the only brave thing I've ever done. And that was scary beyond belief."

He was smiling now, his thumbs catching the tears that escaped. "Lucy, I'm pretty sure I started falling in love with you the first time I saw you, glowering so suspiciously at me. Not that I had a clue then. But I'll tell you this. Stunned as I was by Sierra's claim, I'd made up my mind before you left after one last glare that I'd be calling you whether I was Sierra's father or not."

"Really?" She despised herself for sounding so needy and...doubting. Hopeful.

"Oh, yeah." He bent his head and brushed his mouth over hers. Gently bumping his nose against hers, he murmured, "I wanted you. I imagined you naked, with all that glorious hair tumbling loose. And I wanted, just as much, to know *why* you were so sure I was a jackass. What man had let you down so badly, you suspected all of us. Or if it was me, who it was I reminded you of."

"I— It was only that—"

"I was a man who had a daughter I'd never had any idea existed. I know." He kissed her again, his lips lingering on hers. His tenderness was palpable, healing the damage he'd done when he'd told her she wasn't to be trusted. "Will you give me another chance, Lucy? Even if I don't deserve it?"

For a long moment she simply drank in the sight of his face, not looking guarded, but instead revealing emotions that made her heart take a long, slow tumble that shouldn't have been physically possible. *I love him so much.* Every small part of him. The lines on his face that deepened when he was serious, as he too often was. The mouth that could kiss her so passionately, could curl with wicked humor, or smile so gently. The nose that was too big but still somehow just right. And those pale eyes that could rivet her with a glance, eyes she'd seen as cold as Arctic ice, and as warm as sunlight glinting on water. The man who had used his grief for good, who had—despite what he said—always put his principles ahead of his ambitions, giving a lonely girl her dream of a real father.

He was waiting, a shadow of fear in his eyes. "Lucy?"

"I love you." She smiled, but it trembled on her lips. "I think *I* fell in love with you that first day, too, when I walked into your office. I looked at you and I thought, *He's perfect*. Except then I was mad at myself because you couldn't possibly be." She made a face. "And maybe you aren't. I mean, you *did* screw up."

He gave a choked laugh.

"But you redeemed yourself today. What you said out there was…right. You're the man I believed you were. And I'd really like it if we could be a family. You and me and Sierra."

He kissed her. Lifted his mouth long enough to say, "Lucy…marry me." Then he didn't let her answer because he was kissing her again.

But the words didn't seem to be needed. Of

course she'd marry him! Of course they were a family. It felt predestined. Sierra hadn't only set out to find her dad, she'd set out to find… everything. The place to belong she'd lost.

"I love you," Lucy managed to whisper again.

He lifted her higher, backed her against the door. "I need you." His voice had gone hoarse again. "Just us. Do you think your mother would mind?"

"Not for a second." She let her head fall back so that his teeth could graze her throat. "Do you suppose all those reporters are gone?"

"Damn." Jon went still. Finally he settled her on her feet, gave her a hot, hungry look, then went as far as the window. "Yep," he said with satisfaction. "They know when they're beaten."

"Are they? They'll find out about Mom, won't they?"

"She's your mother. You love her." He smiled. "I was an idiot."

"Yes, you were."

"Now that we've settled that, can we run away?"

"Absolutely. We just have to tell—"

"The rest of our family where we're going?"

Her "Yes" came out shaky.

Jon's expression held astonishing tenderness, understanding and all the love she'd been afraid to believe anyone would ever feel for her. He tugged her to him for a kiss that was soft and sweet. "Then let's run away," he said huskily.

Lucy said only "Yes."

EPILOGUE

JON LOOKED OUT over the dozen reporters, photographers and cameramen forming a small audience for today's press conference. He'd been surprised so many had shown up, since all he was doing was naming the officers he'd promoted or placed in new positions in the Emmons County Sheriff's Department since he had been sworn in as sheriff.

Ignoring the rest of his prepared statement, he concluded simply, "I have full confidence in the men and women who have accepted the challenge of helping make this a stronger police department." He gripped the sides of the podium. "Questions?"

A man in the back stood up. "Some of your more conservative constituents have to be wondering. What do you think of the color your daughter dyes her hair?"

There was laughter. Jon grinned, too. "Well, it's bright." More laughter. He waited until it had died, and let them see that now he was serious. "I look at the color of her hair as optimistic, and I find that to be pretty miraculous for a girl who lost her mother so recently." After a moment he smiled again. "The truth? I love it." He looked around with raised eyebrows, then inclined his head. "Thanks for coming." He started to turn from the podium.

"Sheriff Brenner, care to comment on your mother-in-law's troubled past? I understand she's a drug addict and convicted felon who's served time for armed robbery, among other crimes."

Jon glanced at Lucy, who stood to one side of the dais with his two captains. The plan was for them to go to lunch when he was finished here. With amusement he was careful not to show, he saw that she wasn't looking at him. Instead, she was glaring at the woman reporter whose voice had rung out.

That was his Lucy.

The question didn't bother him anywhere near as much as it apparently did her. He'd been expecting it for several months now. But election day had come and gone, with Jon winning by a comfortable margin. He'd gotten married. He and Lucy had, just yesterday, put money down on an old house with a big yard in Kanaskat. Sierra could keep a bedroom even after she left for college, and there were a couple more to spare for the family Lucy and Jon intended to start soon.

In all that time, with all those life-changing events, no one had thought to investigate the background of one Terry Malone.

All good things had to end.

Jon turned to the podium. He knew exactly what to say and had almost been looking forward to saying it.

"People make mistakes. They get in trouble. They struggle with their own weaknesses. Sometimes they overcome them. I've only known Terry Malone for a short while. A few months ago, I was cynical enough that I would have told you she was bound to stumble and fall. But I've come to believe she's stronger than she ever knew she was. Having family willing to forgive makes a difference. My wife's love has made a difference." He looked over the small crowd, smiled slightly, then turned a wider smile on his Lucy, who had given up glowering to listen to him. Her eyes were warm, milk-chocolate instead of bitter. Her love did make all the difference. Once again he focused on his audience. In finishing, Jon suspected he didn't sound like a cop. He didn't care. "You asked for my comment, and this is what I have to say. My daughter and any children

Lucy and I have will be lucky. They'll have two grandmothers."

If there were any more questions, he didn't hear them. His wife was waiting.

* * * * *

LARGER-PRINT BOOKS!
GET 2 FREE LARGER-PRINT NOVELS PLUS
2 FREE GIFTS!

Harlequin

Super Romance

Exciting, emotional, unexpected!

YES! Please send me 2 FREE LARGER-PRINT Harlequin® Superromance® novels and my 2 FREE gifts (gifts are worth about $10). After receiving them, if I don't wish to receive any more books, I can return the shipping statement marked "cancel." If I don't cancel, I will receive 6 brand-new novels every month and be billed just $5.44 per book in the U.S. or $5.99 per book in Canada. That's a saving of at least 13% off the cover price! It's quite a bargain! Shipping and handling is just 50¢ per book in the U.S. or 75¢ per book in Canada.* I understand that accepting the 2 free books and gifts places me under no obligation to buy anything. I can always return a shipment and cancel at any time. Even if I never buy another book, the two free books and gifts are mine to keep forever.

139/339 HDN FC69

Name _____

(PLEASE PRINT)

Address _____ Apt. #

City _____ State/Prov. _____ Zip/Postal Code

Signature (if under 18, a parent or guardian must sign)

Mail to the **Reader Service:**
IN U.S.A.: P.O. Box 1867, Buffalo, NY 14240-1867
IN CANADA: P.O. Box 609, Fort Erie, Ontario L2A 5X3

Not valid for current subscribers to Harlequin Superromance Larger-Print books.

**Are you a current subscriber to Harlequin Superromance books
and want to receive the larger-print edition?
Call 1-800-873-8635 today or visit www.ReaderService.com.**

* Terms and prices subject to change without notice. Prices do not include applicable taxes. Sales tax applicable in N.Y. Canadian residents will be charged applicable taxes. Offer not valid in Quebec. This offer is limited to one order per household. All orders subject to credit approval. Credit or debit balances in a customer's account(s) may be offset by any other outstanding balance owed by or to the customer. Please allow 4 to 6 weeks for delivery. Offer available while quantities last.

Your Privacy—The Reader Service is committed to protecting your privacy. Our Privacy Policy is available online at www.ReaderService.com or upon request from the Reader Service.

We make a portion of our mailing list available to reputable third parties that offer products we believe may interest you. If you prefer that we not exchange your name with third parties, or if you wish to clarify or modify your communication preferences, please visit us at www.ReaderService.com/consumerschoice or write to us at Reader Service Preference Service, P.O. Box 9062, Buffalo, NY 14269. Include your complete name and address.

HSRLP11

The series you love are now available in

LARGER PRINT!

The books are complete and unabridged—
printed in a larger type size to make it
easier on your eyes.

Harlequin®
Romance

From the Heart, For the Heart

Harlequin®
INTRIGUE®
BREATHTAKING ROMANTIC SUSPENSE

Harlequin®
Presents®

Seduction and Passion Guaranteed!

Harlequin®
Super Romance®

Exciting, emotional, unexpected!

Try **LARGER PRINT** today!

Visit: www.ReaderService.com
Call: 1-800-873-8635

Harlequin®

A *Romance* FOR EVERY MOOD™

www.ReaderService.com

HLPDIR11